### A Good Place for the Night

"Leading Israeli author Liebrecht has written a collection of extraordinary stories illuminating contemporary Israeli life.... [She] infuses these stories ... with a profound sense of humanity ... a supreme wisdom is found. Highly recommended."
— *Library Journal*

"A mesmerizing new collection. . . . Blending the conceits of science fiction with deeply resonant character studies, [in the title story] Liebrecht presents a new creation myth for the apocalyptic age."
*Jewish Literary Supplement*

"I read these stories with bated breath . . . a wondrous and thrilling human and literary experience."           — *Maariv* (Tel Aviv)

### A Man and a Woman and a Man

"A finely wrought novel . . . strikes an original note."
— *Washington Post Book World*

"Insightful and compelling. . . ."           — *Bloomsbury Review*

"Universal and yet intensely Israeli . . . displays great originality, and Liebrecht's simple style ... makes her accessible to the general reader."           — *Jewish Book World*

"Liebrecht mines her material to great and rewarding psychological depth. . . . A true and resonant and meaningful story ... [told] with a sure storyteller's skill."           — *Jerusalem Post*

### Apples from the Desert

"Liebrecht has perfect pitch. . . . She takes you places you have never been before."           — *New York Times Book Review*

"Rich, exciting, believable stories . . . that take you through the lives of real people, into the heart of their emotional and moral being."
— *Washington Post Book World*

# THE WOMEN MY FATHER KNEW

ALSO BY SAVYON LIEBRECHT

Stories

*Apples from the Desert*
*A Good Place for the Night*

Novels

*A Man and a Woman and a Man*

# The Women

SAVYON LIEBRECHT

# My Father Knew

Translated from the Hebrew by SONDRA SILVERSTON

A Karen and Michael Braziller Book

PERSEA BOOKS / NEW YORK

First published in the original Hebrew in 2005 by Keter (Jerusalem).
Published in the English language in 2010 by Persea Books (New York), by arrangement with Savyon Liebrecht and The Institute for the Translation of Hebrew Literature.

English Translation © 2010
by The Institute for the Translation of Hebrew Literature

Persea Books, Inc.
853 Broadway
New York, New York 10003

Library of Congress Cataloging-in-Publication Data
Liebrecht, Savyon, 1948–
[Ha-Nashim shel aba. English]
The women my father knew / Savyon Liebrecht; translated from the Hebrew by Sondra Silverston.—1st ed.
    p. cm.
Originally published: Ha-Nashim shel aba. Jerusalem: Keter, 2005.
"A Karen and Michael Braziller book."
ISBN: 978-0-89255-356-3 (alk. paper)
I. Title.
PJ5054.L444N37513 2010
892.4'36—dc22
                    2009053243

Designed by Rita Lascaro
Typeset in Minion
Printed on recycled, acid-free paper
Manufactured in the United States of America

First Edition

# Part One

November 17–29, 1990

MANHATTAN–STAMFORD

For the entire time that his father was dead, Meir's memories of the first seven years of his childhood were also buried, especially the five months when he and his father wandered together among his father's lovers. Twenty-three years later, when Meir found out that his father was alive, ghosts began to stir, frightening him with secrets from that far-off time. A longing for what had been—or perhaps for what had not been—was resurrected with them, arousing tastes and smells and voices from a previous life that were surprisingly intense. It was as if these sensations had lain hidden inside him, silent as stones, while he grew the image of a new Meir over the skin of the old, until the day when they were summoned and could burst out and shock him to the core.

Meir heard the news of his father's existence from his mother, in her Manhattan apartment. Uncharacteristically, she spoke haltingly, with long silences. Her eyes downcast, she asked him a question, one that he'd been waiting twenty-three years to hear: "Do you remember your father, Meir?" And now that it was finally being asked, he was struck dumb, the way it sometimes happens when things are late in coming. She looked in alarm at his lips moving silently in front of her, repeating her words. When he finally spoke, he didn't answer yes or no. He simply told her what he knew, and she immediately denied it, then was quiet, waiting, her eyes pleading. Meir never found out what she was pleading for, because he got up abruptly and left, saying he had an urgent meeting. He walked down one floor, then took the elevator another twenty-two floors down, got into his car and sat at the wheel, unmoving for a long time, staring at the brick wall in front of him; he was filled with guilt for leaving like that, despite her entreaties, too stunned to start the car, too stunned to decide where to take himself from there. When he awoke from his trance, his eyes were fixed on a random picture in the photo album his mother had shoved under his arm on his way out the door. The picture showed a baby cradled in the arms of a stranger, a man so like him that he might have been Meir's twin and was, apparently, his father.

The black parking-lot attendant waved his arm, guiding him toward the exit. Meir pushed the open album onto the passenger seat, started the car, and drove to the Twenty-fourth Street exit, toward the river of cars streaming downtown on Second Avenue. Since he hadn't decided which way to turn, habit kicked in, and his car turned left at the first intersection—as if it had a will of its own—and left again onto First Avenue, going uptown. At the traffic light on the corner of First Avenue and Fifty-ninth Street, he stared into the window of a children's clothing store. His eyes lingered on an outfit that looked like the one the baby was wearing in the old photograph from Tel Aviv.

Agitated and confused, Meir was compelled to look at the picture again, but he still could not take in the information that had landed on him without any warning, and he felt lost in an unreal world, the kind he found himself in when waking from a dream. Meir mustered all his strength to control the old trembling of his thumbs, and gripped the wheel with both hands. He drove onto the FDR Drive beside the East River, took the Willis Avenue Bridge into the Bronx, passed the huge Yankee Stadium, and headed out of the city and out of the state, until he finally turned onto the lovely, many-bridged road that led to his house in Connecticut. Suddenly, his car filled with a smell that was neither familiar nor unfamiliar, and surprising tears rose in his throat. He immediately pulled onto the side of the road without signaling, and sat there for a long while, eyes closed, until he could identify it: the smell of vanilla.

Years before he'd encountered it on women's necks; the sweet, innocent smell of vanilla made the tip of his tongue long for the rough, chilling contact with a scoop of ice cream perched atop a cone. He used to gobble it all down in an instant, including the sticky streams that dribbled over his fingers, and then down the cone itself.

All at once, he remembered his mother's eyes when, less than an hour ago, she asked him: "Do you remember your father, Meir?" Seeing how he froze in the middle of a gesture, his lips moving soundlessly, she had added, "The one from Tel Aviv."

"He died a long time ago," Meir had said, his heart clenching. Not once, since the day he ran as fast as he could toward a fat woman in a wheelchair in the arrivals hall at the New York airport—he'd recognized her by the sign she was holding over her head with both hands—not once since that day had his mother ever mentioned the man from Tel Aviv.

"Well, that's just it," she said with astonishing gentleness—and he saw her lower lip twitch—"he's not really dead."

That was the moment when he must have jumped up and run to the door, not noticing the album she'd shoved under his arm, imagining he heard her call after him that she'd hoped he'd stay for lunch. He didn't remember opening the door, going down the steps to the next floor and ringing for the elevator at a safe distance from her apartment. It wasn't until the elevator arrived that he noticed he was on the twenty-second floor and that the photograph album was pressed against his body.

He opened his eyes now and looked around at the scenery. Autumn trees, their colors beginning to change, lined both sides of the road like cut-outs made of fire and copper, and the smell of vanilla in the closed car gave way to the seemingly artificial scent of pine trees. In the distance, he saw a sign announcing a gas station and a restaurant, and although he wasn't the least bit hungry, he decided not to drive to his lonely house but to go to the restaurant so that the strangers there would unknowingly protect him from himself. While he looked through the album, they would shield him from the photographs' power to drag him back to another time, another place.

Carefully, he put the thick album, with a picture of the Wailing Wall inlaid on its worn cover, on the restaurant table. He ordered coffee and blueberry cake, and after the waiter had gone, moved the album closer and stared at the stones of the Wailing Wall for a while before daring to open it.

There was only one photograph on the first page, a picture of him, the baby, wearing a shirt with a round collar, like a girl's. Two of the three photos on the next page showed a tall, attractive, young man with a wide forehead and a shock of black hair that fell to the side. Like a peacock, the man showed off his virtues to the camera, aware of his charm and elegance despite his clothes, which were plain except for a small silk scarf tied jauntily around his neck—his father. In the photo on the right, he was with a fat young woman whose light-complexioned face was forgettable, but whose chestnut hair was luxuriant and tempted your hand to reach out to it—his mother. The man leaned against a beautiful ironwork railing and was pulling the woman toward him. It looked as if their weight was about to overwhelm the delicate railing and that they'd land on the sidewalk. In the picture on the left the man leaned against an imposing white car with diplomatic plates that he'd impulsively appropriated for the photograph. As Meir studied the picture and the triumphant expression on his father's face, his order arrived. But instead of the aroma of coffee and blueberries, a remembered smell of fried garlic and onion filled his nostrils, and he turned away.

His glance fell on the photo below the other two, in which— he now noticed—his father was smiling broadly and a grimacing boy sat frozen on top of a desk, holding onto the edge with his small fingers. He looked as if he'd been thrown from a distance and happened to land among all those books and was afraid to move because he might lose his balance and slip onto the floor— Meir, about two years old.

He looked into the depths of the picture, trying to dredge up invisible shapes, and suddenly, as if there'd been an earthquake, Meir clutched the table with both hands and the cup jiggled, causing coffee to run over the sides into the saucer. But that desperate grip didn't stop the adult man from being swept toward the frightened baby boy sitting on the edge of the desk among piles of books threatening to topple. Meir's slightest movement might cause the boy to collapse and make the books fall to the floor, which seemed as far away as the bottom of an abyss. And there, at the bottom of the abyss, Meir clearly saw bloodstains, and then he regained his composure.

The earth settled, and as if he'd just escaped disaster, Meir rubbed his knuckles, pained from gripping the table. A distant memory had struck in him the fear he'd lived with in childhood. It had pierced him like the pin in a mounted butterfly. His right index finger hesitated on the edge of the page, but he quickly decided to close the album: it would be better to look at the photographs one by one and not to run through them as if he could catch up the twenty-three years—and the forgotten first seven years, too—in an hour. He looked up, his gaze drawn to the back of a man at a table sitting opposite a woman. The man was leaning over, whispering a secret in the woman's ear.

At that moment, Meir knew with absolute certainty that he'd seen that sight before, a long time ago in another life, and it stirred in him now what it had stirred in him then: the sense of a fateful encounter between a man and a woman in which every movement of their heads, every hint of a smile, every lowering of a shoulder— was a sign in a mysterious language that had been his native tongue in childhood; the feeling of helplessness that came from knowing that his life depended on the connection between them; and his annoyance that the man and woman were exchanging those secret signs in full view of everyone, as they conversed, while he held his breath in suspense, waiting to see if they rose together and the man took the woman's elbow and led her to the door or if the tension between them erased their smiles, and the man got up abruptly and moved to another woman's table, where the courting ritual would be repeated until the man and woman rose together, the man took the woman's elbow, and they walked toward the café door, past Meir, who was still holding his breath, his eyes tired from staring, his body aching from anticipation.

The man at the nearby table must have sensed the penetrating stares on his back because he turned around and glared at Meir like a dog who's been disturbed while eating. Then, after taking a good look and apparently deciding he didn't know the solitary man, he turned his back again. Meir, under the spell of the memory, kept staring, afraid that the memory would vanish if he took his eyes off the couple for even a moment. His staring finally drove them out, but Meir kept watching them through the window until they got into their car. Like a dream that fades upon waking, the vision they'd summoned up grew fuzzy, and only then did he get up and leave, too.

In his quiet house, Meir tried to calm the stirring of wellsprings within him that threatened to overtake reason. Under the sharp eye of his dog, he paced the wooden deck, staring at the grove across the way, where, as a child, he had believed the Olympian gods lived. *The edge of the floor near the railing is squeaking again,* he said to himself, *and I have to call in that guy who does sloppy work.* He tried to calm the anxiety he felt about the smells locked in his memory; soon they might escape and he would drown in the sights and sounds that followed in their wake. Yet despite his anxiety, he also felt a kind of joy, a growing, quiet, potentially intoxicating happiness. He stopped abruptly, midway along the length of the deck, suddenly realizing the reason for his happiness: in the midst of his agonizing writer's block, he now had a story with living roots, a story as powerful as the survival instinct that would not be thrown in the wastebasket like dozens of earlier efforts. There was a couple torn apart, a boy raised in a distant country by his mother, a dead baby girl, a boy living for decades thinking that his father was dead until one day, close to his thirtieth birthday, his mother tells him that his father is alive.

Meir hurried into the house and into his study. He closed the door and abandoned himself to a new, exciting thought: finally, something real was happening to him, something that could make the heart pound and become a written story; a story taken from his own life, that could be told in the first person, not the kind borrowed from other people's lives and told in the third person. It would be the end of the painful writer's block that had haunted him every day and tortured him every night for three years. He turned the idea over in his mind eagerly but with suspicion. The fleeting thought that he'd pounced on the material like a buzzard on a carcass left him feeling uncomfortable.

Meir had written his first book in one burst during a summer and autumn when he became friendly with a sportswriter whose pregnant wife left him without explanation and went back to her parents' home in Atlanta. The pain of their separation had kindled Meir's imagination. Meir was a copyeditor at the same newspaper, and it was from his office that the sportswriter had carried on his emotional conversations with his wife, her sister, or the lawyer. Meir had been drawn into supporting his friend's struggle. When the abandoned husband realized he couldn't persuade his wife to come back, he fell into a depression that produced heartbreakingly poetic sentences, and Meir found himself surreptitiously writing them down. At night and on weekends, he would write the story of how his friend and his wife—whom he'd only seen once, dressed as Pocahontas at a newspaper costume party—fell in love, grew jealous, separated, and ended up hating each other. While he was writing the story, which took up all his free time and imagination, Meir experienced feelings he'd never had before: excitement that intensified until it burned; shortness of breath, like after a run; an overflowing heart; an addiction to the sweet pain; furor that aroused his passion until he felt the desire to masturbate; a yearning to be with the loved woman; the joy of learning of the pregnancy; the shock of her increasing remoteness; the profound sadness of separation; the desperate attempts to understand why she'd left; the vast emptiness of loss. He wrote compulsively, causing the managing editor to complain that Meir was neglecting his work, but Meir was engrossed in his writing, as if it were life itself and he had no choice but to live it.

He finished the first draft in the middle of the fall and quickly completed the little editing it required. Entire pages needed no changes, and he invested most of his efforts in altering details about the protagonists to disguise the source of his story. He gave the manuscript to a publisher-acquaintance, who made a face, hinting in a quashing tone that there was no point in hoping for a response before spring and recommended—with indifference camouflaged as generosity—that he should send the manuscript to other publishers as well. But by the end of that week, the man called, excited about the story and happy to hear that the manuscript hadn't yet been sent out. He was ready to publish it soon, he told Meir. Two days later, a messenger brought a contract with numerous clauses, one of which obligated the author—Meir's eyes lingered on the magical words—to give him his next book, too. The publisher put the first printed copy of Meir's book into his trembling hands, and looked with mocking affection at Meir's thumbs drumming on the cover. And on the nights that followed—he never told anyone—Meir would fall asleep hugging the book, unwilling to take his hands off it even when he slept.

Most of the reviews praised it effusively. Meir kept them in an envelope along with a vitriolic letter from the sportswriter, who had moved to Atlanta around the time the baby was due and been sent the book anonymously by one of the staffers. For a long time after receiving the abusive letter, Meir tried to compose a reply that would be moderately friendly, explanatory and not apologetic. But after he'd thrown the eighth letter into the wastebasket, he got up to make a cup of tea and had to admit that although he'd done something contemptible, he didn't feel guilty. He also wondered whether delving into other people's lives and peering into their thoughts, some of them embarrassing, wasn't part of the literary act. He went back to his desk with a fresh cup of tea, knowing that's how it was: art was exempt from apologies.

The surprising abundance of reviews; the readings at bookstores that ended with book signings; the flirtatious fan letters from women who liked to read; the many interviews, two on television—were all part of the hullabaloo surrounding the book's publication. And while all of this was going on, the publisher told him that a talented young director and a group of actors, graduates of the Yale School of Drama, were so excited by the book that they wanted to turn it into a movie. Suddenly pursued by two beautiful actresses and surrounded by enthusiastic young interns and volunteers, Meir now wrote, dreamed, and lived his story in the form of a screenplay. Within a few months, the movie—albeit a low-budget one—was edited and finished, and for two weeks it was screened daily at the university, then at community centers in Stamford. And though the responses to the movie were fewer and more restrained than to the book, Meir decided he would also write screenplays in the future.

Later, when the noise surrounding the book died down and he was forced to edit articles about the successes of other new writers, Meir found himself alone in his study, futilely searching for a new story and missing the exciting months he'd spent with the actors. Dejectedly, he stared at the Post-It notes on his corkboard, listing the director's good suggestions: "The plot must move ahead through a series of conflicts;" "What the main character knows, the viewer must also know;" "Put a subtext under every text."

Every once in a while, the publisher would call, report on sales, say how sure he was the next book would be a national bestseller, and ask off-handedly how the work was going. Meir would assure him—and sometimes even believe—that he'd soon find a subject and settle down to write. But three years passed and nothing happened. He was often filled with a sense of despair, irritated that although the publisher's doors were open to him and the film director was interested in his next screenplay, his imagination seemed all at once to have dried up. His antennae searched for a story, for the merest thread of a plot—and found total barrenness. Sometimes his imagination would trick him and send him a scene, a character, or a sentence that inspired him with sudden hope, like a hunter who's been lying in wait for hours when a deer suddenly appears in his rifle sights. And Meir, feeling the scene become clearer, the character rounding out, and the sentences taking on meaning, would get ready to dive into a new story. Sometimes, in his imagination, he'd even write the opening words of a screenplay, describe a place or a character, and then gaze with pleasure at the professional style:

> *Interior. Sunday noon. André's garden.*

Or:

> *Exterior. Night. The sidewalk in front of the door of a nightclub on Eighth Avenue.*

But in time, he understood that those were mere illusions. The scene was ordinary, the character drab, the sentences meaningless, none of those brilliant suggestions hanging on the corkboard were being followed, and he had no idea what was happening in André's garden or who was walking on the sidewalk in front of the nightclub on Eighth Avenue. And he'd go back to sitting for hours before the blank screen, foraging around inside himself and not finding a single event in his life worth writing about.

In this hunt for material, Meir discovered that his boring life offered no story. He was distressed that his life was so dreary and arid, and that his only source of inspiration was the stormy lives of strangers. He found himself pillaging other people's lives, ransacking the stories he heard, but again coming up with nothing of value.

As a last resort, he decided to write about relationships he'd had with women. In his sophomore year in college, he remembered, he'd been besotted by them, had fallen in love with a different girl every month and immediately proposed to her. But he wasn't faithful to any of his prospective brides, and even before they had time to give him an answer, often only a few days later, he was already in love with another woman. It wasn't until the end of the year, when he saw that his grade point average was very low, that he sat down in his room, like someone who's just gotten off a roller coaster, and admitted to himself that he hadn't really loved any of the women he'd proposed to. He'd lied to all of them, sometimes out of necessity and sometimes out of childhood habit. They'd all refused him, and in retrospect, he was suddenly hurt by the rejections. He didn't miss any of them after they stopped seeing each other; some didn't even say hello when they passed him on campus. Also—he had to admit—he hadn't actually chosen any of them, had never pursued them. They'd given him their phone numbers, and when he didn't call, they called him, invited him to their rooms, and seduced him in their beds. His falling in love was never genuine: it happened only in his imagination, aroused his body but sidestepped his heart.

After college, when he took a job on a local newspaper and moved into his grandfather's house, he'd find women mainly where he worked and sometimes in the restaurant at the Stamford railroad station. From time to time, he'd go there on his way home from the office, hold a glass of beer between his body and the paper he pretended to read, and steal glances at the girls and women passing by with suitcases and travel bags, on their way north to New Haven or Boston, or south to New York and New Jersey, looking for someplace to spend the time until their train arrived.

Here, too, he waited for them to talk to him, to ask him for a pen or directions to the payphone, to keep an eye on their things. And occasionally—when he told them he worked at the newspaper—they promised to visit him there, and some of them actually called.

The women, he realized in a moment of cruel self-awareness, would ask him into their lives and he'd be swallowed up in them, disappearing as if he had no life of his own. With the sportswoman, he ran and swam and exercised and rowed; with the poet, he went to poetry readings and book signings; with the painter, he went to museums and art supply stores; with the woman who practiced yoga, he bought white cotton clothes and went to yoga lessons; with the fashion designer, he went to fashion shows and bought chic clothes in trendy boutiques; with the inventor of children's games, he'd played board games for hours, and had even created a move for a game she'd developed; with the bridge player, he'd read the how-to-play-bridge books she gave him and once he went to a tournament with her in Baltimore. Their hobbies and occupations became his hobbies and occupations, changing, as if he were a human chameleon, with every change of girlfriend.

As for the women he knew after college, he adopted their habits just as he'd adopted those of the girls he knew in his youth, but these women did not induce the birth of a story either. He had nothing in common with any of them, he told himself. He'd devoted himself with equal ease to young and older women, married and single, virgins and mothers, good-looking women and ugly ones, tall and short, white and black, placid and tempestuous—as if women were all the same to him. Except for those whose odor put him off, he had no trouble responding to them all. Sometimes the relationship lasted a few weeks and sometimes a few days. He refused to meet their families and never initiated a night out or a meal, and he certainly never asked them to spend the night in his house. Sometimes, after seeing an exhibition or a play in Manhattan, he'd invite them up to his mother's apartment, not to taunt or mollify her, but mainly because he'd gotten tired and wanted to be alone for a while. Most of the women refused, but the willing ones were as excited as if they'd already been asked to become members of the family, and after he introduced them, Meir would go into his old room and close the door like someone who'd just retired from the world. He'd lie on his back on the bed of his youth, sometimes hearing the murmur of their conversation or the sound of their laughter, and discover time and time again the extent of his loneliness, the gaping chasm between himself and his mother, himself and the woman he slept with at night. His colleagues at the paper thought he was a sociable guy who lived a wild bachelor life. In contrast to the pseudo abandon of his lifestyle, his inner life was an arctic wasteland. He was never elated by any new encounter or distraught by any parting. He never bothered to finish reading any of the nasty letters written to him by women who accused him of leading them down the garden path; he threw them into the wastebasket without even tearing them up.

Only once was his heart truly awakened, by a vivacious young woman called Holly, the unmarried mother of a boy named Tyson. But he couldn't construct a story around her and the boy, although thinking about them stirred his soul.

She came into his office at the paper one day with a dark-skinned girl in tow, sat down across from him, and seated the girl in a chair next to her. It turned out that Holly was a teacher in a school for the mentally challenged and also a volunteer at the community center in Waterside, one of the poor neighborhoods of Stamford, and the girl was Martina, a very talented dancer. Before he could explain that he was the paper's copyeditor and that she should be seeing the arts editor, Holly had already warmly invited him to the school end-of-year recital, so he could see the girl dance and then print her picture in the paper. When he pointed out her mistake, he thought he saw a slight flush of embarrassment spread under her dark skin, but she continued rummaging around in her bag, pulled out an invitation and put it down in front of him, saying with a charming smile that he was still invited and would surely enjoy the evening, and she urged the girl to invite him herself. He was so surprised by Holly's audacity and moved by her support for the girl that he promised to come.

Two days later, at the entrance to the Waterside community center, she welcomed him with outspread arms, as if he were a cherished relative, and pulling him along behind her, she introduced him to the center's director. Only later, when he sat beside her in the first row, did he learn that she had a son, the boy who was standing a short distance from her, his legs crossed as if he were trying not to pee. During the performance, Holly held Tyson on her lap, her sparkling eyes fixed on the black girls dancing on the stage. Suddenly, Meir felt the boy's hand, small and warm, on his arm, creeping towards the crook of his elbow like a small mouse searching for a safe haven. Holly was now completely engrossed in watching the next act, a children's choir, and Meir in looking at the boy moving his hand along his naked arm, eyebrows contracted in concentration. Meir choked up with the sweet pleasure of it. A week later, Holly called to thank him for the piece in the paper about the young dancer, and he asked how her son was.

"You can come and see him, if you want," she said and gave him her phone number and address. For a few days, Meir walked around bewildered by the new excitement that she and the boy had aroused in him. One evening, he departed from habit, called Holly, and invited himself to their home; he brought the boy a present, a frog that croaked and also floated on the water when you pressed a button. Holly gave him a hug when he came in, took off her stained apron in his honor, and called Tyson, who immediately appeared at the top of the stairs, flew down to the door, and buried his head in Meir's stomach. In an instant, Meir found himself sitting in front of a bowl of soup, Tyson on his lap. Holly talked about her volunteer work at the community center and Meir recounted how, many years ago, he'd worked as a volunteer to help immigrant Latino children in his high school. That night, Meir told Tyson a bedtime story and spent the night in his mother's warm bed.

For a few weeks, he was drawn to Holly and Tyson and went to see them sometimes at the community center, where he sat next to Holly as she read stories to the blind or helped non-English-speaking immigrants puzzle their way through the tangles of forms. Tyson sat next to him and listened to the stories, too, or played with the immigrant children. And one day, watching her cover the table with letters that a Colombian girl had received from the bank, it occurred to him that her life was so full that she didn't notice how empty his was, and he suddenly realized how her life was devouring his. Here she was, already filling his evenings and his thoughts at work, and soon he wouldn't have a corner left to hide in. Alarmed at having been drawn into her home and at having fallen in love with Tyson, he vanished from her life one day without explanation or apology, and didn't answer the urgent messages both she and the boy left him. A few days later, his heart almost stopped in fear when Holly called him at at work, wondering about his behavior. Without hesitating, he lied and said in an unfaltering voice that his fiancée, from whom he'd separated after a fight four months earlier, had come to see him and now they were going to get married. After two more weeks of missing them, Meir pushed mother and son out of his mind and went back to the comfortable, barren tranquility of his previous life.

When hope of getting inspiration from real women had disappeared, it occurred to him to write screenplays about the women in Greek mythology. As a child in Tel Aviv, he'd spent a great deal of time looking at the illustrations in a book of myths, and kept doing so during the first few months in Connecticut, maintaining the only connection to the boy he'd been in Tel Aviv. Years later, in college, he wrote papers on mythological heroes and even gave highly praised lectures on them to his classmates.

One night, he had a daring thought: to write a series of screenplays on goddesses and women of Greek mythology who find themselves in New York at the end of the twentieth century. He could see the opening lines:

*Interior. Daylight. Macy's.*

Medusa, who has snakes for hair, rides up the escalator from floor to floor, and people run away from her. Anyone who looks at her turns into stone. All the live people quickly evacuate the store. Now the store is full of merchandise and stone people. The manager comes out of his office. Medusa looks him straight in the eyes, and he turns into stone. She goes into his office, sits down in his chair, looks at the family photographs on his desk. Everyone in the photos whose eyes she meets turns into stone.

Once, driving his car very late at night, he tuned into a radio call-in show where listeners ask a psychiatrist with a deep, warm, confidence-inspiring voice for advice. A fifteen-year-old girl, who confessed that she'd been sexually active from the age of thirteen, said in a whisper that she'd been sleeping with her father for a few months and enjoyed having intercourse with him more than she had ever enjoyed it with any of her boyfriends. The psychiatrist cleared his throat and spoke cautiously about long-term damage and a fatal blow to any future relationships with men and also to her relationship with her mother, but the girl kept claiming stubbornly that she enjoyed what she was doing with her father and had no reason to stop. You could tell that she hadn't called for help, but for approval. When approval wasn't forthcoming, she stopped whispering and said in a raspy, belligerent voice that she wouldn't take his advice and slammed down the phone. Meir's imagination was ignited by the scene of a house shrouded in silence after midnight, doors opening slowly onto a long hallway, darkness filled with passion and the sounds of breathing—

*Interior of a house. Night.*

A suburban, middle-class home. Total silence. The camera moves up the stairs in the darkness to the top floor and the hallway leading past the bedrooms. Two doors open soundlessly. The figure of a man appears in one: Robert. In the other, the figure of a young girl: his daughter Zoey. They're both barefooted, in nightclothes. He walks out first and she follows him along the hallway and down several staircases, to the cellar.

*Exterior. A parking lot in front of a high school. Afternoon.*

Robert is sitting in his spacious car. He is visibly excited. His fingers move restlessly on the wheel. Zoey stands out among the many students coming out of

the gates. She sees the car, smiles, turns toward it in
a slow, mincing walk.

*Interior. A motel reception desk. Afternoon.*

Robert and Zoey are at the reception desk. The clerk
hands Robert a key and gives Zoey an unreadable look.

Meir's imagination was still inflamed by the girl and her father
when the next listener came on and in a quavery voice said that
she was fifty-four and had recently discovered a few gray pubic
hairs. The psychiatrist cleared his throat again and kept his tone
of voice serious as he said that there was nothing abnormal about
that. She interrupted him, presumably afraid they'd cut off the
conversation because her question wasn't abnormal, and said that
she'd plucked the gray hairs and put them in a small jewelry box.
There was a short silence, in which the psychiatrist was perhaps
searching his memory. When he spoke again, it was clear no one
had ever confided such a thing before. There was nothing wrong
with collecting pubic hair, he said, but she should try to stop the
habit before she got carried away into uncontrolled behavior.

*Interior. Bathroom. Day.*

A fifty-year-old woman is standing in front of the sink
in her bathroom. On the marble counter next to the
sink is a jewelry box inlaid with turquoise stones. She
opens the cover and studies the contents of the box.
In a close-up shot of the inside of the box, we see a
few curly, silver hairs.

Excited by the two stories he'd heard and wanting to retain
what he'd written in his mind, Meir turned off the radio.
Suddenly, he remembered the story of the princess of Cyprus,
who had been cursed by Aphrodite and made to fall in love with
her own father. Every night, the young girl would steal into her
father's bed and make love to him. Unlike the story told by the girl

on the radio, when the king of Cyprus found out that he'd slept with his daughter, he decided to kill her. But the gods saved her by turning her into a tree, and nine months later, the beautiful baby, Adonis, was born from that tree.

For a long time after he got home, and in the following days, Meir tried to develop a screenplay from the two cases, then a short story. He gave up on the story of the girl who was so keen on sleeping with her father when he realized he was unable to describe what they did after they closed the basement or motel room door. However, he did manage to write a moving description of the older woman removing the signs of old age from her pubic hair and of her sorrowful thoughts on the devastation of time. But no plot emerged. He couldn't move the story forward, couldn't even imagine the fate of the curly silver hairs in the jewelry box.

Other people's life stories, however tumultuous, no longer aroused his imagination, he said to himself despairingly, and there was absolutely nothing in his own life to write about because he didn't remember anything about his childhood in Tel Aviv before the age of seven, except for fragmented scenes, most of them of an old man with a tremulous voice who lived in a house filled with piles of junk, who once fell down on the sidewalk, and once screamed in fear. Whenever he considered the possibility of digging down and forcing those days out, an image flickered as if in warning: a large bloodstain on a light background. His throat would become dry and burn as it had done with illness in childhood, so he'd stop and retreat, letting the doors of memory close.

Every once in a while, Meir was drawn to write about Arnie, his mother's friend in childhood and her secret lover as an adult, who had embraced Meir wholeheartedly, acknowledging that beyond his visible life, in which he had a wife and daughters, was another hidden, equally real life in which he was strongly bound to Meir and Meir's mother. Of all the people he knew in America, only Arnie could touch the depths where the soul of the story lived—and time after time, Meir would stop himself writing about him, afraid that Arnie would read the book and discover that the seven-year-old boy was still stuck where he'd been then, when he arrived in Connecticut burning with fever, terrified by his mother's enormous size and the fact that she rode around in a wheelchair. Then, Arnie had knelt in front of him and checked his tongue and his eyes, forging an everlasting bond when he put his warm hands on Meir's shoulders and asked his mother to translate what he said: "Don't worry so much. Tomorrow is a new day."

While all this was happening, as if one of the Atlanta sports-writer's curses had come true, on a rainy day, while he was making a left turn onto the Bruckner Expressway on his way to New Haven, his car turned over. A policeman, who came to the hospital to take his testimony, told him about the accident—the only thing Meir remembered was the slow, prolonged squealing of tires that sounded like the roar of a beast of prey. But even before that, in the split second when he woke up to the glare of the street-lights, his body completely paralyzed, Meir thought that this must be what dying is like: the light, the soft sounds, the numb body, the pleasant blur that made him feel as if he were floating. Then his head cleared and he realized that it wasn't scenes from his life that were flashing through his mind, but the thought that he wouldn't be able to write his second book or screenplay, and that there were so many other things he'd never get to do in his life. Then, from within a glowing circle, he saw Arnie's head bent over him, like in his childhood when he was sick, and he knew that Arnie wouldn't let him die. He thought that maybe now he could write a story that began with a car accident, and, at the same time, it occurred to him that the small production company couldn't afford to stage a car crash and it might be better to look for a richer company.

During the next five weeks at home, his mother came to look after him and to take care of his dog. Her presence so disrupted his peace of mind that Meir tried hard to show how quickly he was recovering so she would leave his house.

During those weeks, remembering the pleasure of writing his first book, he tried again and again to construct a story that began with a car accident, but on the first page, he had already come to a dead end. Sometimes he thought he felt a story growing inside him, climbing like a silent pain. Then he'd stop, trembling, recalling that this was how the blessed period of writing had once begun. But days of expectation produced nothing, until he became ill, either from exhaustion or disappointment or because of the fierce argument that was raging between his mother and Susie, a lecturer in film studies he'd been sleeping with at the time, and with whom he'd gone to see European films at the Bleecker Street Cinema. The argument resonated from the ground floor to his room on the first floor, where he lay in the throes of a high fever, stories drifting in and out of his mind, among them, one about a blood feud between a woman and her son's lover, whose English had a slightly Italian lilt. He thought he'd retain bits of the stories, but when he recovered, he found they had all disappeared, dispersed like fog.

Even though he hadn't succeeded in getting a story down on paper, the whisper of the words asking to be born never stopped. They wandered in his imagination like evil spirits, seeking a shape, eating away at him. Sometimes he would discover that a thought charged with emotion was forming in his mind, straining to be put into words. The next day, in a moment of alertness, he'd look at what he'd written and be embarrassed. Amazed, he'd remember the stirrings that had gripped him and delete what he'd written with the touch of a key. Then he'd go back to staring at the blank screen, the desire to write burning inside him. But he had no story, he had no feelings, and he had no words.

It was exactly then that Meir learned his father was alive. As if fate had looked at him and, seeing his distress, decided to hand him a story. Now he was about to discover it, like a childless person who finds an abandoned baby on his doorstep.

From the age of seven, when he'd been hustled onto a plane, his backpack filled with his few clothes, two notebooks, and a book

of Greek myths for children, Meir had known that his father was
dead. He couldn't remember who'd told him about this death. It
was as if the news had always been part of him; as if even when his
father was alive, danger had followed him like a shadow. So it was
not surprising when the shadow swallowed up the man: he vanished, and the knowledge stayed frozen somewhere in the back of
Meir's mind. Only now, when it was still unclear how great a threat
the news was, did the light suddenly shine on unasked questions
that had been buried in layers of time.

Sitting at the desk, he pulled the album toward himself and
began looking through a series of photos taken on the Tel Aviv
beach. His father, against the background of the white lifeguard's
hut, probably wearing a bathing suit, but looking naked because
he's hugging his mother—who is wearing a dress—from behind,
and Meir curled up at their feet like a puppy, covered with sand.
And here's his father, in the water up to his shoulders, waving
both hands like Columbus sighting land; and in another picture,
his mother is sitting on the sand, her arms around her raised
knees, her beautiful hair pulled up in the back. Her eyes, wide
with admiration, look at the handsome man standing above her,
his legs spread, a towel across his shoulders, like a victorious
Olympic athlete. Next to them is Meir, engrossed in building a
seashell fort, and behind them the Mediterranean, as flat as a mirror all the way to the horizon.

Stealthily, the water began to churn beneath the surface, and
Meir found himself drifting in it, so pleasantly, so furtively, that
he forgot about the ever-more-distant shore. Then suddenly it
swallowed him up, and he was swept away rapidly, caught
between tumbling walls of water that closed in on him, blocked
out the glow above him, dulled his senses, and quieted his fren-
zied movement until he stopped struggling; then, after a while,
Meir was swaying in a soothing, lulling hammock.

Now he trembled, his body experiencing what had evaded his
conscious memory. Was it a drowning? Was he the one who
drowned? Did the body remember first? And then: Had his

mother known all these years that his father was alive? Had they corresponded? Had his father sent him messages that she had kept from him? Why had she let him believe his father was dead? Why had she persisted in the lie for so many years? Why had no one bothered to tell him how his father died? Why had his grandfather or his uncle or Arnie never mentioned him? Why had his father allowed them to make him disappear? Why hadn't he announced his existence? Why hadn't he found ways to reach his son? Why hadn't he come to look for Meir himself? Why did his mother decide to tell him now that his father was alive? Why did she give him the album, which had apparently been hidden all these years in the Manhattan apartment he grew up in? And he himself, why hadn't he ever asked a question about his father? Why hadn't he been curious about his death?

Around midnight, Meir felt an old longing to relax in a warm bubble bath, as when he was teenager in his mother's house and would masturbate there. He stood in his clothes and watched the whitening water rising toward him. Then he undressed quickly and slid under the layer of foam as if he had to hide from scrutinizing eyes. His hands went straight to his penis and he trembled at the gentle contact of his practiced fingers, which knew how to touch himself far better than any woman's did, knew how to brush over his testicles floating in the water, to push them away from his stiffening penis, a finger lightly stroking its length and both hands sliding along the vein on its underside as it swelled like an arrow being shot from his testicles. He didn't try to delay the eruption, which came very quickly and elicited a faint, cracked sound from the depths of his body. He peered from under his eyelids at the floating semen blending with the vestiges of foam, already feeling the beginnings of the sorrow and emptiness that would soon engulf him, drawing him into the oblivion of sleep.

Slowly, over the following days, scenes from his childhood rose from the depths, and he was amazed at how the scenes had been submerged and frozen in silence for all those years, how the image of the bloodstain had blocked the memories, and how he'd locked the questions about those seven years inside him.

While sitting with his dog in the vet's waiting room or walking through the aisles of the supermarket or standing next to his car at the gas station, a scene flashed through his mind, flickered, and faded: a glaringly lit floor of ochre diamond shapes; a desk piled high with books, where he'd posed for a photograph; shutter handles he could see clearly, although they didn't appear in any picture; a group of people sitting around a table in a café, and at the far end of the room, a man in an apron drying glasses lined up in a row. At quiet times, when Meir was alone, the memories would linger, opening like a door opening on a door opening on a door, as he sat for hours in his reclining armchair in front of the huge window in his silent home, staring at the spectacular trees turning gold, and he let the memories come, frightened of what they would bring, but nonetheless waiting for them like a patient suitor: a floor of ochre diamond shapes in the foyer of the house, iron shutter handles in the shape of people, a man and a woman leaning towards each other from either side of a low table in a café.

During the day, the scenes came into his consciousness slowly, but at night, they would leap up and assault him. Just as he was falling asleep, a scene would materialize suddenly, appear like a diver bursting through the surface of the water in a moment of distress, driving away the bloodstain, which always rose first. Bits of scenes that had been blocked for twenty-three years appeared now like the blurred scenes of a very worn film, some of them in black-and-white, some in faded colors, the murky forms becoming clearer and taking on shape: people who were as alike as twins were trying to create faces for themselves, insisted on separating, differentiating, showing their uniqueness; a woman he didn't know asking him if he'd had lunch yet; an old man cursing the Nazis, his eyes feverish; the edge of a bed with rumpled sheets; a man—his father from the photographs—bursting out of the door of a building, muttering to himself, "Whore. All women are whores;" a shriek coming from a parched throat echoed like the screech of a bird of prey and shattered against the walls of a closed room.

Then he would jump out of bed, soaked in sweat, terrifying the dog out of its sleep. He would turn on all the lights in the house and go down to the deck, drawn to look into the memories opening up inside him.

A persistent memory: A man sitting at a desk, his shirt pulled tightly across his back, his hand racing fervidly as he writes line after line from right to left. Pages fall to the floor of ochre diamond shapes. There had to be absolute silence during those moments of intense concentration when the man was writing and erasing, and suddenly, with the wave of an executioner's hand, he'd rip out the page, crumple it into a ball, and toss it to the floor. The man had a serious face, deep-set eyes, very dark short hair, elegant movements: his father.

Another memory: A room in which small iron people grasp the shutters. A window. Under the window, a large bed, plump pillows at its head: his parents' bed. His parents' bed is soft and warm from their bodies lying on either side of him, and he sees his mother's hair, the ends igniting like match tips in the first light, and his father's handsome nape emerging like a tree trunk from between his shoulders—his father posed like a peacock even in his sleep—and he himself is buried up to his ears under the protective blanket, waiting for the moment the magic would fade suddenly and the ceiling would fall on them. He could never remember the moment he got out of his bed—a boy of three and five and six—opened his door, felt his way down the narrow hallway that had a heater standing in the corner, opened his parents' bedroom door, climbed into their bed, and pushed his way between them as they slept. He would fall asleep at night in his own room and in the morning, without any rational explanation, find himself in the double bed in the next room.

A third memory: An empty kindergarten, and he's hanging on the gate, his knees stuck between the iron posts, waiting for someone to come for him. Abandoned and alone, he's wetting himself, crying bitterly.

A clear memory: A sun-drenched Saturday morning, his father is holding his hand and they're walking together like soldiers, stopping on the sidewalk in front of the synagogue, listening to the prayer that's drifting out to the street. His father tells him that the name of the synagogue is "Meir," and one day, many years later, the day of his bar mitzvah, he will be called up to read from the Torah here and the women in the gallery will throw lots of candies onto the heads of the children and men below.

Another memory: He's jumping on the sidewalk, moving forward along the row of gray blocks with his legs spread, hopping ahead on one foot, his arms out to the sides like a scarecrow. His eyes skip with his feet to the next square, and he's careful not to look up from the row of blocks that stretches onward forever.

Still wondering at how his memory played its hiding games, the image of Mnemosyne, the goddess of memory, rose in his mind. Meir had given a lecture about her to his classmates, and the teacher had been impressed with how much knowledge he'd shown. At the end of the lecture, he passed around the children's book of Greek myths open to the page with a drawing of Mnemosyne surrounded by her nine babies, the nine muses, and the children were amazed at the sight of the square Hebrew letters.

Like someone who has found a treasure and wants to keep it for himself, Meir was in no hurry to share his new memories with his mother. He was afraid that speaking of them aloud would drive the images away. Because of his habit of keeping her out of his life, he never considered the possibility that his mother's life might also be in turmoil. Sometimes, the thought would cross his mind that he should call Arnie and tell him the news, but since they hadn't spoken for weeks, he decided to put off the conversation until he'd calmed down.

A week after he'd been told of his father's existence, he had an urge to hear his mother's version of things. He was troubled by the growing number of riddles posed by his fragmented memories, so he called and asked her if he could come over. Most of the important conversations they'd had since he left home at the age of eighteen had taken place on the phone. If he didn't have to meet her eyes, Meir could lie easily, tell her about classes he'd completed and grades he'd gotten, and she couldn't see the twitch of a grin on his lips. Whenever they were about to have a crucial conversation, she'd beg him to meet her, as if she suspected that twitch of a grin, and he would evade it with various excuses, insisting that they talk on the phone instead. Now that he'd suggested coming to her house, he was shocked to hear her refusal, spoken in a faint, hollow voice.

"You don't want me to come?"

"I already told you: not today."

"Why not?"

"Because I can't see you today, I just can't."

"I don't understand why."

"So you don't understand."

"Explain it to me."

"Not everything can be explained."

"What about tomorrow?" he persisted.

"I can't tomorrow either."

"Is it because I didn't stay to have lunch with you? I had an important meeting."

"I believe you."

"And I didn't call all week because I was confused and needed time to think quietly."

"I can understand that."

"So why are you punishing me?" he asked.

"I'm not punishing anyone. I just can't see you now."

"Why not? Did something new happen?"

"Yes."

"What?"

"I'll tell you when you come."

"When?"

"I'll let you know when."

*   *   *

She stayed holed up in her apartment for another three days, apparently swept up in her own memories, hardening her heart against his entreaties to let him come and see her, to hear what new thing had happened. He pictured the expression of profound sorrow on her face that matched her voice on the phone. Sometimes, he imagined her standing at the southern window of the guest room, watching the bustle of life below, her eyes drawn downtown to Seventeenth Street, to Stuyvesant Park, which she liked and where she used to go during lunch breaks to scatter crumbs for the pigeons. Sometimes he imagined her standing in the bedroom, next to the western window, looking down at Twenty-third Street where it crossed Third Avenue, and at the more distant intersection with Lexington Avenue, where Baruch College stood, the school her brother had attended in his youth, and rising on the right, the golden dome at the top of the insurance building that had been the inspiration for Meir's first story, written when he was ten. From there, she looked further, at the intersections of Madison, Broadway, and Fifth, and of Sixth Avenue, where the street sign on the corner read "Avenue of the Americas," a sign that made Meir's heart leap. Then she focused on the place furthest away, where, on a clear day, you could see the river beyond the edge of the city, and maybe the sight would move her the way it had moved her when they'd both stood at the window for the first time, even before they'd gone to live there, when she had pointed out the sights they would soon see every day from the windows of their new home. That was when he had seen the golden dome for the first time, glittering in the sun.

On the fourth day, she called him early in the morning and invited him over. And he, as excited as a thwarted lover whose darling suddenly warms to him, had an attack of generosity and arrived at her doorstep the very same morning with a box of chocolates and a large bouquet of flowers.

Through the crack in the door, he could see her face was haggard and gloomy, sadness deepening the lines from her nose to her chin. There were dark crescents under her eyes and she peered at him suspiciously, as if she might change her mind and slam the door in his face. And then, as if reconsidering, she turned around, and he could see her hair gathered messily at the back of her neck with numerous hairpins. He followed her inside and gave her the box of chocolates and the bouquet of flowers, and she took them silently and pointed to the armchair, as if this were his first visit to her home. He studied her as she put the stems, one by one, into a vase and then when she made them both coffee and placed the sugar bowl, a pitcher of milk, and a box of paper napkins on a tray. Something about her movements was different, suggesting that her thoughts were far from her hands as they slowly groped around in the back of the cabinet again and again, searching for the napkins that were already on the tray.

Finally, they sat in silence behind their coffee mugs. They were unused to speaking face to face and shot quick glances at one another, glances that revealed how aware each was of the other's distress.

"Did they let you into the parking lot?" she asked.

"Yes. The Polish guy's okay. The black guy's the one who makes problems."

She was quiet for a while, as if she were thinking about the black guy and the Polish guy, and defeated, finally said, "We have to talk, Meir," seeming to confirm that against her will, the time had come to do something painful and there was no avoiding it.

"Maybe I should've talked to you a long time ago, I don't know, maybe I should've done it right after you came from Tel Aviv so that you'd know everything from the beginning. But I didn't have the courage. I was afraid that you were too young, that you wouldn't understand, that you'd react badly. There are things that, if you don't say them right away, you never find the right time to say them. Arnie told me to go with my intuition, so I decided not to bring it up, and the longer I postponed the conversation with you and as more years passed, the harder it was to talk, because you were starting to get used to life here, after so many problems, and I was afraid that the memories would just upset you. But maybe that was a big mistake."

She seemed terribly tired, exhausted from twenty-three years of inner conflict, and it suddenly occurred to Meir that she'd been a very young woman then; he calculated quickly: she was twenty-three when he was born, thirty when he came to the United States, and she lost her baby daughter before she turned thirty-one.

Meir looked at her with new eyes, spellbound. If she had spoken to him like this years ago, his life would have been different, the malignant sense of loneliness that had gnawed at him all those years might have been less. If he had seen that concern, that pain on her face, the anger he harbored toward her might have dissolved, and they might have had a normal relationship, like in his uncle Simon's family. Instead, there was always a distance between them, disguised as politeness, and he was always well-mannered in front of his grandfather's friends, in front of the few friends his mother had, and in front of strangers.

"Why did you decide to tell me now?"

"I didn't decide. He did."

"Who?"

"Your father."

The two words stood in the air between them for a while, as if they both had to get used to the new phrase.

"Why now, of all times?"

"Because he's very ill."

Meir was silent, aware of a sense of joy that had been kindled in him. He managed to suppress his smile, but he couldn't stifle the coldhearted but exciting thought that illness, especially a very serious illness, would be a major dramatic addition to the story he was going to write.

"And why wasn't I allowed to know that he was alive when he was healthy?"

"I tried to explain that to you before, Meir."

"You thought I'd react badly," he quoted her, unintentionally sounding disdainful.

"Maybe I made a mistake. I already said that, too."

"What was it? Were you afraid I'd want to go back to Israel to live with him?"

"No. I wasn't afraid of that."

"Then why?"

"I explained that to you before."

"But I still don't understand."

"I guess not everything is understandable."

He was quiet, gathering his strength for the next round.

"If you're not a widow, then are you still his wife? Are you two still married?"

"I suppose that, formally, I'm still his wife."

"That means he didn't remarry." What am I asking? he wondered. Am I asking whether the small family circle had suddenly grown and I have siblings? A stepmother? Step-grandparents?

"No, he didn't get married."

"And what does he expect me to do now that I know he's alive and ill?" He rebelled against the responsibility thrust on him, a responsibility he'd never felt toward his mother.

"Ask him yourself. He's planning to come here."

"Where?"

"Here. To New York."

"To visit? As sick as he is?"

"He's very sick and in a wheelchair, but that's what he wants. Arnie'll look after him, take him to his surgeon friend in the hospital in Boston."

Meir choked. A husband meeting his wife's lover, maybe even a husband whose wife's lover is present while he's being operated on and then takes care of him—that's a story full of great emotion: Will he recover from the surgery, how will the relationship between his parents develop, and the relationships between Arnie and his mother, between his father and Arnie? If he doesn't recover or even dies on the operating table, how will that affect his mother's relationship to Arnie? And how would the encounter between father and son go? That alone was worth sixty or seventy pages.

"Why is he in a wheelchair?"

"He has a weak leg, after a few operations."

"And where is he thinking of staying?"

"He'll go into the hospital in Boston, but I assume that he'll live here for a few days before and a few days after."

"And you'll be able to take care of him? You'll be able to lift him?"

"He doesn't have to be lifted. He can stand. The other leg is fine. He just tires easily."

"Okay," Meir said, shrugging his shoulders. But under his forcibly restrained façade, his mind was spinning with all the intriguing possibilities that were opening up. Like for example, the moment the man and woman meet again after such a long separation: He's limping toward the building, looking for her name on the small bronze plaques, announcing his arrival on the intercom. She tells him what floor she's on and stands at the door of her apartment waiting for the elevator to bring him up to her—

The elevator door opens and his father's wheelchair takes him into the corridor. His mother is unable to choke off a cry of surprise. The picture of the beautiful man she left behind in Tel Aviv shatters before her eyes and, stunned by the poignant sight of the stranger, she extends her hand to him politely—

The elevator door opens. His father, as handsome as the man in the pictures, takes a step toward her and they fall into each other's arms—

The elevator door opens and his father is rooted to the spot at the sight of the woman standing in front of the elevator, the serene woman with the beautiful hair, and she steps into the elevator, extending her hand to him in an aristocratic, supremely gracious gesture, as if declaring that there is nothing personal in all this: this is how guests are greeted here—

The elevator door opens and they stand opposite each other like statues until the elevator door closes and takes him to the top floor, leaving her helpless in front of the lighted display of numbers, her finger pressing the button until the elevator stops again on the twenty-third floor, the door opens, he emerges and they burst into laughter—

His injured leg betrays him and he collapses onto the floor, hurt, and she kneels at his side, alarmed—

He's standing at the door to the apartment looking around at the elegant rooms—

His eyes linger on the flowers—

He bursts into tears and shaken, she hurries to call Arnie—

He bursts into tears and she hugs him tightly, soothing him—

They're sitting at the table like two polite strangers—

She's suggesting that he put his things in Meir's room.

"He's staying in *my* room?"

"I thought . . ." she said, flinching at his cry.

"Without asking me?"

"Asking you? I didn't think you still considered it your room. You have a whole house of your own."

"Some of my things are still here."

"I don't think he'll pry."

Then his father would stand at the western window in exactly the same place where nine-year-old Meir had stood, where Meir had cried inconsolably at the view of the urban landscape—never imagining that one day, he would fall in love with that landscape—longing for the grove that surrounded his grandfather's house in Connecticut and never imagining that one day, his father would stand in that same place and look out at the same bustling streets of New York. And when he'd had his fill of looking at the streets, his father would start walking around the room and stop to look at the old tape recorder, Arnie's first gift to Meir, at the photograph of the trophy from the last baseball tournament Meir had played in, at the commendation for his community work with the immigrant Latino children at school, at the invitation to the production of *The Wizard of Oz* put on by the drama club in Meir's senior year of high school, at the picture of him being awarded second prize in a short story contest for teenagers—milestones in his son's life that were previously unknown to him. And maybe his eyes would fall on the tattered, faithful book, *Greek Myths for Children*, that had wandered with Meir from the time he was a child, and maybe he'd pull the book out of the row of new-looking volumes and run his fingers over the illustrations: Athena bursting from Zeus' forehead; Zeus disguised as a swan, making love to Leda, the wife of the King of Sparta; Pegasus, the winged horse, emerging from Medusa's slit throat; Pan, god of the forests, dancing among the trees on his goat's legs; the winged sandals the gods gave to Perseus.

"I'll take everything out before he comes."

"I don't think that's really necessary."

"I don't want him to touch any of my things. When's he planning to arrive?"

"He has to get a visa, reserve a flight, and collect all the medical documents."

And maybe his father would continue his journey around the room, stopping in front of the face of Eleanor, the girl created from his seed in Tel Aviv, but who'd been born and died far away from him. She was about six months old in the picture, a few days before she died, sitting in her carriage, completely engrossed in an ice cream cone bought in the Carvel ice cream store shown in the background, the store with the pink awning, located on the ground floor of the building. He might stand for a while in front of the daughter he'd never met, searching for his own features in the child's intent face. Then he'd unpack and put his clothes in the closet that held his son's school and sports uniforms, and sit on the rocking chair his son had sat on (scratching his knees until they bled, during the first few years), and at night, the father would lie in the bed where his son had dreamed and masturbated for years, until he'd left the house at the age of eighteen.

His mother, as blind to him as always, didn't see the glitter in Meir's eyes and said in a pensive voice, "I was always curious about what you remembered from Tel Aviv."

"But you never asked."

"To protect you," she said, her eyes growing moist, and he almost blurted out: And not to protect yourself?

Instead, he said seriously, "I remember very little. Many of the things in the photographs you gave me look familiar, but I haven't even had time to go through them all. My head fills up with memories, with scenes, most of them blurred. I'm not always sure they're even mine. Maybe I saw them in a movie, maybe someone once told me something like that."

"But Meir," she said, "back then, when you came here, you talked a little . . . about your friends, about the kids in the neighborhood, about Jerusalem. Your memories were full of details."

"They must have been wiped away right after that."

"That seems impossible."

"But that's what happened."

Here it is, within my grasp, he thought, this was the place that held the secrets, the place that had been locked to him under the bloodstain. And now, he was standing on its threshold.

At that moment, he was surprised to recognize the aroma of garlic and onion: it was the same aroma that wafted out of the neighbors' kitchen window in Tel Aviv and then, carried on a sea breeze, spread over the street and the boulevard. All at once he remembered the boulevard: the sprawling tops of the trees (whose trunks were so thick and with so many exposed roots coiled around them that they looked like giant balls of wool), the ground always shaded, and at the end of the boulevard an imposing concrete building, the Mann Auditorium, with tall palm trees lined up like a row of soldiers in front of it.

"I talked about Jerusalem?" he asked.

"You were very excited about the trips to Jerusalem."

"I was in Jerusalem?" he asked, surprised.

"Of course you were. When we lived in Israel, we used to go to Jerusalem every summer."

"With me?"

"Of course with you. We took you everywhere."

He felt a surge of bitterness. The casual remark—maybe spoken innocently, maybe not—the façade of normalcy she was trying to impose angered him; the attempt to deceive him was so obvious, it was insulting. Suddenly now, after so many years of never mentioning even the smallest detail about his father, she was painting a picture of familial happiness: "We took you everywhere."

"Who took me?"

"Your father and I, of course."

"What's so 'of course' about it?"

"I understand," she stated, "you're angry at me for not telling you about him, but as I explained, for the first few years, we decided not to mention him because we thought it would be easier for you to start a new life here. And there were hard times, I'm sure you remember. Maybe it was a mistake not to tell you what really happened, I don't know. I thought that if you wanted to know, you'd ask. But you never did."

"I forgot him completely," Meir said, suddenly sorrowful.

"Maybe it was right for you to forget," she said, gently.

"And what about you? Did you forget him, too?"

"No," she said, "I didn't forget, and you're one of the reasons for that. The older you get, the more you resemble him. I'm not the only one who sees it. Everyone does."

"Who's 'everyone'?" Did she think she could mislead him into forgetting that his life had been derailed abruptly and that "everyone" was now split between the people who knew *them* and the people who knew *him*?

"Anyone who sees photos of him says it," she said, perhaps alluding to the long limbs posed so nonchalantly, the dark hair falling to the side, the wide forehead. "You know, whenever you went through a crisis in college—and there were some before college, too—I was sure that your mental state had something to do with that first period, with the fact that you never talked about what happened, that you never asked." Her voice was suddenly a whisper that hinted at her frailness, and though he clearly heard her waiting for him to deny her words, he chose not to say anything.

She blinked rapidly, then spoke with effort. "You said on the phone that you're starting to remember now and that you have a lot of questions."

"Yes."

"So you can start," she said, moving her hand unconsciously to her face as if shielding herself, and when he remained silent, she lowered the shield slightly and said, "You can ask."

As confused as a child standing in front of a huge selection of candy, who can only take one, he quickly organized the muddle of questions in his mind.

"Maybe we'll start at home," he said. "What did it look like outside, what did it look like inside? Remind me."

"The house was an old house on a street called HaNevi'im," she began. As she spoke, Meir felt an entire world that had always existed inside him was being revealed, an archeological find appearing under the gentle probings of the digger's brush. She spoke slowly, occasionally mixing Hebrew words into her speech, and his dormant feelings from that time seemed to be awakening, aroused by the force of her voice.

**The whitewashed brick wall built during one of the wars to protect the entrance from bombs, the wide entranceway with one corner filled with bicycles and baby carriages, the elongated windows at every turn of the staircase, the wooden door with its flimsy lock that sometimes opened when you shoved it with your foot, the ochre diamond shapes in the apartment floor, the desk always covered with piles of books threatening to topple, the old kitchen with its ancient streaks of dust ingrained in the cracks at the bottom of the sink and the edges of the marble counter and the ceramic tiles, the foreboding dimness that never lessened, not even in the middle of summer, the dimness that darkened the rooms with a constant pre-rain feeling and turned blue to black and red to crimson, the plants that refused to thrive no matter how hard his mother tried, so that finally she gave up on her dream of filling the kitchen balcony with countless colorful flowers so it would be like her parents' garden in Connecticut, which she showed him a picture of, and on Saturdays, when she wasn't rushing off to the law office where**

**she worked, she would go out to the backyard, wearing rubber boots, her hair gathered at the back of her neck, and become completely involved in cultivating the garden beds far from the wall, where the sun lingered until afternoon.**

"And I liked the house?" he asked, suddenly picturing himself standing at the window like an anxious guard on duty. Where were his parents, maybe they wouldn't come, maybe they'd leave him there alone and disappear, maybe they'd forget where the house was, maybe they'd find a different place and a different boy.

"Yes. I think you liked the house very much. And so did your father and I."

"What kind of child was I?"

"A child with imagination," she said after a pause.

A child who lied, he said to himself, at first making up lies to survive, then out of boredom, and finally out of habit. He didn't lie maliciously, but he understood very well how much damage lying could cause. And his habit of lying, wide-eyed with put-on innocence, persisted when he came to America.

"You were a quiet boy, sweet, sometimes a little mischievous. You usually looked as if you were busy thinking deep thoughts. I'd say, a serious boy."

The face of the boy standing at the window became clear.

An anxious, worried boy, quick to cry—he said to himself in a moment of insight—a constantly tense boy, waiting for disaster despite his father's declarations of love, which made him wonder whether his father loved him as much as writing poetry, and despite his mother's declarations of love, spoken in English, the language in which she herself had heard declarations of love as a child but in which, for him, the words separated from their meaning and became a curtain of empty syllables that dulled his awareness.

**Late every afternoon, when the door opened and his mother came home from work, Meir—in an act as regular as a ritual—**

would hurry to the bathroom, whose window looked out onto the back balcony, and sit, fully clothed, on the toilet. From there, he could hear his parents' voices coming from the kitchen, whose door opened onto the same balcony, and he would eavesdrop on their conversation, believing that this time, he would find out their malicious plans for him, the ways they were plotting against him. Also when he was in his parents' bed, he thought he was close to discovering something. Whenever he woke up, he listened furtively to their whispered conversations. Maybe they were planning to send him away like Hansel and Gretel were sent away, and he didn't even have a sister to share his fear with.

Everything he did—Meir suddenly realized from the distance of time—everything he did, including his nocturnal walks to his parents' bed and his eavesdropping from the bathroom—was aimed at uncovering a secret he was sure existed. He suddenly remembered himself clearly, sitting on the toilet, his body constricted, his hands torturing the plastic man his ill grandfather had sent him from America, swiveling its hinged joints until it turned into a beetle. His parents' quarreling voices fueled his anxiety, and in his panic, he put together facts that boys his age couldn't even imagine: if they don't pay the rent, they'll have to leave. Will they find another apartment? And if not, what will happen to him? His mother is planning to go to America. Will she come back? And if she doesn't, what will happen to him? Will she take him with her? And what about his father? His father doesn't want her to go, but she insists. Will his father join her? And if so, what will happen to him? She promises to send money for the rent, and the office owes her a month's salary anyway. But if she doesn't send money, where will they live? Every few days, he brought himself up to date on the details his parents never imagined he was secretly collecting: the lease is almost up; his father still hasn't received the money for an article Meir himself had been sent to deliver to the man in the small room on the third floor of the *Davar* news-

**paper office—he'd gotten a sour candy for making the delivery; his mother's father is very ill and might die soon; his uncle Solomon sends telegrams from Connecticut, urging his mother to come to see their father. Something about his mother's condition occasionally causes an argument to flare up. Is she ill, like her father, and will she die soon, too? Then what will happen to him? His father claims that she shouldn't travel to America in her condition; she replies that her condition is not a disease and the last time she was in this condition, she worked until the last minute. At night, Meir would go over these words in his mind until he fell asleep, exhausted from so much thinking. And in the morning, he'd find himself in his parents' bed.**

"Do you remember your father and me together?" she asked.

"When you were in the kitchen, I used to listen to you from the bathroom."

"So you do remember."

"I'm not clear about how, but I know things, all kinds of small details."

"What did you hear from the bathroom?"

"The yelling. You fought all the time."

"And that's what you remember?" she asked sorrowfully, peering into the bottom of her coffee mug, her face somber, a fortuneteller reading bad signs.

**The contentious voices from the kitchen were so different from the pleasant languidness of his parents' bed. He suddenly remembered his father's arm drawing an arc in the air as it moved toward the gold-kindled hair. The stroking fingers lingered on the hair and then the hand slid onto the blanket or under it, ignoring Meir, who was so crushed between them that he almost choked.**

"You don't remember our going out together? For instance, for ice cream? We went to Whitman's for ice cream very often, the place on the big street called Allenby that had a lot of stores," she said, pouring coffee into her empty mug. "They had a few flavors there, but you only liked vanilla."

**Even during the winter months, when eating ice cream wasn't allowed, he could taste the vanilla ice cream they sold in Whitman's on Allenby Street. He and his parents used to go there together, a lovely picture of familial bliss. The minute they left the apartment, the bickering was replaced by contentment and Meir was flooded with a sense of calm that he felt in the presence of his parents only when they were out of the house. Then he was handed the ice cream cone, and he'd finish it off even before they reached the sidewalk. His mother would give him a cloth handkerchief so he could wipe the sticky smears off his hands, which he did while covetously eyeing his parents' cones. His father would give in and offer him a spoonful, but his mother would shield her ice cream with her hand like a child and say, "I told you not to eat so fast."**

**His parents would walk along the street, their arms around each other's waists, their heads touching, like young comrades, and he thought they sometimes kissed.**

**But a short time after they were back home, Meir heard them become angry with one another all over again.**

"I also remember that you used to kiss in the street," he said, thrilled by the clarity of the scene that rose in his memory.

"You mean you saw?" his mother asked, and he thought he saw a flush blossom on her cheeks. She took a sip of her coffee, pausing as if to clarify the matter for herself. "So there *was* love there," she said, almost in surprise.

"You shouldn't trust a six-year-old boy's memory too much," he said cruelly, and he saw her face darken. Why did he insist on withholding a good memory from her?

"But we can trust a thirty-year-old woman's memory," she said, recovering immediately.

"So there was love, so what?" he said. His head jutted forward as he spewed out the words: "It was short and it ended badly."

"That doesn't change the fact that for a while, there was love," she said, standing her ground.

"There were mostly other things," he said, seeing a new scene of his mother sitting at her desk in the office.

"What things?"

"If you have such fond memories, maybe I shouldn't ruin the picture for you," he said, watching the expression of the woman sitting at the desk.

"Tell me," she said. "Let's hear some other things you remember."

"There was suspicion, there was anger, there were secrets," he said, reading the expression of the woman in his imagination.

"Whose secrets?"

"You both had secrets," he replied, suddenly remembering the snapshot of Arnie she kept in her desk drawer.

**They kept their secrets from each other, but they shared them with him, instilling a sense of betrayal in Meir from the time he was a young boy and intensifying his fear of the moment they would reveal their secrets to one another. His mother's secrets were in her locked desk drawer in the law office: photographs, some in nice frames, letters with beautiful stamps from America, and many small, ornate gifts—all neatly arranged.**

**Sometimes, on the days his father was late and he remained alone after the other children had been picked up, he heard the annoyed kindergarten teacher calling his mother on the phone. He'd wait for his mother, hanging on the gate, until he saw her cross the street in a dangerous run. On the way to her office, she held his hand in a tight grip that felt good, and she wouldn't drop it until she had to pay the kiosk owner for the take-out sandwich she bought for him instead of a real lunch. Then she'd hold his hand again until they went into her office, where she'd clear away the piles of papers and make a place for**

him at the edge of her desk. Then she'd put the sandwich down in front of him next to a cup of tea she made. When he finished eating, she'd replace the plate with blank paper and colored pencils. When he got bored, she let him look in her drawer. In the right-hand corner was a pile of pictures held together with a rubber band, pictures she took with her when she went to America to say goodbye to her father. Meir had spent a lot of time looking at them, even after he went to live in America: some of the photos were from her childhood, a different hairstyle in each one, but her face lit up by the same smile that moved from one shot to the other. He loved the pictures of her as girl—in one, standing with her legs apart, sandals sunk into the mud of the recently watered back garden, wearing a dress with a sailor collar; and in another, with her hair wet, wearing a red bathing suit. In other pictures, she was with classmates, and in most of them, there was a mischievous boy standing behind her, holding his index finger and pinkie over her head like horns. For a long time, she let Meir believe that the boy was her brother, Solomon, but finally she gave in and told him that the boy was Arnie, her childhood boyfriend. Without her saying so, but maybe because he saw the gentle way she gathered the pile of photographs and put them in her drawer, Meir knew that he wasn't supposed to tell his father about Arnie and the drawer of secrets, because if he did, the yelling would start again in the kitchen.

The first time he had picked up Arnie's picture, his mother had snatched the whole bundle away from him, but right away she calmed down and seemed pleased that she'd found someone to share her secret with. Later, she would willingly share with him, open her drawer and show him with a hint of pride: here she's sitting at the same desk with Arnie in class; here she's with Arnie on the school swimming team; here she's playing a duet on the piano with Arnie; here, she and Arnie are leaning against a road sign on the way to Salem, the city of witches; here's a gold necklace Arnie sent her for her birthday; here's a jewelry box; here's a heart-shaped key chain; here's a framed photograph of them together. Sometimes, when Meir was angry at her, his need for revenge was so strong that he came close to telling his father her secret, but he always stopped himself, satisfying the need with the knowledge that his father had a secret too: their regular visits to his relative.

"What secrets did I have?" she asked.

"Arnie's letters, the picture of Arnie."

"Those weren't secrets."

"So why didn't you keep them in the house? Why did you leave them in the office, locked in a drawer?"

She shrugged like a rebellious child, and her voice also sounded childish when she asked, "And what secrets did he have?"

Meir hesitated, as if it were still possible to ruin their relationship or save it, becoming in an instant that child maneuvering his way between his parents.

"There were women?" she asked, unable to hide the insult under her pretense.

"There were no women then. At least I didn't know about women. There was only . . . Look, all of a sudden I remember his name: Berl. His name was Berl."

"You remember Berl?" she asked, astonished.

Most of his Tel Aviv memories were shrouded in darkness, but the image of Berl, his voice, and his screams as he fled from the Nazis were kept in a separate compartment, illuminated, as if Meir had been ordered, from the time he was a young child, to inscribe the man in his memory and save him from oblivion. He also remembered their first meeting very clearly. One afternoon, walking down the street with his father, just as they passed the window of a lingerie store, Meir suddenly saw an old man dressed like a beggar collapse onto the sidewalk a few steps away from them. His father immediately dropped his son's hand, hurried to the man and knelt beside him. Berl's face and the sound of his voice had been etched in his mind for all those years, but his name had vanished from his memory.

"Yes, I remember him and his cellar and how he fell down in the middle of the street . . . . He was Father's brother-in-law."

"Brother-in-law? He was no brother-in-law. He wasn't even a member of the family."

*Exterior. A summer day in 1965. A street in Tel Aviv.*

> Berl (an old man reaching out and touching
> the head of a young man bending over him):
> Aharon?

> Aharon (the young man):
> Berl?

(Aharon helps Berl to his feet, and they cry and embrace. Passersby stop and gather around, and some of them wipe away a tear. Aharon looks for his son and gestures with his head for the boy to follow him. He takes the old man to the nearby bus stop and sits him down on the bench. The old man strokes Aharon's face. They speak Yiddish to each other. The boy, although he doesn't speak the language, understands what's being said.)

> Berl:
> Aharon, I thought that you . . . with all the others . . . I didn't know you were alive.

> Aharon:
> I didn't know you were alive either . . . . Where do you live, Berl?

> Berl:
> Here, in Tel Aviv. On Shlomo HaMelech Street

in Tel Aviv. And are there . . . Maybe you know
if anyone else from our family is alive?

Aharon:

My mother's family is in Jerusalem from before the war.
And there's my father's cousin, Yakov—

Berl:

Yakov, Miriam's husband?

Aharon:

Yes, but Miriam . . . There's a new wife now, Pnina.

Berl (sadly):

And that's it?

Aharon (sadly):

Yes . . .

Berl (happily):

But you're alive, what's important is that you're alive.
And who's this? Your son?

Aharon:

Yes.

(The old man reaches out to the boy. The boy recoils.
The old man feels the boy's face and looks at him.)

Berl:

He looks a little like my Issachar, doesn't he?

Aharon:

I don't know . . .

Berl (shouting):

Sure he does. And no wonder. Family! Tell me, Aharon.
You and your father ran away to Russia, right? They
didn't catch you at the border?

Aharon (glancing quickly
at Meir and seeing his alarm):
You know what, Berl? This isn't a good place to talk.
Come home with us and we'll talk quietly. There's a lot
to talk about.

Berl:
You come to my place first. (To Meir) You like
chocolate, right?

"Why do you say he wasn't family?"

"They used to adopt families for themselves, those people who went through the war in Europe. Every classmate and every neighbor became close family, nothing less than a brother-in-law."

"He really was family," Meir said, quick to play the role imposed on him as a child.

"That's what *he* said," she replied, shrugging.

**From where he was, sitting on the toilet, Meir heard them that evening, arguing more loudly than usual. His father was babbling excitedly, trying in vain to imbue his wife with the excitement he felt, but her coldness was unshakeable, and she answered him mostly in English. Even before she met Berl, she wanted no part of this sudden relative. Over and over again, she objected in an accusing voice, saying that if this man was so close, why hadn't Aharon mentioned him before, implying he'd made up the story of Berl to deceive her. His father explained that all these years, he'd been sure Berl hadn't survived the camps, and he raised his voice—ignoring all her interjections—and insisted that he was a very close relative who had survived. Berl had been married to his older sister, who died a few months before the war broke out, and his two small children had died of disease during the first year of the war. Now Berl was about sixty years old, all alone, and he'd invited them to his house on Shlomo HaMelech Street. His mother announced that she wouldn't go. His father pleaded.**

"I promised him," he said, his voice shaking.

"So what."

Berl, wearing a white shirt, his combed, wet hair plastered to his scalp, was waiting for them at the door to the house on Shlomo HaMelech Street, and from the way his back arched against the fence, he had clearly been standing there for a long time. When he saw them, he reached out for Meir's father with open arms and was about to swallow up his mother in his embrace, too, but she quickly stretched out an arm to keep him at a distance. Berl, not the slightest bit offended, hugged the hand that was pushing him away and said excitedly, "Come in, come in. I was starting to think that you forgot."

Berl took the hand of his young brother-in-law, who was a head taller than he, and led him along as if he were a child. He walked toward the backyard, looking back every once in a while to see the woman in her light-colored dress trailing behind them. She walked gingerly along the dirt path, holding the hem of her dress in one hand and her son's hand in the other, an expression of disgust on her face. On the steps leading down to the cellar, she stopped at the sight of Berl and her husband, now busy moving a tub across the floor in the depths of the cellar.

"Come here, Meir," she called to him after he'd dropped her hand, run down the steps, and stood in front of the secret cave that extended back deep inside the room.

She raised her voice again, and when Meir didn't respond, she tiptoed into the cellar, grabbed his arm and pulled him out of there, over his objections. At the door, she shouted in English, "I'm taking the boy," and was already sailing toward the street, dragging Meir behind her, squirming and crying.

Hurt and angry, Meir rejected her offer of ice cream and at home went straight to his room. After he stopped crying, he still fumed, refusing to listen to her explanations about the terrible diseases lying in wait for children in a contaminated place like that, where rats scurry around in the corners. When he heard the front door slam shut, he slipped into the bathroom.

His father berated her furiously for leaving without a word of goodbye and for taking the boy with her, leaving Berl in tears because he'd bought Meir so much chocolate and had been so excited about their coming that he hadn't slept the whole night.

His mother protested vehemently, as if they'd tried to set a trap for her, telling her about an apartment on Shlomo HaMelech Street, where people lived, and then taking her—and even worse, her little boy—to an apartment that wasn't meant for people, but looked like a cellar from the Holocaust, full of rats and disease.

That night, his father slipped into his room just as Meir was about to fall asleep, shoved a small package under his pillow— a present from Berl—and whispered in his ear that tomorrow, after kindergarten, they'd go to visit him. Meir ate some chocolate and looked at the moon smiling its enigmatic smile at him, and didn't know whether he was really looking at the moon and eating chocolate or only dreaming that he was looking at the moon and eating chocolate.

"So he used to take you to that Holocaust cellar without telling me?"

"Yes."

"And you never got bitten by a rat?"

"No."

"And it didn't turn your stomach?"

"No. I liked going there."

"You liked going there? A dark cellar full of garbage, with wet walls and a terrible stench."

"In the eyes of the beholder, I guess. For me, it was a cave out of a fairy tale, Ali Baba's cave."

The cellar, it turned out, became a crawl space, about half of a person's height, and continued to the foundation walls. There, where even Meir had to crouch, was where Berl hid his treasures: broken chairs, car tires, frying pans without handles and dented pots, women's clothes, scraps of cloth, bottles of all sizes and shapes, laundry lines, plastic bags, metal pipes, ragged pillows, huge spools of electric wire, torn slippers. Meir used to forage around among those treasures while his father and Berl talked together in Yiddish. Protected in the depths of the cellar, as if he were invisible, he'd see Berl burst into tears and his father hug him and soothe him in his embrace the way he soothed his son.

"I loved Berl and I loved his cellar."

"I realize now that I didn't know what you really loved then," his mother said sorrowfully. She fell silent for a moment and then, her jealousy aroused, said, "So you two had a whole life without me."

"Right."

"And after I left, you didn't have to hide anything anymore."

"Hide Berl?"

"Berl and the whole world. And after I left . . ." she said, her voice dropping, "Do you even remember that I went?"

One night, Meir had a dream. His mother was bending over him, wearing an unfamiliar outfit, giving off a scent he didn't recognize. Her mouth was open above him, as if she were about to devour him, and he shrank when she kissed him in places he'd never been kissed before: at the base of his neck, under his chin, on both his closed eyes. Then her mouth opened wider and sucked him in, and he slid between her teeth, to the side of her tongue, into her throat, and was swept down along her vocal chords into her hot stomach, where he landed gently on the bottom of it, as if on a mattress.

In the morning, he found his father bending over him exactly where his mother had stood, as if they'd changed places and now it was his father's turn to devour him. He heard his father say, "Good morning, Meir. It's time to get up. You didn't sleep last night because of your mother, so I let you sleep another hour, but you have to get up now."

That's how he learned that his mother had left at three in the morning and that his dream hadn't been all a dream.

"You didn't come back like you promised," he said, hurling that child's pain at her, ignoring her face, softening now with the memory of the parting.

"I couldn't come back," she explained slowly to the child in words he could understand. "I was pregnant then and the doctor made me stay in bed until I gave birth. I wasn't allowed to move."

"You left me alone with him."

"He always took care of you. You both got along very well without me, didn't you? Even when I was there, he was with you often. He was the one who went with you to buy your notebooks for the first grade, you must remember that."

They bought the schoolbag, notebooks, stickers, pencil, eraser, ruler, pencil case, and book covers in the store on Nahalat Benyamin Street, where all the books and objects, even the new ones, were layered with dust. When his mother came home from the office in the early evening, the notebooks were already covered and displayed on the table, the name MEIR ROSINBERG gleaming on the stickers. She stood at the table for a minute, looking at the neatly arranged notebooks and row of writing implements, as if she only now realized that her little boy was going from the kindergarten on Netzach Israel Street, from which they used to summon her urgently when his father was late, to the school where—and this she didn't know—he would barely finish out the first term.

On the morning of the first day of school, his father took him to the gate. He was waiting there at the end of the day, when the boy walked toward him, exhausted from four hours of sitting in a chair, and fell into his arms, sobbing. The three of them celebrated that day with Whitman's ice cream again. For the next few days, his mother was busy finishing up her work in the office, getting ready for her trip, packing up the large, new suitcase that eventually blocked the hallway to the kitchen.

"He took care of me okay."

"But when you got here, remember, you were a little like a wild boy. Your table manners, personal hygiene. . . . And I blamed myself for leaving you that way with a man I thought was responsible, but obviously was not. I had to go, I hope that at least now you understand that. I had to say goodbye to Grandpa because I missed the chance to say goodbye to Grandma."

"So you said."

"Grandpa was very ill."

"I know."

"Did you get to school on time every day? Do you even remember school?"

"I remember a green gate."

For the first few days, his father would take him to the school gate and come to pick him up when he was finished with his work. Sometimes, he finished his work a long time after the school day was over, and Meir would wait next to the gate, playing with a dog that came to eat the leftover food the children saved for it, or, when the dog didn't come, he'd study the decorations on the gate, counting aloud over and over again the petals of the flowers, the circles and triangles. In the afternoon, he'd play in the yard with other children, maybe the religious neighbor's children, and sometimes—the image of a boy with darting eyes popped into his mind—sometimes, his only friend would come to his house. They'd clear a space on the desk and do their homework together and examine the shell collection with interest. Sometimes, Meir would go to his friend's house—he couldn't remember his name now—but they never managed to do their homework there because his friend's baby brother would come over every once in a while and tear pages out of their notebooks, and the friend would smack the brother in the head. Then his mother would send the boy and his guest outside to sit on the front steps.

"So why do you say you don't remember? Look, you remember all these small details."

"I remember while I'm talking, but I'm not completely sure how much of it I actually remember and how much I'm imagining."

"You really did have a shell collection," she said, then after a moment of silence, she added hesitantly, "And apart from school, how was it after I left?"

As soon as he heard his mother's footsteps entering the house, announcing that she was home from work, Meir would feel depressed, filled with a yearning that gradually seeped into the rest of the day. After her first letter came, he went to the mailbox a few times a day, would stick his fingers into the slit and sometimes pull out a postcard or a blue envelope and run back into the house, waving it over his head, looking for his father to read what it said. Later, he would beg his father to read the letter over and over again until both of them knew it by heart, the part written in Hebrew that was full of spelling mistakes and the few lines written in English. His mother wrote again and again that she dreamed about them at night, and Meir, as if wanting to communicate with her in a new language, began dreaming about her, too, seeing her always busy with things that had nothing to do with him: filing letters in a law office, browsing through American magazines, hoeing and pruning and turning over soil in the backyard flower beds.

He felt her absence most strongly on Saturdays, the day when all three of them used to go out to visit friends or stroll on the beach. His white shirt, his special Sabbath shirt, fell off its hanger one day and was finally found on the closet floor, crushed under a shoebox. Annoyed, his father straightened the

sheet on his bed and started ironing the shirt on it, then left the
iron on the collar too long and scorched the edges. A long while
later, after Meir's tears had been wiped away and he'd been
promised a new shirt, they went out and walked toward the sea:
he in the everyday shirt he wore to school, and his father, more
elegant than usual, in a nice suit and with a silk scarf around
his neck.

Near Pnina and Yakov's house, his father began to walk more
quickly, also hurrying past the park where they sometimes met
his friends and their parents, and when Meir asked why they
weren't going into the park, his father replied that he felt
uncomfortable about them seeing Meir in his school shirt. He
walked briskly toward Dizengoff Street, where there were many
outdoor cafés, and slowed down in front of the Kassit, the café
frequented by poets.

"We were waiting for you to come back."

"Who's 'we'?" she asked, avoiding his eyes.

A short time after his mother left, it seemed to Meir that his
father began to drift away, too. Occasionally, his father would be
late waking him up in the morning, and sometimes he'd forget
his promises. Meir was waiting longer at the gate after school.
Often, he would stop talking in the middle of a sentence, surprised and hurt to see his father completely immersed in
thought, not listening to him at all. The first few nights, Meir
found himself in his parents' bed, as usual, but his father
insisted on ending that bad habit and threatened to punish
him by locking the door if he didn't stop his nocturnal wandering. Frightened at the sight of his father's steely eyes, Meir
burst into tears, and his father went back to being his father
and hugged him with a warmth that was filled with remorse.
But the bedroom door was locked that night. In the mornings
that followed Meir would wake up in his own bed. It was one
day during lunch recess at school that he suddenly began to

suspect that someone was with his father behind the locked door. There were little signs, and his ability to recognize them sharpened with time: in the bathroom, a reddish hair snaking along one side of sink; a cigarette holder hidden under the edge of an ashtray; a pair of the fancy goblets kept in a separate cabinet for special occasions suddenly sitting on the counter in all their splendor on an ordinary day; the unfamiliar scent of eau de toilette floating in the air.

Once, lying awake in his bed at night, he heard hushed voices coming from his father's bedroom. A strange murmuring special to the hours of darkness drifted in from the small balcony that the bedroom doors opened onto: sighs, gurgles, muffled cries, whispers. He slipped behind the door made of square panes of glass, where he was closer to the sounds. The sighs turned into moans, the whispers into a jumble of fragmented words. He stood there until the sounds died away, finding it hard to believe that his father was making them, wondering whether his father was dreaming and talking in his sleep. Meir stood there a while longer, wondering whether he should knock on the door, yet knowing that you should never rouse anyone from a dream. When finally he heard his father's gentle snore, Meir went back to bed.

One day he came home early from school and found a strange woman standing next to the window, looking through a booklet. Her purse hung from her shoulder.

"Your father went to buy a typewriter ribbon," she said.

His eyes were drawn to her red hair.

"Tell him that Orna finished the work and left," she said, putting down the booklet and walking past the boy to the door.

All that afternoon, his father tried to convince Meir, for some reason, that Orna had come to help him choose poems for a booklet he was editing for the Writers Association. But a trace of the now familiar, sweet scent lingered in the air, or in Meir's imagination, and hardened his heart.

And two months later, when his mother's letters stopped coming and Meir started pulling lawyers' letters out of the mail-

**box instead, for some reason, he couldn't stop thinking about
that snaky red hair.**

"What do you mean, 'who's we?'—Daddy and I waited. He used
to water your flowers on Saturday, and we read your letters a
thousand times, until all of a sudden, you stopped writing."

"And why did I stop writing—do you know?"

"Really, why did you?"

"Your father didn't tell you why I stopped writing?"

"He said you didn't love us anymore. That you'd forgotten us
forever."

She jumped up, agitated. "That's what he said? So he didn't
give you the letter I wrote especially for you. I want you to know
that I never stopped loving you for even a moment."

They both stopped, aware that he hadn't heard such an explicit
declaration since the time they lived in the house on HaNevi'im
Street. Only now it had the bad taste of something that had come
too late.

"And what was that love worth?" he asked. "You didn't send us
money."

"You're blaming me?" Her eyes reddened. "Does that mean
you're condoning what he did?"

"I blame both of you. But right now, I'm talking to you, so I'm
blaming you."

"Because you don't know the truth. I couldn't come back
because there were complications with my pregnancy. And later,
I heard all kinds of rumors about things you couldn't know. I
wrote him a pretty harsh letter accusing him, and he wrote a very
insulting, unfair one to me. He wrote that he could manage without me. So I wrote back: go right ahead. Support yourself for a
few months. It won't hurt you to live real life for a change. And
then I really did stop writing for a while. Later on, though, I wrote
almost every day, but my letters came back because you moved
away and I didn't have your address."

"He didn't know how to make a living, you knew that."

"I wanted to teach him a lesson."

"And me, too? Because they threw me out of the house along with him."

"Who threw you out?"

"That guy from your office, a policeman, and the landlord. You didn't know?"

"The office told me that you'd left the apartment . . ."

"We didn't leave. They threw us out."

"I was sure you could live with Pnina," she said and, chastened, sat down again.

**Sometimes, on Saturdays, the three of them would go to visit Pnina and Yakov, his father's cousin, and eat candy from tiny paper baskets. And there—even though his mind was occupied mainly with the delectable sweets—he would discover another side to his parents. His mother would try to charm the hosts, entertain them with stories from the law office where she translated contracts into English, her native tongue, showing off now to prove that she was worthy of their handsome cousin, the poet who spoke four languages fluently.**

**After the visit to Pnina and Yakov, his mother would hurry home, as if she'd used up all her strength in the living room they'd just left. Sometimes Meir and his father would go to the beach and collect seashells that they brought home. He played with them for a long time afterward, pressing a shell to his ear to hear the whoosh of the waves that sometimes drowned out his parents' arguing voices.**

"I didn't like going to Pnina's," he said.

"Really. She made all those sweets especially for you."

"Whenever we came home from there, you and Daddy always fought."

"You noticed that?" she asked sadly.

"Yes."

"But we used to make up right away and go for ice cream, and on the way, Daddy would tell you how we met. You really loved hearing that story, and he told it to you a thousand times. You must remember that."

Meir's father had decided to move from Jerusalem to Tel Aviv so he could spend time with the circle of poets whose poems he read in the weekend supplements. His cousin Yakov rented him a small, inexpensive room in the apartment of a doctor's widow, who didn't need the money but was afraid of staying alone at night with her elderly mother. He had only one suitcase of his belongings and a carton of books. For the time being, he left the carton in the storeroom of the bookbinding shop where he worked, and he took the suitcase with him on the bus. Once, a group of noisy American youngsters took up most of the bus. Sitting in front of him was an Israeli woman carrying on a halting conversation with one of the American girls, and he learned that the group had come for the celebration of Israel's tenth anniversary, that the girl had just graduated from New York University and was planning to stay in Israel, even though her family was opposed to the idea. She had a pleasant voice, and even before he saw her face, he decided to do something daring that would be in keeping with his decision to live in Tel Aviv. He would introduce himself to her. When the bus stopped at the Tel Aviv central bus station, he quickly pushed his way in front of her and shoving open the resistant door, extended her his hand gallantly, saying, "Me Tarzan, you Jane." Years later, in one of their kitchen quarrels, Meir's mother threw that up to him, saying all he wanted was an American passport.

"Was he sad after I left?"

"He was quiet and the house was quiet."

"Was that good or bad?"

"Bad, because it was boring and good because there was no fighting."

"And how did you manage after . . . after HaNevi'im Street . . . What did you do with all the furniture?"

"We moved most of it to Berl's place."

"You mean that cellar?" she said sorrowfully.

"Yes."

"There was enough room there?"

"We didn't take everything. We gave your bed to the religious lady next door and we threw a few pieces out on the street."

She fell silent, bidding farewell to the furniture that had once held her clothes and lingerie and her parents' pleading, admonishing letters, the furniture she polished so lovingly, the furniture that had been witness to sweet times and bitter times, abandoned long ago on the rainy street.

"The office promised me that they'd give your father more time to get organized."

"Maybe they did, I don't know. They yelled a lot."

"Who?"

"The landlord would come and there was yelling. Also that guy from your office."

"And where did you go that day, where did you sleep?"

"The religious neighbor said we could sleep in their house at night."

"With all the children they had, there was enough room for you?"

"Yes. They had beds that folded up onto the wall."

"How long did you stay there?"

"One night."

"And then?"

**The belongings that the mover took in a cart pulled by a tricycle to Berl's cellar were piled one on top of the other: a desk, two cabinets, a kitchen table and three chairs, a single mattress without a frame, suitcases full of clothes and linens, housewares packed in boxes, tablecloths and towels bundled into pillowcases, a box overflowing with papers and photocopies, a carton of books (most of them large and heavy, bundles of books tied together), a carton of Meir's things: a few books, school workbooks, color-**

ing books, colored pencils, the shell collection. They wrapped it all in enormous plastic sheets and waited for the rain to stop.

Berl welcomed them joyfully, shoved aside his packages to make room for the mattress that was put on the floor and the blankets spread next to it to be used as another mattress. He rubbed his hands together and hopped excitedly from one foot to another, looking as happy as a child whose loneliness has so suddenly and happily come to an end.

"Then we went to live in Berl's house."

"To that smelly cellar of his?"

"It was his home. I don't remember it being smelly."

"Without a shower or hot water, with the neighbor's sewage outside, that's where he took you?"

"He took me to Berl's house."

"And what about school? Wasn't it far from school?"

*Interior. Night. Berl's cellar.*

(Meir, Aharon, and Berl are lying on their beds. All three are having a hard time falling asleep, Berl, because of the intensity of his excitement, Meir and Aharon because of the upheaval in their life and their proximity to each other. Berl is muttering. Meir is listening to the echoing footsteps of the people walking on Shlomo HaMelech Street, and watching the shadows painted by the bushes on the other side of the cellar's high windows.)

Meir (sitting up in alarm):
Daddy, I didn't do my homework!

Aharon:
Never mind. You won't be going to school tomorrow anyway.

Meir:
Why not?

Aharon:

Because it's far and I have all kinds of errands to do in the morning.

Meir:

So where will I be all day?

Aharon:

You can stay with Berl or you can come with me, but you can't cry that your feet hurt, because we have a lot of walking to do and lots of steps to climb.

Meir:

Will you have time to take me to school the day after tomorrow?

Aharon:

I hope so.

Meir:

But I won't have the homework for the day after tomorrow.

Aharon:

I'll write your teacher a note. She'll let it go this time, she'll understand.

"And that's how you lived there with those two?" she asked.

"It was fine," he said heatedly, going out of his way to defend their honor, suddenly remembering a little mouse scurrying across his blanket that night.

"One crazy and the other one irresponsible, what can be fine about that?"

**For the next two days, his father was still busy with errands, but before he went out in the afternoon, he taught Meir one page of his school workbook and gave him homework to do. Sitting at the desk, its sculptured shape standing out in its new home,**

**Meir sat in front of his open notebook and read from it, and Berl sat next to him, crying out in amazement at every word.**

*Interior. Evening. Berl's cellar.*

(Meir and Berl are sitting at the desk. Meir is filling a line with the letter "צ," straining hard. Berl accompanies every new "צ" with a cheer of encouragement. Meir stops writing the letter in the middle and his eyes fall on a long scratch on the edge of the desk. The scratch had been carved in the wood a long time ago, when his mother was cutting a rope from around a package that had come in the mail, and the knife had slipped, cut her finger, and scratched the desk. Meir's head drops suddenly to the notebook and he bursts into tears.)

Berl (alarmed):
What's wrong, Meir'ke?

(Meir is crying. Berl strokes the back of his neck.)

Berl:
Is it because of me?

Meir (shakes his head and
touches the scratch on the table):
It's because of this.

Berl:
You're afraid your father will be mad because you spoiled his desk?

Meir:
My mother spoiled it.

Berl:
When?

Meir:
Once.

Berl (happy):
So he won't be mad at you.

Meir:
But it hurt her. She was bleeding.

Berl (stroking Meir's head):
Little boy, she doesn't even remember it anymore.
What you don't remember doesn't hurt you.

Meir:
What if she comes back all of a sudden? She'll go to
the old house and she won't find me. She won't know
I'm here.

Berl:
The neighbors will tell her. Everything will be fine.

Berl goes to the cabinet and takes out a bar of chocolate, breaks off a square and gives it to Meir.

Berl:
Here, Meir'ke, have some chocolate.

(Meir, his eyes filled with tears, eats the chocolate
hungrily.)

"They took care of me. They made me feel that I was important
to them, that they loved me," he said, attacking her more than he
was defending them.

"I'm not saying they meant to harm you. I'm saying that under
those conditions, they couldn't give you everything you needed."

"I didn't lack for anything."

**Two days after they left the apartment on HaNevi'im Street,
Meir took a bath in a tub like Berl did, because he didn't have a
shower. He sat down in the tub full of lukewarm water, and his
father shampooed his hair and rinsed it with water from a ket-**

tle, and then both washed their clothes in the same water and hung them outside on a cotton rope that stretched from the trunk of a palm tree that grew at the far side of the garden to a piece of iron that protruded from the wall of the shed where the garbage bins were kept.

After Meir had been absent from school for a week, his father promised him that now, after he'd done all his many errands, he'd take him to school on Sunday. Meir begged him to take him to his friend's house so he could copy the homework, and his father agreed. The friend was happy to see them, and told them that the teacher had asked every day whether any of the kids knew what had happened to Meir. She'd sent the friend to Meir's house to find out how he was, but when he got there, he found a man painting the walls who told him that the old tenants had left and wouldn't be coming back. Meir's father said that, for the time being, they were living with a relative and no one could come to visit there, but they'd be in their own place soon, and then friends could come to see Meir. After looking through the notebook, he said that Meir was ahead of the class, and then Meir copied the homework and the children said goodbye, promising to see each other the next day.

They took the long way back to Berl's cellar so they could walk along Dizengoff Street. His father stopped next to the tree and looked across the street at Kassit.

"Alterman isn't there today," he said, almost relieved.

"And if he was?"

"Then I'd go inside and say hello."

"But there are other people inside," Meir said.

"No one interesting," his father said and started to walk away, pulling Meir behind him.

"And how did you manage at night?"

"There was enough room for the three of us."

"On the floor?"

"No, we each had our own bed," he said, lying easily.

"And your father slept there every night? He never left you there and disappeared?" She asked the explicit question in a calm voice.

"He never disappeared," he said truthfully.

"And you stayed in that cellar all those months?"

Once, walking along the street hand in hand, they bumped into a woman his father knew, a long-time clerk in the Writers Association, and stopped to talk. During the conversation, Meir sensed the change in his father, in his voice and his posture, as if he were pretending to be someone else. The woman's eyes stayed on the boy the whole time, as if she couldn't pull them away. Her expression must have given his father an idea, and he asked her if she happened to know of a place they could stay for a few days, take a shower, and cook a hot meal for themselves—until they found something permanent. Even before he finished stammering out the question—her eyes were still on the boy—she invited them to come and shower in her apartment because her soldier son stayed at the army base for weeks at a time and hardly ever came home.

That evening, Meir splashed around in a bathtub full to the top. He dived over and over again, his face on the bottom of the tub as if it were the bottom of the sea, until his skin whitened and wrinkled. Then, washed, with his wet hair combed nicely, he was invited to eat pot roast and potatoes, whose aroma filled the house. They sat around the set table, once again a man, woman, and child eating from plates that were all from the same set.

"Berl's probably worried about us," Meir suddenly said.

"You're not going to any Berl today," the woman asserted. "I took out the sheets already."

Meir slept on the convertible couch in the living room for two nights, getting used to the lengthwise crease in the mattress, to the sounds drifting in from the street, to the heavy beat of the music coming from the neighbor's apartment. Since he fell asleep before his father and woke up after him, he couldn't know whether his father had slept next to him all night or only lay down for a minute when he woke him in the morning, but he sensed without proof that his father had been in the bedroom of the clerk from the Writers Association.

On the evening of the third day, the soldier son suddenly appeared, dragging a giant duffle bag and a carelessly rolled up sleeping bag. His mother, who had already sat down to dinner in the kitchen with her two guests, jumped up and went over to him, alarmed. The soldier took a quick look at the table, at the man and the boy, cut them down with a glare, and went out to the living room balcony with a banging of doors. The Writers Association clerk changed instantly, shrank, mumbled an apology, and hurried out to the balcony. Then they heard the son shouting.

His father's face clouded over and he asked quietly, "Do you want to take the picture you drew yesterday?"

"Yes."

"I'll go get it. Finish your tea and we'll go."

Berl was overjoyed to see them, trying in vain to hide the signs of frailty in his voice and his eyes. From that day on— not knowing yet that they were preparing for the days of wandering that would follow—they made a habit of taking Meir's schoolbag and clean clothes with them in case a welcoming home came their way. When they encountered one of his many women friends, his father would ask with a hesitation that disappeared with time whether they could go to her place today because the boy hasn't bathed for a few days. The women rarely refused.

"Where do you know them from?" Meir asked, surprised at the number of women.

"From the Writers Association, from the book publisher's, from the newspapers, from the Artists Association, from the theater. You get to know a lot of people when you wander around the city."

"We only lived with Berl at the beginning. Then Daddy started looking for a place of our own."

"So you did have an address?"

*Interior. Early evening. Berl's cellar.*

(Meir and Aharon enter the cellar. Berl is sitting squeezed between the sink and the wall, his chin between his knees. He looks up at them with terrified eyes, and then gets up and asks them voicelessly, with wildly gesturing hands, to close the door quickly, making circular motions with his hands for them to lock it from the inside. Aharon and Meir hurry over to him.)

Aharon:

What's wrong, Berl?

Berl (whispering):

They were here.

Aharon:

Who?

Berl:

You know.

Aharon:

No I don't.

Berl:

The Gestapo.

Aharon (shocked):

That's ridiculous, Berl! (To Meir) Bring some water, fast. Berl had a dream.

Aharon lifts Berl, pulls him gently and sits him at the table. Meir goes to the sink and fills a cup with water.

Aharon (softly):
There's no Gestapo, Berl. We're in Israel! They were here.

Aharon:
Don't be silly, Berl. (Takes the cup from Meir.)
Here, drink this. (Aharon helps Berl drink as if he were a baby, holding the back of his neck with one hand and pressing the cup to his lips with the other.) Think of the boy, Berl. We want him to grow up without fear, don't we? You had a bad dream. Show him how calm you are now. Drink a little more.

Berl:
Not a dream . . . not a dream. I know when it's a dream and when it isn't. They were here. With their hats and shoes.

Aharon:
How many were there?

Berl:
Two.

Aharon:
And what did they want from you?

Berl:
They were looking for you.

Berl points at the table. There's a letter on it. Aharon goes over and reads it.

Meir:
What is it, Daddy?

Aharon:

From the police station here on Dizengoff. (To Berl)
What did you tell them?

Berl:

That you're not even in the ghetto. That you're not
here.

Aharon:

That was no Gestapo, Berl, and this is no ghetto. That
was an Israeli policeman. He wants our new address,
that's all. Here, the policemen watch out for us. That's
their job in Israel.

Berl:

He had a pad.

Aharon:

Of course, he did. Every policeman has a pad.

Berl:

You have to escape, Aharon. They'll come back and
catch you.

Aharon:

I'll go, Berl. But not today. It's Friday. They don't work
on Fridays. And definitely not on Saturdays. We'll leave
tomorrow night.

*Interior. Night. Berl's cellar.*

Meir and Aharon are lying next to each on the cellar
floor in the dark. They're whispering.

Meir:

Will they come to get you, Daddy?

Aharon:

No, of course not.

Meir:

They really only want the address?

Aharon:

They want it, but for the time being, they won't get it. When we have a real address—when they pay me for the articles and we get ourselves an apartment—then we'll go to the police and take care of it.

Meir:

Are we really leaving here tomorrow?

Aharon:

Yes. Because Berl is so scared.

Meir:

So where are we going?

Aharon:

We'll find something. Don't worry. But Meir...

Meir:

What?

Aharon:

You won't be able to go to school on Sunday.

Meir:

Why not?

Aharon:

Because they can go to the school and look for you. And we don't want that to happen before we have an address.

Meir:

Why would they look for me?

Aharon:

To get to me.

Meir:

And what'll they do to me?

Aharon:

Nothing. They'll hold you until I come to get you.

Meir

And what'll they do to you?

Aharon:

Nothing. But the best time to do it is when we have an address.

Meir:

So how long will I be out of school?

Aharon:

A few days. Meanwhile, you have Sunday's homework.

Meir:

And we'll go to get the homework?

Aharon:

I think that, for the time being, we shouldn't go anywhere.

Meir:

Why not?

Aharon:

Because we don't have an address yet.

Meir:

Are we really leaving here tomorrow night?

Aharon:

Yes.

Meir:

Do we have to?

Aharon:
Yes. It's not a good idea for the policeman to find us
before we have an address. But we can come to sleep
here at night. They won't look for us at night.

Meir:
Where will we be during the day?

Aharon:
I don't know yet. . . . But we'll know soon. There are
lots of places.

"We didn't stay in one place. We lived here and there with all
kinds of people. And we wandered around a lot."

"Where?"

"In Tel Aviv. On the streets of Tel Aviv."

"On the streets! What do you mean, you wandered the streets?"

"We were looking for places."

"And that's how you found them? By wandering around?"

"Yes. He knew a lot of people . . ."

She suddenly withdrew into silence, bent her head until her
chin touched her chest, as if she were talking to her heart, and
grew sad.

Then she looked up. "What about school?" she asked.

**For a few days, they walked around together until evening.
Then his father persuaded him to start going to a different
school that the policeman wouldn't be able to find, and so
began a period of switching—from one school to another,
four times. Every week or two, his father would carefully iron
Meir's shirt and go to register him in a new school. He'd sit in
the principal's office, his legs crossed elegantly, and explain
in polished language that they had just moved to Tel Aviv
from Jerusalem or Afula or Eilat, and he still didn't have the
papers. They would arrive, he promised—his hand on his
heart—within a few days, but until then, it would be a shame**

to fritter away the time of a boy who was such a diligent pupil and loved school.

Meir and his father would leave the principal's office, hand in hand, joined in the brotherhood of criminals. Sometimes his father would burst out laughing the minute the principal could no longer hear or see them, put his hand on his chest and say, "The boy loves school, Sir. Why make him wait until the papers come from Afula?" And Meir would become uneasy: this liar, pretending to know his way in the world, this man was holding his hand and dragging him to a bad place.

One principal adamantly refused, claming that the boy wasn't insured, but the three others were impressed by the serious expression of the father so concerned about his son's education, and let the boy into class after they were promised that tomorrow or the day after, he would be registered at city hall. Over and over again, Meir would sit in a class of strangers, getting used to responding to different names, Yossi or Motti, names he'd chosen from a list his father had given him, learning a story, a bit of arithmetic, careful not to get friendly with the other children, choosing remote corners for himself at recess, afraid that someone would recognize him, frightened that every time the door opened, it would be the school secretary coming to ask when his father would give them the papers he'd promised to bring, staring at the braid of the girl sitting in front of him or at the foot of the boy in the next row, cut off and isolated, stammering something a long time after his name had been called, causing even one of the teachers to stifle a laugh. A few weeks later, when he finally realized that the chances they would have their own place were slim, he asked his father to stop moving him from one school to another, and his father quickly replied, "You're absolutely right. What's the good of another ploy? You're in the school of life now." Then he seemed to regret his grandiose declaration and chose a more modest approach: "We'll study together. One private lesson is worth more than a full day at school. And in the end, we'll have a place of our own, too."

\* \* \*

"I switched to a few different schools and in the end, I stopped going altogether."

"Meir, Meir," his mother said. "You never talked about this."

"I didn't remember it. I didn't remember anything from that period."

"You didn't want to remember?"

"I couldn't," he said, the bloodstain appearing before his eyes.

"And how is it that you remember now?"

"I don't know, but that's what I've been doing this whole last week." He said no more, unwilling to share his amazement at the miracle of remembering.

"Nothing is simple," she said, reaching out for the first time and covering his hand with her own. "Is it hard for you, Meir?"

His hand burned under hers, not with warmth, but with the sting of fire.

"It's like watching a movie," he said. "It's me and it's not me."

"And what is it doing to you?"

"That depends on what I remember," he said, pulling his hand away.

"You're angry at me, aren't you?"

"I'm angry, yes. Not just at you."

"There are some things you don't understand. A child can't understand all of that."

"There are a lot of things I don't understand. For instance, I don't understand how you don't know that I wandered the streets. In winter."

"I thought you'd go to live with Pnina until your father started working and could pay rent. I wanted to teach him a lesson. I admit that maybe I was wrong. I was sure that he'd take you to Pnina. She really loved you."

"Why did you send the police to look for us?"

"The law office where I worked sent the police. And they did it because they were worried about you. They couldn't find you. I didn't send the police, but I was very scared that he was neglecting you."

"He took me everywhere."

"So where did you live all those months?"

"Months? How many months was it?"

"Five."

"Five?" he said, amazed at the memory's ability to expand and contract time.

"Yes. Where were you then?"

"I told you. With Berl, and with other friends of Daddy's."

"Men friends or women friends?" she asked with uncharacteristic directness. But before he could answer—as if she'd mustered all her courage to ask the question, but wouldn't be strong enough to face the answer—she turned pale and moved her hand to her heart.

"Are you tired?"

"Very."

"And you want me to go now."

As usual, in farewell, they touched cheeks. It was a recognition that certain customs would always prevail. Also as usual, Meir wasn't surprised to find that her sorrow didn't move him.

In the elevator, he felt uneasy about the way the visit had been cut short and decided that, before he got into his car and drove home, he'd stay outside for a little while to let the sting of having been thrown out fade. He crossed two streets and went into the restaurant whose eastern windows were visible from his mother's apartment. The whole time, his imagination kept playing the game of possibilities for his story, and a revelation gripped him: this would be the place from which he would spy on them this time. The boy wandering the apartment hallway as if moon-struck, squeezing between his parents as they slept; the boy sitting on the toilet, ears perked to pick up their voices—that same boy would now be sitting in a different place, at a different time, again focused on where they were, never to know what they're saying to each other, never to learn the secret of the man's charm. It would be as if almost a quarter of a century hadn't passed since the Tel Aviv nights, as if the man were again insinuating himself into a woman's home. And, despite the many years Meir had lived alone,

he was overtaken by a feeling of loneliness when he thought about
what he'd do on the first few days after his father's arrival. Maybe
he'd ask for some vacation time and stay holed up in his house.
His imagination would overflow with images, raising questions
that would not let go: his mother would probably tell his father
that he could bathe at her place after the long flight. Would she fill
the bathtub for him, adding bubble bath, and would he immerse
himself in the water scented with lilac, the only scent she used,
and rest languidly in the fragrant water, a cigarette in one hand,
the other on the back of his neck? Would she dare to go into the
bathroom like she used to sometimes in their apartment in Tel
Aviv to scrub his back, and would he shift his back slightly and lift
the hand holding the cigarette toward his mouth, and would she
tilt her head to the side and laugh? Would she tell him to throw
his underwear and socks into the wicker hamper, where they'd
mix with her underwear and socks the way they did in the hamper on HaNevi'im Street? Would she make the bed for him or
leave the sheets on the bare mattress as a declaration that she
wouldn't be serving him beyond what courtesy required? Would
the man stand at the window half the night, staring wide-eyed at
the wonderful strings of the city's lights lying at his feet as if he
were at the top of a Ferris wheel? And then would his mother put
on one of her fancy nightgowns and invite his father into her
huge bed? Would his father reach for her body at night, and
would she let him touch her? Would they make the same whispering and sighing sounds that had escaped from the rooms his
father had been in with other women? Would they talk all night,
lying in each other's arms, reminiscing? Would they laugh when
they remembered that fateful bus ride from Jerusalem to Tel Aviv?
Would they find the right moment to remember the "Me Tarzan,
you Jane"? Would they talk about their son? Would she tell him
the truth about the boy's first period of muteness and how his
strangeness had repelled the other children the first few years;
would she dare to tell him about the years he'd sat and dug his fin-
gernails into his bleeding knees? Would she boast about the two

prizes he won in writing contests? Would she tell him about the women he invited into her living room? Would they mention Eleanor? Would they mourn their little girl together for the first time? Would they mention Arnie? Would she tell him that, in his nightmares, their son would shout Arnie's name?

It suddenly occurred to him that he didn't know anything about his father's past, except that he was born in Poland. Where had he spent the years of the war, how did he get out alive, and when did he go to Israel?—Meir was suddenly eager to know.

Tired, despite the two cups of coffee he'd drunk, he got up and left the restaurant. On his way home, leaving the city and heading north to Connecticut, the questions his mother had asked kept buzzing around in his mind: "Where did you live all those months?" And, "Men friends or women friends?"

That night—as if the questions opened a window into the tunnel of his memory, giving access to the time when he first became aware of transience, suspicious even of his benefactors and antagonistic toward all those women—Meir remembered wandering through long office corridors, down paths in public parks and streets leading to endless staircases; he also recalled the many women—his father's lovers, friends, and acquaintances— who had opened their doors and sometimes their hearts to offer a bed to the man and shelter to the boy. But, unlike his memories of the house on HaNevi'im Street, those sights rose chaotically, splintering and skipping through time. Then suddenly he pictured a line of women passing by, one after the other: a clerk with a beehive hairdo from the Writers Association office; the lover of an important poet who'd died; the owner of a kiosk on the Boulevard; a movie theater cashier who wasn't there in the evenings; a kindergarten teacher whose living room was cluttered with toys; an opera singer who clicked her tongue in amazement at the sight of Meir's fingers; and numerous other women, strangers he knew nothing about.

Without his mother's words to awaken his memory and conjure up images, he was swept into a whirlpool of sights and jumbled sounds: Berl sleeping with his mouth open, as if ready to scream; a well-lit café and his father sitting with graceful nonchalance, his legs crossed; the start of a downpour, and Meir running to the bus stop shelter; a woman fluffing a pillow and then stretching a sheet over a mattress lying on a carpet; he and his father on a park bench, one order of pita with falafel and two apples between them; he and his father sitting in a dark theater watching a choir singing on the stage; his father moving away on a dark street, arm in arm with two women; long corridors that go on forever between two gray walls; his father sitting at a table between two women, holding a hand of cards, the sounds of a storm and tremendous claps of thunder outside; his father making his way between the tables in a café toward a woman sitting alone at a table, browsing through a magazine, and Meir praying to God with every fiber of his being; water rising in a bathtub, threatening to overflow; a policeman's shirt close to his face, and a policewoman stroking his head, whispering, "You only have a mother"; his father dancing with a woman in the dark, his hands under her dress, pulling it up over her thighs, and they're laughing softly, whispering into each other's necks.

From the fragmented scenes, there suddenly arose one clear, detailed memory: his father walking along a path in a public park, Meir Park—the name flickered in his memory—far from the corner where the famous murder had taken place years before. They sit down on a bench together and his father reads to him from a used children's book, *Oliver Twist*, or maybe *Huckleberry Finn*. As Meir listens, his eyes follow with longing two children playing with a hoop.

And once—the memory came as swiftly as a slap: three of them are sleeping in the only bed in a small studio apartment, his father in the middle, a woman on one side of him and Meir on the other, his back to his father, not moving a muscle, even when the mattress starts moving under him the way he imagines it would in an earthquake. He buries his nose in the pillow, closes his ears to the suppressed moans coming from behind him, sounding like a conversation between two stutterers, and he remains wide awake even after the thrashing stops.

Another memory pushed its way into the memory of the shaking bed: Meir is curled up in a recently made bed, and his father lies down next to him fully dressed. He pretends to fall asleep in his son's bed, but Meir knows that he's awake, waiting for Meir to fall asleep, so he deceives his father, who's deceiving him, and starts breathing slowly, watching through the slits of his eyes as his father gets up carefully and tiptoes to the woman's room.

And a new, heartwarming scene intrudes itself into this memory of his father slipping into the woman's room: a pleasant house belonging to two women, sisters. One is clinging to his father, standing behind him as if they were in a beauty salon, combing his hair; the other is tending to Meir, feeding him as if he were a baby, whispering into his ear that he is the beauty king of Tel Aviv. Suddenly, he remembers walking hand-in-hand with his father down the street and sitting with him, side-by-side at a piano that stood between the apartment's front door and another door and—his heart stopped—behind that door was the bed covered with the bloodstained sheet.

Meir sat for hours in front of the computer at his house in Connecticut, dizzy with the sights of rooms and streets and women's faces, thinking of himself as a seashell that had rolled into the desert but still held the whoosh of the waves. He tried to push the images aside, dilute the profusion, focus on the first words of his story which, like a sheep leading a flock, would bring the first sentence, the first paragraph, then the whole story. "The sign to J. F. Kennedy Airport could be seen in the distance." The memories, like strong waves surging up from the depths, broke on the shore and spit out his flesh-and-blood father who, as soon as he got his visa, would land at the New York airport in his wheelchair. His son, Meir, would be waiting for him in the arrivals hall, and maybe there, in the airport cafeteria, or in some other random place along the way, he'd slam the wheelchair into the wall. His father would tremble and beg and burst into tears, but his humiliation would not mollify the offended boy waiting inside him for the kick of his life. The son would seek vengeance for the crimes committed against him when he was too young to defend himself, and he'd vent all the fury, all the pain and horror that had lived inside him from the time he was seven.

With a burning hand and with all his senses attuned, Meir wrote a full page describing his father's arrival at the New York airport. As he wrote, he could hear the bustle of the place and smell the special smell of the strangers waiting in the hall, he among them, to greet the passengers from Tel Aviv. He'd hear Hebrew all around him, recognize words he once understood and surprisingly, he'd understand even words he didn't know, suddenly feeling his heart beating faster, the beats becoming blows pounding against the walls of his body. When the first passenger appeared at the door, opening his arms from a distance to his waiting loved ones, the thunder of Meir's heart would already be exploding in his ears and he'd long to run away to a quiet place, but his legs would stay rooted to the spot. Dozens more people would emerge into the hall. Then a flight attendant pushing a wheelchair would appear, and Meir's heart would stand still: here was his father.

The man in the wheelchair would look nothing like the man from his memory or from the old photographs. Pale and shriveled, his eyes gaping as if in shock, he'd be shrunken in the chair, pushed like a baby, and Meir, despite the sudden weakness he felt, would hold up the sign that said ROSINBERG, and he'd be gripped by a strange feeling, as if he were a child again, accompanied by a tall and determined flight attendant, as if he were trying to suppress the strange trembling of his thumbs so that she wouldn't be alarmed. His feet were standing on the same floor, maybe even the same tiles, and as if he were watching an old movie rewinding, he'd see clearly a seven-year-old boy approaching the wheelchair rolling toward him, slightly calmer when he realized that someone was actually waiting for him, as promised. He looked at the fat woman stuck in the chair, knowing that they were mother and son but feeling only that they were strangers, until he heard,

"Welcome home, my darling," whispered into his ear, and he recognized the voice and burst into tears.

Around midnight, while he was sitting unmoving in front of the computer, his mother called.

"Is it too late? Did I wake you?"

"I'm awake."

"So you didn't manage to fall asleep either."

"Did something happen?"

"Arnie called. He's worried about you. He says you're avoiding him."

"I'll call him tomorrow."

"Good . . . So I didn't wake you?"

"No."

"Do you have guests?"

"No."

"I thought maybe Holly was there."

"No, she's not here."

"Are you still seeing each other?" As usual, she dared to ask him things on the phone that she wouldn't ask him face to face.

"No."

"It's over between you?"

"Yes, it's over."

"Too bad. I saw what a good relationship you had with the boy."

"But it really bothered you that they were black."

"That's not . . . But you say it's over . . . and there's someone new?"

"No. No one."

"Too bad," she said, then suddenly went quiet.

"Okay, listen, I—"

"Your loneliness makes me very, very sad."

He said nothing, didn't let the sadness in her voice touch him.

"I wanted to ask you something," she said, her pensive tone becoming urgent now, as if all the questions until then and all that had been said were only a ruse to get to this question: "I wanted to ask whether you've given any thought to what we talked about."

"Yes, I have," he said, deciding to take advantage of the moment. "And I have a question, too."

"All right," she said, hesitation in her voice.

"When exactly did he go to Israel and where was he during the war?"

"Ah," she said, almost in relief. "You're finding out now that you don't know much about him, right? Yes, there are things you have to be told . . . so it's like this: When the war broke out, he was about seven. Before the war, they lived in Poland, in a little town near the Russian border, and they escaped to Russia when the Germans went into Poland. During the war, he was in Russia with his father. His mother stayed home and died from complications of a pregnancy. After the war, they went back to Poland for a few years. Later, he went to Israel alone, because, in the meantime, his father died, too."

"I thought that, for a while, he was in a ghetto in Poland with Berl."

"Apparently not."

"How old was he when he went to Israel?"

"Fifteen. He went to a kibbutz, but it didn't suit him because he wanted to go to school and they didn't approve his studies. So he moved to Jerusalem. Someone from his mother's family lived there and helped him get set up. Sometimes, he talked about his time in the kibbutz and in Jerusalem, but you don't remember that either."

"No."

"So, did you remember other things?"

"No," he said, seeing clearly the image of two women who looked alike, sitting in a dark room, singing in high, screechy voices.

"You know, I still haven't told you everything."

"Like what?"

"What's been happening to him all these years," she replied, then she waited a long minute until she was able to say, "He was in prison."

The answer to the question of why he hadn't gotten in touch all those years suddenly became clear, but it took a while for Meir to ask, "For all those years?"

"Almost. Eighteen years, or something like that."

"For murder?" Meir asked, finding that he wasn't at all surprised, remembering the iron fingers closing around his arm, almost pulling it off as he was dragged across the stone floor in front of the bedroom with the bloodstain on the sheet.

"Now you understand why we didn't talk about him."

"Why didn't you tell me this when I was at your place?"

"I was waiting for the right moment, and the moment didn't really . . . I think that . . . But now you have to know."

He got up, as if he were running away, crossed the kitchen, went down the iron steps to his garage, got in the car and started it, raised the electronic garage door, drove out in reverse, lowered the door, and found himself driving toward the railroad station.

At the station restaurant, he gradually calmed down. A woman walking by moved her thighs in a way that caught his eye, but she hurried to the steps without glancing at him, busy transferring her traveling bag from one hand to the other, and slowly disappeared, losing her legs, her torso, her arms, until the back of her neck and her head vanished, too. He kept his eyes fixed on the empty space for a minute, then turned around, searching for another woman to look at.

All at once, he was struck by a memory of his father standing at the door of a café, and he got up and went home without examining the still unformed memory.

That night, old mysteries were solved and fell into place in the picture of his life, like the pieces of the giant puzzle his uncle from America had sent him when he was a child. His mother had allotted him a square on the living room floor of their Tel Aviv apartment, and every once in a while, one of them would forage around in the pile of a thousand pieces, pull one out and add it to the picture that was taking shape. Now he understood why he'd stayed in his shell and only Arnie had been able to look inside, and that only rarely; why he'd felt eternally marked as an outsider and had kept his distance from his classmates, especially from the girls who tried to have a relationship with him; why he'd let the girls in college do the pursuing; why most of the relationships he'd had for the last five years were with married women and unmarried mothers; why when he slept with them, almost mechanically, he held back his feelings, even for the ones he liked.

Then, as he waited in vain for his fury to vent, waited for the thrill of understanding to abate, the pain arrived. In front of the luxuriant trees glittering in the dark, Meir sat mourning the child who'd lost his innocence in a few short days and the years he'd wandered outside the boundaries of time. He now remembered his childhood that had been no childhood, and the youth that had been no youth, and the adulthood that had nothing adult about it because something had been thrown out of kilter too early and could no longer be fixed. He wondered whether that part of him, so good at erasing memories, was also good at miraculously transmitting to him things that had never been said in words. Had he always known that his father was alive, that his father was a murderer and not a victim? Was it that knowledge that had thrown Meir's life into disarray? Had the things he had seen and heard during those months of childhood destroyed his relationships with women forever? Could he start over again, as though he had no past?

When the trees in front of him glowed with the first light, Meir told himself that the boy who was dragged along by his father on his wanton journeys, who never experienced what other boys his age did, but knew other things, like the sounds of sexual intercourse made by his father and his lovers—that boy could have grown to be like his wayward, devil-may-care father or his punctilious, controlling, perfectionist mother. He could have grown to celebrate indecency and tolerate the obscene, or the opposite, to a desire for perfection and a life of control and order. But he did neither. Instead he was drawn to blandness, fearfully avoided all contact—neither despised nor accepted, neither wild nor prudent. And the constant feeling that something was missing, he knew now, was his longing for the boy who had stayed in Tel Aviv, for that missing part of himself that had been split off in an instant, when he was put on a plane to a different world.

And he understood something else: that he was completely frozen, his feelings and memories and longings as fossilized as his life. Was it any wonder that his pen had frozen over the page, that even the letters had become ice on the computer monitor?

*If there was an Olympics for thinking, I'd win a thinking gold medal because my head is always full of ideas inside ideas inside ideas, each one so much better than the other that it could drive you crazy but once Dr. Susskind told me that as an exercise I should try to chase the thoughts out of all the corners of my mind get out get out the way you chase away cats and not think about anything and just leave the place for thoughts empty like for instance a stage without scenery or a curtain or people so I said to him what kind of stupid idiocy was that not to think and is that what he spent all those years studying to be a doctor for because it was a real waste of time and if someone was already alive why should he waste his life on not thinking after all I have to get so much done and examine all the thoughts that come into my head like the eruptions of a hurricane or a volcano that's also a very nice description and arrange them like soldiers parading on Independence Day and also write the story I've already started and this time I'm going to finish it because when Ola my little sister was around she always bothered me and I didn't have a head for writing and I never finished the stories I started but times are different now and I plan to finish the story and it's going to be a very beautiful story about Abraham from the Bible but not about how he wanted to slaughter his son because ever since what happened to Ola my little sister I can't sleep on white sheets and I can't look at blood or think about blood or write about blood except for Abraham's goats that I'm writing about now which had the sweetest eyes in the world and on the day I finish writing the story I have to start a diet because I can't get into dresses with these slabs of fat all over my body especially on my knees and I have to get back to a size forty-two like Ola and I always wore because after we invested our all in our performance dresses with the lace and ribbons and belts they brought us from abroad and with the buttons just right she wouldn't let them make me a new one especially because she stayed a size forty-two then anyway so she couldn't care less. But now I don't worry about my dresses but about the boy's clothes I never saw a boy as handsome as that and as thin and as sad as that and I tell him to stop worrying so much because he's already in our house mine and Ola's and we have a big heart for him because our heart is double and that's a secret but I only tell him and Dr. Susskind about it and he has a good bed and a bath whenever he wants and soon we'll buy him everything he needs especially clothes and a new blanket and it's true that he can't go to school because it's very dangerous and the bad policemen are looking for him day and night as if he was some dangerous criminal but I can teach him at home because what schoolteachers know I know plus French and piano and they don't know a thing about French or piano and I can show him that if he studies a little and manages with the clothes then better times will come because he's going to be the beauty king of Tel Aviv like his father and it'll be so nice in our home with our French and our chocolate and we'll live happily ever after like it says in books because what more do I need if I have my little sister Ola who I love even when they say she's prettier than I am and plays the piano better and now we've found ourselves a man and a boy so what reason in the world do I have to do something bad to her and I forgot to mention the café we can go to and sit with all the actors and poets and Bohemians like we used to once in the days of the café and remember how it was a very important place in our history because the first most important thing is writing books and the second most important thing is history because how do we even know who and what we are without our history and our memories that live deep down in our bodies whether we like it or not—*

# Part Two

December 12–19, 1990

TEL AVIV

The man lying on the bed near the eastern window of room number six of the internal medicine department in the Tel Aviv hospital bore not even the slightest resemblance to the man lightly sketched in Meir's memory or the one looking directly into the lens in the old photographs. Eyes closed, pale, and frighteningly gaunt, he lay with his face to the window, the contours of his skeleton pronounced under his transparent skin.

Meir, feeling suddenly weak, thanked the head nurse and tiptoed to the head of the man's bed. He was gripped by a strange feeling, as if he'd gone back to a life that he'd already lived, and in it, he was a boy accompanied by a nurse: she was tall and determined, and his small steps quickened to keep up with her as he tried to suppress the odd trembling of his thumbs so she wouldn't drop his hand in alarm. The boy approached the bed next to the window in the maternity ward and peered at the crumpled purple face of the tiny stranger who was his newborn baby sister.

Now Meir looked at the man lying in the bed, aware of their familial bond but unable to overcome the feeling of discomfort. He was mesmerized by an image flickering in his mind's eye: a good-looking man, his hand stretched upward, holds a lit cigarette over his head in the way that an Olympic athlete would hold a torch, and dances between the crowded tables of the café on his way to charm the next woman. A moment later, the dancing man faded and Meir found himself scrutinizing with concern the bones that delineated his father's skeleton and the mouth pursed in pain. Then he imagined saying the two words that made his body shudder: "Hello, Father."

Startled, as if he'd heard the unspoken words, the man opened his eyes. Meir drew back in alarm. One of his eyes was a very light purple, like the background color of wallpaper that might be in a little girl's room. The man opened both eyes wide, the seeing one and the blind one, and strained to lift his head from the pillow, the tendons in his neck becoming pronounced as he moved closer to the young man standing over him. For a long moment, they stared at each other, perhaps wondering what the other was thinking or whether this emotionally fraught moment was different from others, first-rate raw material for the writer: how it would differ from the ordinary moments that would soon follow, from the questions about the pain, the drugs, the doctors, the food, the flexibility of the visiting hours. Or perhaps each was wondering what would be the other's first memory from twenty-three years ago, one clamoring to be remembered, another begging to be erased. Would this be their last parting, the casual, ordinary "good night" that no one ever imagines will be the last? Would this be a fleeting view through the crack in the door of the white, rumpled sheet with the long bloodstain on it that looked like a giant Chinese letter? Or would it be a random, forgettable moment like the one when Meir's father had stopped in the middle of a street to double-knot a trailing shoelace, kneeling in front of Meir like a servant before his master?

"Shalom," Meir said in Hebrew, hearing a clear whisper in his mind, "Welcome home, my darling." Watching the darting eye that looked up at him, Meir reached out his hand and was surprised by the solid grip of the emaciated hand that took his. Strong fingers closed around his fingers, and pulled him downward. For a minute, the movement seemed like a joke, like the rope-pulling game they once played on the beach, and Meir was dragged down until his face was directly in front of his father's. It occurred to him that if the man planted a kiss on his lips, he'd shake him off and back away, but his father only looked at him with his staring eye, examining his face in amazement, and whispered in Hebrew in a familiar voice hoarse with cigarette smoke,

"You've grown so much." The voice held neither pride nor surprise, only deep sadness, as if this boy's growth symbolized the flight of time, the flight of life. Meir continued to stand there, bending over and not moving, as if he were waiting for the touch of the hand that had once ruffled his hair.

"Do you still understand Hebrew?"

"Yes."

"So I have a request," the man whispered in his ear. Meir's heart hardened. He straightened up abruptly, moving out of the range of the hand that did not reach out to touch his hair. They'd only just met again, and he already had requests.

"Take me to the toilet," he said, pointing to the wheelchair standing in the corner. "I have to make pee-pee."

"The nurse'll take you," Meir said, retreating into English as if escaping to a safe place, shocked, for some reason, by the man's childish language, as if this were a sly attempt to return him to their past. "I'll go call her," Meir said, horrified by the sudden thought that he might have to support his father when he got out of the wheelchair or pick him up, chest to chest, the way you pick up a child, or pull his pajama tie or unbutton its buttons, or even hold his penis when he peed.

"Bring the chair," his father said, kicking the blanket off his legs and pulling himself up into a sitting position. He watched Meir, who reluctantly rolled the chair toward the skinny, white-as-plaster legs that swung over the edge of the mattress. Used to moving from the bed to the wheelchair, the sick man pulled the chair toward himself until it was right up against the side of the bed, then agilely shifted one leg and slid his withered body skillfully onto the seat. "Come with me," he said.

Walking behind his father's wheelchair in the corridor bustle unique to hospitals, past nurses in starched white uniforms, patients in blue print pajamas, and visitors carrying candy boxes and fruit, he suddenly remembered a time they'd both been in a hospital before—this hospital, apparently, perhaps even in this very department.

It was on the day he'd gone to the newspaper office with his father to see the literary editor on the fourth floor. After they'd climbed the first flight of stairs, his father suddenly declared a race, and they'd charged up the remaining three flights, Meir lagging far behind, and arrived at the literary editor's desk, out of breath. After the grown-ups had exchanged a few words of greeting, the friendly conversation suddenly heated up and turned into shouting. Before he understood what they were saying, Meir saw his father collapse onto the floor. Immediately, there was a commotion. People ran out into the corridor from the nearby offices and gathered around the man who was lying on the bare floor. One of the clerks poured a glass of water on his face cautiously, as if she were watering a plant, and some people shouted in alarm when the man didn't move or open his eyes under the shower. They made way for the boy, who was crawling along the floor through the crowd of legs.

Until the ambulance arrived, and in the ambulance itself, Meir held his father's hand in both of his as if he were holding a chick, looked at his face, which was as pale as a dead man's, and cried bitterly, arousing the pity of the newspaper people and later touching the hearts of the medical team. In the Internal Medicine Department, a bespectacled doctor held Meir on his lap as if he were his own child and patted his back gently to comfort him, promising that his father would soon be completely healthy, and they'd once again be able to play the games that all boys play with their fathers. A young nurse wiped Meir's tears, coming so close that he was enveloped by the lemony shampoo scent of her hair, and then she handed him a small bowl of candies.

Meir spent a few quiet, safe days in that room, which was heated to exactly the right temperature. His father was delirious with fever, and Meir stood at the window near his bed for hours, staring at the rain pouring down diagonally outside. At night, Meir slept in the armchair squeezed between his father's bed and the wall, and during the day, shared meals with him. Moved by the boy's devotion to his father, the nurses gave him a towel and a pair of too-large underpants and sent him to the shower. They heaped his sick father's tray with enough food for both of them and indulged the boy with toys and sweets. One day, Meir's temperature rose, too, and the nurses began to pamper and joke with him, saying that the fever was a sign that he loved the department. They then called a doctor from pediatrics. For a long time after his father had recovered, the two of them would occasionally walk hand in hand along David HaMelech Boulevard to their department in the hospital to visit their friends, the nurses, managing to arrive at noon to get a free lunch.

Now, in the bathroom, which had a lower ceiling than he remembered from childhood, Meir was standing in front of the wheelchair, fiddling with the brakes to gain some time, trying to decide whether to reach out and help his father up. But his father didn't wait. He grabbed Meir's forearms, hung on them, and pulled himself up until the two men were standing chest to chest and both could see that they were the same height. Looking into each other's eyes, they saw the resemblance. As if he'd read the younger man's fears, his father chuckled and said, "I'll manage from here. You can wait outside."

Waiting for his father, Meir shifted his weight from one foot to the other, alternately pressing the tip of one shoe to the heel of the other. Suddenly, he was flooded with an old feeling. He remembered clearly that once he used to wait for hours for his father, pressing the tip of his right shoe to the heel of the left one, then the tip of his left shoe to the heel of the right one. When they hadn't managed during the day to find a place to spend the night, they'd go to the Kassit in the evening. They'd stop at the tree across the street from the café and look at the carefree people sitting there so casually, amid plumes of smoke and gales of laughter. His father would scan the place. First, he'd check the poets' table to see if Alterman had arrived and who was lucky enough to be sitting next to him. Then he'd make a quick survey of the other people at the tables to find someone he could scrounge a cigarette or two from. Finally, his gaze would move more slowly from table to table, linger on the women sitting alone, but not ignoring the ones sitting in couples, sort the people like a magician preparing his accessories, using his instincts to locate the woman, who, within an hour, would offer her house key to the handsome man she had just seen sitting with the poets, the woman whose heart would soften upon hearing the story of the little boy who carried all his earthly possessions in his school bag. At a particular moment, his father would tense up, and catch his breath as he imagined what would follow, and Meir would become infected with inexplicable excitement. Then, without taking his eyes off the café, his father would say, "You don't move from here, Meir. Even if it takes a long time—you wait here for me and you don't take even one step away." Then he'd briskly cross the street to the café, and without turning to look back at the boy standing near the tree, he would signal Meir with a small movement of his hand. And Meir, breathless with happiness about the secret sign, about the pact with his father and about their adventure, would prepare himself for a long wait. A knob that jutted out of the tree like a growth touched the back of his neck and he rubbed against it, moving his head from side to side like an eternal nay-sayer, and at the same time, he'd shift his weight from one foot to the other, pressing the tips of one shoe against the heel of the other, until he got tired and slid down to sit at the base of the trunk.

Sometimes people walked by him and Meir would panic when he saw a boy from his class or an old neighbor. He'd scrunch up against the tree, tucking in his head like someone who'd fallen asleep sitting up. Most of the time, he kept his eyes on his father and, already familiar with the entire courtship dance, Meir saw him working hard to provide them with a place for the night, for the Sabbath, for a few days, a decent place where they could take a shower with hot water and sleep between clean sheets. On rare occasions, his father gambled on the wrong woman. Once, a woman had asked for the boy to come into the café. Meir crossed the threshold of the café like a beggar who'd been invited into the king's palace, and at his father's instructions, sat down across from the woman. He heard them order a mug of hot chocolate, and for a moment, they looked like a small family, a couple reveling in the sight of their son sipping hot chocolate, his eyes closed in pleasure. Until the woman sprang to her feet as if she needed to go to the ladies room urgently, then grabbed her purse, and instead of going to the ladies room, walked decisively to the door and left. Meir saw the puzzled look on his father's face, and the illusion of ordinariness dissolved.

From the other side of the door, Meir heard the flow of his father urinating and the memory of a very old image came to his mind: his father, completely dressed, distractedly running his hands over his crotch as if he were naked. Meir could follow the hand stroking the penis, the fingers sliding down between the top of his thigh and his groin, gliding under the testicles and rocking them, cupping them as if to weigh them, proud of their heaviness. At that moment, Meir felt movement in his own testicles as if they were trying to get smaller, to contract into the size of seeds, to squeeze into a safe place to hide inside him. He heard his body, like a distant echo, pleading to crawl inside itself: a seven-year-old boy, shaking as if he had a fever, his head buried under the pillow, pressing his hands as hard as he could over his ears, trying to ignore the woman's laughter and the whispered moans that were growing into shrieks. But the sounds pursued him. He couldn't push them away, he couldn't even make them fainter, they seeped into his ears and descended with the flow of his blood into his constricting loins.

Meir noticed now that behind the door the stream of urine had stopped. He approached, listened hard, and called out, "Do you need help—?" The word "Father" hovered on his tongue, then vanished.

The bathroom door opened wide and his father, seated on the wheelchair, stared at him as if he knew everything that had passed through his mind, as if he'd heard the word that had hovered on his tongue and then vanished. A young nurse walked past them, and with a rapid movement that reminded Meir of the flash of a lizard's tongue, his father grabbed the nurse's hand. She stopped and gave his father a look of revulsion when he lifted her hand to his lips and kissed it in a style from other times and other places. The nurse stood motionless, tolerating what he was doing, yet not hiding how much she wanted the moment to end. When it was done, she pulled her hand away and walked off without looking at him.

Confused by her brusqueness, his father said apologetically, "Israeli manners," as if Meir was the one who should be insulted. Meir did feel offended for his father, but was also angry at him for what he'd done, and he was disconcerted by the intensity of the feelings his father's actions had aroused in him.

"Follow me," his father ordered, waving his fingers. Meir immediately quickened his steps behind the wheelchair, maneuvering it skillfully in the hospital corridor between people and objects until they reached a small, sunny glass-walled room filled with potted ferns placed between the few wicker chairs to provide privacy for patients who wanted to be alone with their visitors. In one corner sat an older woman with a hairdo that had gone out of style decades ago, holding the hand of sad young girl wearing pajamas from home. The wheelchair rolled to the opposite corner and spun around in front of a chair that was buried between the plants. After glancing quickly at the woman and her hairdo, his father waved his hand at the empty chair in the gesture of a host saying to Meir, "Have a seat."

Meir sat down. In the bright light, his father's good eye wandered slowly over the features of his son's face, studying his eyes, his forehead, his hair, his nose, his jaw, his mouth, his chin, then descended to his shoulders and legs and rose again to his hands to make sure all the young man's features were faithful to his own. His smile, which began at the corners of his eyes and spread across his face, swelled like a cheer of victory, the victory of blood ties over the vast ocean that separated them, the victory of his own image living its life so far away.

"When did you arrive—today?"

"Yes."

"How many hours is the flight these days?

"About ten."

"They say there's going to be a war with Iraq here."

"I know."

"Of course you know. Did you see on television how America is sending soldiers and water over on airplanes?"

"Yes."

"They say we're going to be attacked by missiles, and millions will die."

"I don't believe it."

"Still, they distributed gas masks. I want you to take mine. It's in the nurses' room."

"I don't think I'll need it."

"There's also a box with a hypodermic needle that you can inject into your thigh in case you inhale gas. The nurse will explain how to do it. I want you to promise me that you'll take it."

"Okay," Meir said, a scene flashing through his mind: Daedalus preparing Icarus for his flight of escape, harnessing wings to the body of his son.

"Okay," the patient said, reassured now that the matter of the war had been settled. "So you must be very tired."

"I'm fine. I slept on the plane."

"But you're probably hungry."

"I ate and drank and I'm fine."

A small blood vessel buried in the depths of Meir's body moved at the homeless man's old habit of worrying about where the boy trailing behind him in the street would eat and sleep. Now he was also preparing him for the imminent war.

On rainy days, they'd leave the open parks and look for refuge in the entranceways of buildings. Once, sitting on the steps just inside an old apartment house, waiting for the rain to stop, a tenant came running in, dripping wet, carrying two plastic shopping baskets. They got up to let her pass, and then his father, as if he'd known her forever, reached out a hand and she, as if this was always their way, handed him one of the baskets. Together, they disappeared around the bend in the staircase, the sound of their steps echoing until, according to Meir's count, they reached the third floor. When his father came back, he was holding an apple in each hand, trying to judge their weight as if his hands were scales. He sank his teeth into one of them and handed the other to Meir, and they went back to sitting on the steps.

"Did you ask or did she give them to you?"

"She gave them to me of her own free will."

"And you weren't ashamed to take them?"

"I helped a nice lady, and she found a nice way to say thank you. What is there to be embarrassed about?"

"It's like we're beggars."

"We're not beggars. We just haven't gotten settled yet."

But once, perhaps even before the apple, Meir was standing next to the trash can at the entrance to a public park, his eyes quickly scanning its contents, searching for something worth taking: paper to color on, a frying pan, a partially eaten piece of candy. His father, seeing what Meir was doing, pressed the boy's head to his body and pulled him away.

"We'll have our own place soon, Meir."

"When?"

"Soon. I didn't want to tell you because it isn't definite yet, but it almost is: someone's arranging a teaching job for me."

"In a school?"

"Yes. A literature teacher in a religious school. Then we'll be all set up with a regular salary."

The position of literature teacher joined the long list of glamorous jobs he'd been promised, including editor of a literary supplement, regular columnist for a well-known weekly, translator for a large publishing house—and it too, like all the others, inspired hope for a while and was never mentioned again.

For the entire time that Meir was sunk in memory, his father watched him with his one, glittering eye. However, Meir found that he was mesmerized by the blind eye, wondering when it had lost sight, wondering why the nurses hadn't bothered to cover it. For a moment, it seemed as if his father was straining to see through it, trying to better take in every one of his features, every fleeting expression.

"I brought you something," Meir said, handing him a nicely wrapped box he'd bought in the duty free shop in New York. His father reached for it eagerly, unused to receiving gifts. He unwrapped it with his nimble fingers with a child's excitement, then saw the picture of the rectangles of chocolate on the box and, with a child's disappointment and disregard for manners, said, "Next time, bring cigarettes instead."

When he turned his probing eye on Meir again, he saw Meir's discomfort.

"You're saying to yourself: this foolish old man thinks there's going to be a next time." His father chuckled, exposing the gap where a tooth was missing. It lined up with the blind eye, both marking the side that had been punished as opposed to the right side, which had been granted clemency.

"I'm not."

"Sure you are," his father said, putting an end to the subject and turning to a different matter. "Why did your mother say you don't speak Hebrew?"

The word "mother," Meir thought, trembling inwardly, was uttered naturally, as if this wasn't one of the many words in their private dictionary whose meaning had been distorted.

"When did she say that?"

"A while ago, when we talked."

"You talked?"

"We had three long phone conversations. They cost me a fortune. They cost you, actually. Half your inheritance went on those calls," his father said, letting the thought of his inheritance sink into Meir's mind, and added, "That's when she told me that you can barely speak Hebrew, but your Hebrew is fine."

Meir was silent.

"I confused you with that mention of inheritance, didn't I?" A mischievous spark flashed in the depths of his eye.

"Absolutely not," Meir said, working to overcome his distress. "I studied Hebrew every Sunday and I had an Israeli friend for a few years, so I understand everything, but it's a little hard for me to speak."

"You speak a lot more than I imagined you would . . . I thought we'd have to speak English, so I started reading some English papers to brush up on the language, but . . . What were we talking about? I confused myself too—Yes, so you ate and you drank and you arrived today and came straight here."

"Not straight here. First I went to Shlomo HaMelech Street to look for Berl's cellar."

His father looked shocked. "You remember Berl?"

"Yes."

"Because your mother said you hardly remember anything," he said, "and that most of the memories you have are bad."

Meir was distracted suddenly by an odd movement his father made: he reached out with both hands, grabbed his right leg, lifted it, as if it were an object, and placed it on his left leg so that he was sitting with his legs crossed gracefully as he had in the past, one hand over the other on his raised knee. Meir's eyes were drawn to his father's hands, the hands women had loved, with knuckles that protruded like those in the pictures of saints. Sometimes his hands lay still next to each other or on top of each other, but usually they moved like a magician's, lighting a cigarette or reaching for a woman's nape under a cloud of hair or clenching into a fist to knock on a door. Now they were lying on his kneecap, white and aimless.

"I remember only Berl clearly."

"You forgot everything else and only remember Berl?"

"I have many fragments of memories, but most are blurred. I remember only Berl clearly."

"Is that so . . . So you went to Shlomo HaMelech Street?"

"Yes."

"And what did you find there?"

"Nothing. I couldn't figure out which building was his. Is he still alive?"

"You remember *only* Berl..." His father stretched out the words, enunciating them clearly, and blinked his blind eye as if he no longer believed Meir and wanted him to know that his ploy hadn't worked. "Why Berl, of all people?"

"I don't know why."

"Because there were many—"

"Maybe because I loved him most of all, or because he loved me most of all."

"There were many people you loved and who loved you."

"Apparently not, because I don't remember them," Meir the adult said, hurrying to the aid of Meir the child, so he wouldn't be duped. "What about Berl, is he still alive?"

"Berl died years ago, in 1973, two days after Yom Kippur. It was the third day of the war, about four months after your bar mitzvah."

Even though Meir had prepared himself for this possibility, now that he heard it spoken out loud, it hit him hard.

"What did he die of?"

"A heart attack."

"A heart attack? And who took care of him in the end?"

"He didn't need anyone. He died in his bed, in his sleep."

"So it was an easy death."

"His death was the easiest thing in his life."

Meir was suffused with the glow he always felt when he witnessed justice being done, but he hid his satisfaction from his father's prying eye.

"So you can rest easy about Berl."

"Yes." Meir wasn't sure he'd managed to elude his father's eye. "Where's his grave?"

"Where my grave will be: in the Kiryat Shaul cemetery," he said, and as if it were the natural continuation of the sentence, he asked, "Where did you put your suitcase?"

"Excuse me?"

"I asked where you put your suitcase."

"At the hotel."

"You found a hotel?"

"Yes."

"Where?"

"On HaYarkon Street."

"Do you have a problem with money?"

"No."

"Good. Are you thirsty? Want something to drink?"

"I'll go get us a Coke," Meir said, jumping at the opportunity, and hurried out, sensing the eye piercing his back. Out of his father's eyeshot, he allowed himself to lean against the wall behind the people waiting for the elevator and he smiled, letting a sigh escape his lips: Berl died without suffering. Berl died in his bed, surrounded by his beloved junk; he didn't die by fire or gas or suffocation or shooting or hunger or thirst. He simply closed his eyes peacefully, as if he were like any other person, and his nightmares and waking visions of horror came to an end. And maybe his funeral took place on the fourth day of the war at one o'clock along with the funerals of the Israeli soldiers, those same soldiers he used to salute when they walked past in the street. Then he would say to Meir in a trembling voice, "Take a good look, Meir'ke. He's one of our heroes, a soldier in our Israeli army."

When Meir returned to the glass room carrying a bottle of Coke and two disposable cups he bought at the volunteers' stand, he saw that the sick girl and her visitor had gone.

"You're used to Coca Cola, aren't you?" his father said, reaching out for the cup.

"Yes."

"And you're not hungry or thirsty, and you feel okay, right?"

"I'm fine, yes."

"So now you can ask," he said, tilting his head back and closing his eyes as a sign that he was listening.

"Ask what?"

"Whatever you want. I think we've talked enough and now it's time for you to ask your questions."

Meir was surprised at how well preserved his father's ancient ability to read his wishes was. "I wanted . . . I wanted to know what's wrong with you and what happened to your eye."

"My condition is bad. We're better off not knowing too much. The doctor is trying to hide it from me, but I know it's bad. And on top of that, my eye went two weeks ago."

"Why don't they bandage it for you?"

"So you want to be Moshe Dayan's son, do you? But that's life—your father isn't such a big hero," he said, opening the purple eye wide.

"And the other eye is healthy?" Meir asked, ignoring the taunt.

"I fought with them about the other eye so I could see you. They wanted to do an emergency operation on it, but I told the doctor: I gave up one eye—Moshe Dayan managed pretty well with one eye, too—but leave me the other one because I have to see someone very important to me, and if I don't have eyes, I'll have to feel him and I'm not sure he'll let me."

Too surprised to react, liking his father, despite himself, for the matter-of-fact, unself-pitying way he had just spoken, Meir looked back at the open eye staring steadfastly at him, studying every move he made.

"I almost went to see you in America."

"I know."

"But my blood pressure started going crazy all of a sudden and the doctor wouldn't let me go."

"I know."

"I almost went to Arnie's colleagues for treatment."

"I know."

"You know everything and you don't know anything," he said, his eye dancing. Meir wondered what his father knew about Arnie, about the childhood photographs and the gifts his mother had received and kept in the drawer of the Tel Aviv law office, about how easily Arnie had slipped into the role of father, about the time Arnie came over every night to bandage his knees, about all the years Arnie took him to baseball games, all the years he'd come to see his mother at the end of the day on his way back to his wife and daughters. Although he'd never seen them embrace, the strong attachment they had was obvious even when they were on opposite sides of the room. And what bound them with ties of guilt was the death of Eleanor. Left with a nanny for the three days his mother and Arnie spent together in Texas, she'd burned with fever for most of that time. They were summoned urgently to the hospital, but it was too late.

"What don't I know?" Meir said angrily. He was thinking, I was there at her bedside in the maternity ward when Arnie held Eleanor; and six months later, I cried in his arms when he picked me up at Eleanor's funeral.

"You don't know what happened or didn't happen, and you don't know why I wanted to go to America."

"You wanted to be treated in an American hospital."

"Is that what you think?" his father asked with a grin, but seeing Meir's embarrassment, became serious. "And Arnie was good to you?"

"Very good," Meir replied, trying to sound casual, surprised at himself for attempting to save his father from the truth instead of saying loudly: he took care of me. He was the one who came in the middle of the night when I was sick. He was the one the school called when I broke my leg. He was the only one I talked to about Eleanor after she died. He took me on trips with his daughters and to baseball games without them. He came to rescue me from my first summer camp after I begged him to on the phone. He secretly gave me a tranquillizer before I was called up to read from the Torah. He explained to me about erections. He took me to college interviews. He gave me a feeling of confidence, something I never felt with you.

"He was good to your mother, too," his father said casually. Meir wondered what was the subtext of this remark that made his heart clench. Was his father affronted that another man had taken his place, or was he protesting against his son and the games Meir was playing with him? Or was it appreciation for Arnie, the man who took upon himself obligations that another man abandoned? Or, simply acceptance of the reality he no longer had control over?

"He was good to you, too," Meir said, relieving the clenching of his heart with a joking tone that had no joke in it.

"How?" his father asked.

"He wanted to help you get well."

"He wouldn't have made me well, and that's not why I wanted to come," he said.

"So why did you want to come?"

His father grimaced as if he were about to burst into tears, and there was something in that expression that suddenly reminded Meir of Eleanor.

"I wanted to come because I never understood from your mother what you remembered and what you didn't."

"That's why?" Meir asked in blatant disbelief.

"Yes."

"I told you before: I have very few memories."

"So that's what I wanted to understand, because we went through things together.... And I wanted to check with you.... She said you remembered the apartment on HaNevi'im Street and the kindergarten on Netzach Israel Street and Whitman ice cream ..."

"It's very fuzzy."

"Do you remember anything about after we left HaNavi'im Street?"

Meir scrutinized the seeing eye. "Like what?"

"We wandered from one café to another, you must remember something like that."

**His father would stop at the entrance to the café, and Meir knew without being told that, from there, he could assess the mood of Alterman and the people sitting at his table as well as how much**

danger he could expect, based on how hungry they were for amusement. Sometimes Meir could sense from across the street and through the café windows how the people at the table mocked his father, not by taunting a strong, dangerous somebody but by disregarding a weak, harmless nobody.

"Why do they always laugh when you talk to them?" he once asked his father.

"They're not really laughing; that's just the way it is among friends," his father said. "Once it was because of a poem I translated and once because Alterman said I don't know how to write in rhyme or meter and now it's because of 'Raisin-Mountain,' which is what Rosinberg means. Alterman likes to call people names and they think it's funny. So every time he calls me 'Aharon Raisin-Mountain,' I call him 'Natan Old-Man,' which is what Alterman means." He raised his chin as if he had retaliated with a double dose and erased the insult. But Meir could sense the hesitation in his posture when he'd stop at the door to check out the mood or level of drunkenness at Alterman's table. If he thought Alterman was in a good mood, he'd walk by them serenely, stop to say hello and take a cigarette he was offered before he headed for the woman he'd already picked out. When he thought they seemed eager to insult, he'd ignore them and sit down at a table that was back-to-back or side-by-side with the table where the chosen woman was sitting. Once, his heart filled with joy when Meir saw Alterman invite his father to the table with a gesture and move his chair to make room. His father sat between Alterman and a handsome young poet from Jerusalem, whose praises he'd sung long afterward. But as the time passed, Meir's sense of pride at the warm reception had been replaced by concern that his father might get so carried away by the conversation, by the liquor that Alterman was pouring, and by the laughter around the table, that it would get very late.

Sometimes his father would be devious: he wouldn't go straight to the chosen woman or even glance at her table.

From the door, he would head for other people, pat three or four of them on the shoulder, exchange a few words with one of them and burst out laughing; sometimes he'd sit down next to them for a while, sip from a shot glass, light a cigarette they handed him, and then call the waiter over amiably and point to a table at the other side of the café, next to the woman's table, where he wanted his coffee to be brought. He'd step lightly between the tables and, still not looking at her, he'd sit down, take out a bundle of papers and begin to write. From where he stood, Meir could see the woman looking out of the corner of her eye at his father, who was immersed in his papers, his elbow on the table, one hand holding a cigarette in the air. When his coffee arrived and he thanked the waiter with a smiling nod, a page slid off his table and landed next to her foot. She looked at it, almost leaning over it, and when his father bent quickly to pick it up, he found himself face to face with the woman. Meir couldn't hear what they said to each other, but he would see the woman burst into joyous, embarrassed laughter. His father picked up the piece of paper, returned to his table, straightened up in his chair, and became immediately engrossed in his writing again. The woman, still smiling, waited for him to look up and then said something to him. His father looked at her with concentration, as if he were still absorbed in distant worlds, but quickly shook himself free of his preoccupation and conversation flowed freely between them until she motioned to the chair next to her and he gathered up his papers and his cup of coffee and moved them to her table. Sometimes they would talk for a long time, sometimes he would reach out to touch her hair or her hand, and sometimes, especially when he was a bit drunk, he'd reach under the table to touch her legs. Sometimes Meir would fall asleep sitting up, and then he didn't know whether he'd actually seen his father's courtship ritual or whether he'd dreamed it: his father's fox-like expression as he silently debated how far he could go with this woman, his hand moving slowly to

**her knees under the table, the way she drew away and froze, the instant comprehension that dawned on her face straining to remain impassive, her eyes slowly beginning to smile, then his wrist disappearing under her skirt, her thighs shifting to the side to shake off his groping hand, and then both his hands emerging onto the table, side by side, as if parading their innocence to the entire world.**

"Which café?" Meir asked.

"Cafés . . . there were a few of them. But not only cafés. There were all sorts of places. And you don't remember anything from the time after we left HaNevi'im Street?"

Puzzled, Meir caught his father's eyes in an effort to understand: Was he asking about the long, cold winter nights he spent near the tree across the street from the Kassit? Was he asking about the homes of his many lovers? About the sounds he heard? About the sights he saw? About the things he understood then and the things he understood only with the distance of time?

"I don't remember any café," he said quietly and thought he saw his father's tense face relax in relief.

"So what do you remember? School? You started the first grade. You had a nice teacher with a pony tail."

Meir fell silent for a moment, taken aback by at the sudden shift from cafés to school.

"I might be getting kindergarten and the first grade mixed up," he said, finding himself drawing a strange, vindictive pleasure from the lies, the straightforward way he managed to speak them, how seriously the sick man accepted them.

"Do you remember the song and dance I used to put on for the principals so they'd let you come to school?" A mischievous smile spread over his face.

"No," Meir said, refusing to cooperate with him on this.

"Not that either. . . And all the months . . . You said you don't remember cafés. That was one thing I was sure you'd remember."

"No."

"There was one called Kassit on Dizengoff Street. Poets used to go there a lot. Sometimes you came inside with me and sometimes you'd wait outside until I finished taking care of a few things . . ."

Once, after his father had drunk more cognac than usual, Meir saw him get up from the poets' table and sit down next to a woman wearing a green coat. It seemed as if they hadn't spoken more than a sentence or two when he got up and crossed the street without looking at the honking cars and gesticulated at Meir, who was sitting in the circle of sand around the tree. Certain of his victory, he was drunker than usual and trembling in a way that his son had learned to recognize. He kneeled in front of him and whispered, "You saw where I was sitting before?"

"Yes."

"Not next to Alterman."

"I saw, the other table."

"The table on the far left with the woman in the green coat. I'm going back there—"

"Where does she live?"

"We're about to find out. Now I'm going back there and you watch her knees."

"Why?" Meir asked, startled.

"So you can see right away whether or not we have a place tonight."

"How will I know?"

"If her knees are together like they are now, then we don't have a place. But if her knees move, each in a different direction, and there's a space in the middle, then our chances are good."

"Why?"

"Because a woman who wants, moves her knees," his father said, coming closer and blowing a smelly cloud of alcohol at him.

"What does she want?" Meir asked.

"What I can give her."

Silently, Meir looked at the woman's knees pressed together.

"Do you understand, Meir?" his father asked, touching Meir's face.

"Yes."

"So wait here and watch. I can't see you from inside, but I know you're standing here and I'll wave to you," his father said and staggered back to the café.

After a while, his eyes tearing from the strain, Meir saw that the woman's knees began to move under the table, pressed together, shifting together to the right and together to the left, not still for a minute, until he could see clearly how they separated, leaving a space between them and remaining that way until his father came out to him and said, "You can go inside if you need to pee. We have a place on Nordau Street tonight, two houses down from where Alterman lives."

Sometimes, when his father was drunk, he would stroke the women's bottoms in Meir's presence, or squeeze their breasts or bury his head in their lap. Once, he even slept with one of them on a convertible couch behind a curtain while Meir, wide awake, his body constricted with cold and embarrassment, was lying on an easy chair on the balcony on the other side of the curtain. Disturbed by the heavy breathing, the small moans and ragged whispers, as if a struggle were taking place, Meir looked down at the street below and saw the flickering blue light of a police car, and he froze at the memory of the policemen driving around in the dark searching for children who'd stopped going to school.

That memory ignited another, a frightening one that also began with Meir waiting for his father, as usual, on the circle of sand around the tree. From where he stood, half-asleep, he saw his father get up to go, accompanied by two women he'd been sitting with. But his father didn't come over to him or glance at him or even send him one of their secret signs, and Meir watched as the three of them turned left and disappeared in the bend of Gordon Street. Meir sat there in the circle of sand under the tree and burst out crying. The flow of hot tears had already reached his chin when his father suddenly appeared above him.

"What's wrong, Meir?"

"I saw you come out and walk away."

"Come on. Follow me. I didn't want them to see you."

"I thought you forgot me."

"How could I forget you? A father doesn't forget his son. Look, we have the key to a large apartment and it's ours for four whole days. That's a good reason not to cry."

"Where's the apartment?" Meir asked, wiping away his tears with the back of his hand and hurrying after his father.

"On Mapu Street near the beach."

"Whose is it?"

"The woman I was sitting with."

"You were sitting with two women."

"She went to sleep at the other one's place because they're getting up early tomorrow to go on a trip. And we have an empty apartment all to ourselves."

"I don't remember that café," Meir said, his throat closing up now.

"You don't remember Alterman either? I talked about him so much. The great poet, Natan Alterman . . . . He was there a lot, too."

"I don't remember."

"You once asked me what kind of cigarettes Alterman smokes and I said 'Ascot'. Do you remember Ascot cigarettes?"

"No."

"I didn't understand why you were asking. You saw him give me a cigarette and you asked. So it must have been important to you," his father said, then fell silent as if searching for another sign. Then he straightened up, attentive once again, and said, "And once you told me you saw his halo. Like light spouting from a showerhead, instead of water—that's what you said, word for word. You were very impressed then. You couldn't stop talking about him. We remember things that impress us better than other things."

"I don't remember any halo," Meir said. But a memory of a night when he fell asleep leaning against the tree flashed through his mind like lightning. A drunk walking past had bumped into the tree and shook Meir, who woke with a start. The drunk, who was startled too, bent over him cautiously and asked if he was a boy or a dwarf. Meir, almost crying with fear, whispered that he was a boy and expected the drunk to hit him or try to kidnap him and then dress him in rags and turn him into a beggar like Oliver, but the man apologized, straightened up and walked away, muttering to himself. Confused, blinded by tears, Meir looked at the café's square of glowing light and at all the people squeezed together around a single table, and he clearly saw an enchantment out of a fairy tale: two glowing diagonals descended from above Alterman's head, encircling it as if at that very moment the laws of nature had changed and the lamp hanging above Alterman's head had turned into a celestial body, shedding primeval, crystalline light in two precise lines to Alterman's shoulders. It spilled around him, and he was in its glow, swaying as if in prayer. Meir sat down inside the circle of sand that surrounded the tree, astonished and awestruck.

"I saw that halo all the time and I told you about it, but you— you said you didn't see it for months, and then one day, I found you sitting next to the tree as if you'd been struck by lightning or something. You were really in shock. You told me you saw Alterman's halo."

"I don't remember anything like that."

"I was sure you'd remember that your whole life, that you'd remember everything . . . So many things happened in the apartment on HaNevi'im Street."

"They say that people don't have memories before the age of two or three because they don't have language then."

"That's interesting," his father said, then grew quiet, and Meir knew he was savoring the new taste of conversing with his adult son. "That really is interesting. But when we went to the Kassit, you were already more than seven."

"I read that memories, even the memories of an adult, are erased sometimes after an intense experience."

"You really did forget," his father said, persuaded. He ignored Meir's comment about an intense experience and showing none of the signs of relief Meir was looking for. "You were a little boy . . ." Suddenly, there was a spark of cunning in his father's thoughtful expression, and he said, "But you do remember Berl."

"Him, yes . . ." Meir said.

"So what *do* you remember clearly?"

"How I arrived in America."

"They sent you by plane, I know. I tried to picture a million times how it was for you, all alone, so many hours, a boy of seven, on a plane for the first time in his life with strangers."

**The pretty flight attendant didn't leave him alone for a minute. She must have gotten a detailed description of the special case and was filled with compassion for the boy whom fate had sent across the ocean, with only his schoolbag; the boy who kept crying softly despite her pampering and the sweets she slipped to him secretly, and despite her invitation to take a peek into the cockpit with all its clocks and dials. When he got tired, she prepared a comfortable bed for him across two seats, covered him, and stroked his forehead. When the plane landed, she cleaned his face with fragrant wet wipes and stood him next to the door of the plane while she bid the exiting passengers farewell. Then, one hand holding his, the other holding his schoolbag, she took him out to the arrivals hall and headed for the very fat woman sitting in a wheelchair waving a placard with the name "Meir" written on it in English and Hebrew.**

"Mother was waiting for me at the airport."

"Really? She came herself?"

"Yes."
"But she was confined to her bed, wasn't she?"
"She came in a wheelchair."

She no longer had the mane of copper hair that had crowned her head and her face was paler and broader than he remembered, but when he came closer, he knew for certain it was her, despite the convulsive crying that changed her expression. He flung himself into the arms she held out to him and met with an enormous stomach as hard as a circle of concrete under the cascade of her soft breasts. Her fingers wandered over his face as if she wanted to make sure they'd brought her the right boy. She stroked his head, buried in her bosom, and said, "Welcome home, my darling," and he burst into tears and was picked up and carried on the shoulders of the man who was with his mother, Arnie.

"And who ran the house? Who shopped, who cooked, who cleaned?"

Frederica walked around the house as if she were invisible. In the morning, she would arrive in her car, raise the metal garage door with her remote, drive inside and go up the steps to the kitchen, almost always carrying a huge paper bag full of groceries she'd bought on the way.

"There was a Latina maid, Frederica."
    "And when you came, who took care of you? Your mother?"
    "She was in bed. Frederica took care of me."
    "From the first day?"
    "Yes."
    "How did you speak to her, in English?"
    "Yes, in English."

Meir was surprised to discover that she spoke a broken English, and within a few months, he was sitting in the kitchen with her,

teaching her from his schoolbook what he'd learned in his
English lesson that day.

"And in general, what was it like for you there, at the beginning?
Did you have a hard time getting used to things?"

The first week, relatives and older friends came to see the boy
from Israel. They looked at him openly and peered at him surreptitiously, apparently trying to match what they'd heard with
what they were seeing. Some spoke only broken Hebrew, but
nonetheless insisted on carrying on a conversation with him,
to determine how bright he was, but he didn't answer them and
there was always someone who said: "Leave him alone. Don't
you see he can't talk?" The first few days, he was stunned by the
size of the house, by the grove of trees around it, like those
around Robinson Crusoe's house, by the squirrels hopping
under the trees and the lovely fawns that emerged from the
grove and wandered serenely in the garden.

When his mother and grandfather were resting in their
rooms, Meir would climb to the top of the thickly carpeted
wooden stairs and slide down on his rear end as if he were on
a playground slide, and he'd go in and out of the many rooms,
the large bathrooms, his mother's dressing room with its
huge mirror. That was during the day. At night, almost every
night for the first month, he'd wake up frightened in the dark,
not remembering where they'd taken him the night before or
how he'd gotten to the large bed that was all his, knowing
only that he mustn't utter a sound. Slowly, objects would take
shape around him and he'd look in amazement at the large
window, the heavy curtain, until he remembered and said to
himself: "America."

For most of the day, his mother would stay in bed and only
when guests came would she walk slowly downstairs, step by
step, to go lie on the living room couch. So Meir spent most of
his days with Frederica and his grandfather, who was weak, had

a shriveled face, and barely spoke, but his eyes followed Meir affectionately, filling with tears at the sight of how thrilled the boy was by the squirrels and the fawns.

Meir was equally fascinated by television. "There is no television in Israel, so he's very taken with it," his mother apologized to the guests when the boy slipped away from them again and again to go sit in front of the mesmerizing screen. And a short time later, everyone was glued to the TV. The news reported on the Israeli army's alert, and then, during the six days of the war, there were daily updates on the brilliant victory and the occupation of the Sinai, the Gaza Strip, the Golan, Jerusalem, and—the viewers' hearts stopped—here was a shot of the Wailing Wall, the only vestige of the Temple, they explained to Meir when one of the women in the room burst into tears, and here was Moshe Dayan, the hero with the black patch over his eye, on his way to the Wall.

"The house was beautiful, my room was full of toys, Frederica took care of me, and Grandpa was nice. There were kitchen shelves full of popcorn and cornflakes and bottles of Coke," he said, thinking: the complete opposite of Tel Aviv. And then he thought: but I wasn't happier than I'd been in Tel Aviv.

"Popcorn and Coke . . ." For a moment, his father seemed to be jealous of him, but quickly continued the comparison, saying, "So you were glad to be in America?"

For the first few days, Meir didn't speak a word. His mother, alternately thinking that the boy was punishing her and fearing that he had a speech disorder, must have called Arnie. The crying sounds the boy made when they met at the airport and the few words he spoke on the way home may have given her hope, but from the moment they crossed the threshold of the house, she couldn't get a single sentence out of him. Silently he sat at the table with them, silently he stared out of the windows, silently he watched Frederica as she invented a sign language for him, silently he stood in front of the TV, enthralled. To people's questions, he reacted with a shrug or a nod, seeing in their eyes that they expected him to say something. He felt that the words amassed in his throat, as if blocked. And one day, about a month after he arrived, when the people around him had grown accustomed to his silence and had learned to read his facial expressions, he got up from the table and said "thank you" to Frederica in English. From then on, as if he were recovering from an illness, the words began to flow from him. No one ever asked him about that month of silence.

"I was confused at first, but I had everything I needed."

"And there was family, too," his father said quickly. Meir couldn't tell whether the words had caused him to feel a twinge of emotion. "How did you manage with the family?—All of a sudden you had aunts and uncles and cousins your own age, something you didn't have in Tel Aviv."

He cried his first tears in America against his mother's neck in the large airport arrivals halls, and at night, alone in his new bed, he cried again. The next day, he cried when his aunt and uncle and their two children, Ronald and Claire, stood in the doorway in a perfect picture of familial bliss: first the mother, tall and brave, facing the dangers in front of them, holding her children's hands as they stood on either side of her, and behind them, shielding them from the dangers at their back, was Uncle Solomon. Only years later, in a conversation with Arnie, could he explain to himself what it was about that picture that was instantly ruined when the children pulled their hands from their mother's grasp and raced inside, what it was about that picture that made his heart ache and set off a tidal wave of tears in him. The picture of those four in the rectangle of the door, bonded to each other in total, self-evident harmony remained forever etched in his mind. And perhaps—he said to himself—

perhaps that picture was such a painful contrast to the memories he'd brought with him that at that moment, he decided to plunge the knife into his Tel Aviv memories and drive them to the depths of redemptive oblivion; perhaps at that moment, he decided that here, in this place, he'd begin his life again, modeled after the one that had presented itself in all its beauty in the doorway.

"At first, they came to visit a lot and Uncle Solomon brought me presents. But after Grandpa died, there was a big fight and there were only phone calls to say Happy New Year at Rosh Hashana, and we only saw each other twice, at the cousins' weddings."

" So there weren't many family ties?" his father asked.

"No. There was a big argument after the will was read, and we didn't see each other until Claire got married and invited us herself."

"So the move to America was fairly easy for you?" his father said.

During the month of silence, Frederica discovered the food he'd been secretly hoarding, preparing for when the days of plenty would end. She found candies in the pockets of his coats, a bottle of Coca Cola under his bed, a roll under his mattress, a jar of peanuts among the shoes in his shoe-closet, a piece of meat rolled up in aluminum foil among the pencils in his in his pencil drawer. One morning, she took Meir by the hand into the kitchen, pointed to one of the pantry shelves and said it was his. For a long minute, he looked at the Coke bottle, the candies, the crushed roll, the peanuts. Then he nodded, went to his room and took a bag of cookies from the back of a drawer and three apples out of a wool hat and put them on the shelf allotted to him. Sometimes, he wondered whether Frederica had reported his hoard to his mother, who then told her what to do, or whether she'd done it on her own, until once, from a casual remark he heard, he realized that it had been Arnie's idea.

∗ ∗ ∗

"It was relatively easy."

"Relatively is good," he father said, shrugging off the responsibility to delve into what was behind that qualifying word. "And after the summer, you started going to school? How was it there?"

**Every day of the summer vacation, an Israeli student, a college sophomore, came to the house to teach him reading and writing so he could skip the first grade. Three months after the Six Day War ended, he passed the tests and went straight into the second grade, where the teacher welcomed him with the respect due to victors. But his excellent test grades and the distant war that so affected the teacher did not impress the children, not even the ones who were Jewish, and for the entire year, none of them volunteered to sit next to the new boy.**

"What was your favorite subject in school?"

"I liked literature and history, especially ancient history."

"Because of the Greek myths," his father said, trying to connect himself to his son's life, wanting to remind him who taught him to love mythology. "Your mother told me that you became an expert in Greek mythology. You can imagine how happy that made me."

"I took that book with me from Israel and kept reading it later, in high school. I even wrote a few papers on it in college . . . . In fact, from the beginning, when I first spent time with Grandpa, it was to read that book together."

**After a few months, the book, which had crossed the ocean with him, was dog-eared from so much use. Since Meir didn't know how to read, he and his grandfather focused on the illustrations. And every day after the month of silence, they'd sit together, Meir's small fingers wandering over the familiar pictures, counting the words he knew in English, and his grandfather would add the names of things he didn't know.**

"Woman, man, flower, sea, eye, mouth, nose, tree, hand, foot, dress," Meir said.

His grandfather pointed and explained, "Forehead, eyebrows, neck, ankle, elbow, grove, seashell."

Two weeks later, Meir said, "The woman is standing on a seashell, the man is flying in the air, the flowers are falling into the sea."

His grandfather said, "The woman on the right is holding a robe to cover the woman standing in the middle. The man on the left is an angel with wings. He's breathing on the woman."

Meir, understanding every word and able to say those sentences himself within a day, said, "The woman is very beautiful."

"You might say I learned English with that book."

"I find that very moving," his father said, his right leg dropping off the wheelchair footrest, and Meir heard the emotion in his voice. "Because I also learned a new language with that book. I don't think I ever told you what happened to me and my family in Europe. When I was about seven, I ran away to Russia with my father. The Germans had invaded Poland and he decided to escape. We lived near the Russian border. And the book I took with me, that stayed with me through the whole war, was the book of Greek mythology, written in Polish. A Russian neighbor helped me learn Russian using the pictures in that book."

Meir recoiled, immediately shaking off this shared experience that had been thrust on him. "It was only by chance."

"Of course," the father said, "and just by chance, I saw that same book in a store in Tel Aviv, translated into Hebrew, and bought it for you. Things are always happening that remind me of the Greek myths. For instance, when your mother told me that you forgot that whole time in Tel Aviv, I remembered that anyone who drank from the river of forgetfulness in the world of the dead would forget his former life."

Meir wondered, Was his father waiting for a confession about the similarity between America and Hades so he could feel better about the contrast between America and Tel Aviv?

"Or was America more like Elysium?" his father asked, volunteering another possibility.

**During his many moments of despair, Meir reread the terrible story of Tantalus, who stood in a pool of water, his throat burning with thirst. But the water receded into the earth the minute he tried to drink it; the juicy pears and figs hanging above his head were swept away by the wind the minute he reached out for them; and a huge stone hung over him, threatening to fall on his head. Wracked by hunger and thirst, his heart filled with despair, he would sometimes pray to Typhon, the flying monster: Come to me, come and drop the stone on me now.**

"It was very rarely Elysium. It took me years to get used to it."

"That long?" his father asked. His voice sounded not a bit sad, and apparently aware of that, he waited a moment before saying, "So you arrived at the end of the year and went straight into the second grade. And all your classes were in English?"

"Yes. It was an American public school."

"And you didn't study Hebrew?"

"Only on Sundays."

"Did you learn to read and write Hebrew, too?"

"Yes. I read a few books for teenagers and some newspapers in easy Hebrew."

"Very good. . . . So at first, you lived with your grandfather. And then?"

**The day after Meir's ninth birthday, Arnie suggested moving from Connecticut to Manhattan so that Meir could go to a renowned special school for children recently arrived in the country, where he'd have a better chance of meeting Israeli chil-**

**dren and making friends. Meir had had his birthday party the
day before, at McDonald's with his mother, Arnie, and four
classmates out of the twenty who were invited. The adults pretended they hadn't been expecting more than four guests and
quickly separated the tables that had been pushed together in a
corner of the restaurant. A short time afterwards, at a relaxed
moment when the initial tension had faded, the children were
busy passing a bottle of ketchup from one to the other and Arnie
was telling them about a funny incident that happened on one
of his birthdays when he was a child, at that very moment, Meir
lowered his forehead to the edge of the table and burst into sobs,
and the children broke into a chorus of laughter.**

"We lived in Grandpa's house for two years. Then we moved to
Manhattan."

"Who's 'we'?"

"Mom and me. Eleanor wasn't there anymore."

Silence fell. The little girl whose father hadn't known her, the
fruit of his seed, his only daughter, to whom he would always be
connected only by one night or one hour of love, that little girl
had been mentioned by name and Meir thought he saw a shadow
cross his father's face, as if the flow of blood through his veins
had momentarily shifted under the cover of his gray skin.

"Who chose that name for her?" he asked, pouring all his helplessness into the question. If he'd dreamed about an ideal family—a mother, a father, a son, and a daughter—the dream had
been destroyed even before she was born, and he hadn't even
taken part in choosing her name.

"I chose the name. It was the name of a friend of Mother's who
was nice to me."

"What kind of baby was she?"

"Cute. She liked to pull my hair," Meir said, trying to find
something to say about the six-month-old baby.

"Your mother sent me her picture. She really was cute. Looked
a little like you when you were a baby."

The old mechanism that collected fragmentary details and put them together into a single picture went right into action: Yes, his father and mother had been in contact over the years. His father had asked for a picture of the baby. Over the phone? Maybe you couldn't make transatlantic calls from the phone in prison. He'd probably asked in a letter. Which means that letters were sent to his mother. Obviously, there must have been regards sent to their child, regards that never reached their destination. His mother didn't tell him about the letters because then she wouldn't have been able to stick to her story about his dead father. So a picture of Eleanor had been sent to him. Had he hung it on the wall of his prison cell? Had he also asked for a picture of his son? Maybe he had childhood pictures of the boy in one of the cardboard boxes they'd moved to Berl's cellar. Had he hung one of them on the wall of his cell? And maybe his mother had sent him a picture of their two children together, maybe the one in which Meir was holding three-day-old Eleanor in his arms and a maternity ward nurse had spread her hands under his small arms as a safety net?

"Yes. We must have looked alike."

"And did you have a hard time with . . . the tragedy?"

"I had a pretty hard time," Meir said, remembering his bloody knees. "Because I'd started getting used to her and also because Mom went into a depression after that, and you could say that she pretty much neglected me for a few years."

"But there was your grandfather," his father said. Meir thought his father seemed agitated, anxious to find the solution to his young son's problem.

"Grandpa was too sick. There was Arnie . . ."

"I understand that you were close to Arnie. To this very day, I'm sure."

**Three days before he flew to Tel Aviv to see his father, Meir went to say goodbye to Arnie. Arnie stood at the door of his clinic, his eyes shining with excitement as he watched Meir**

lock his car. Then his expression clouded suddenly, as if through the present image of the good-looking man stepping lightly toward him sprang the past image of a frightened boy fiercely clutching his schoolbag, releasing his hold on it only in the evening, after he ate and drank and checked out every corner of the house.

They hugged each other tightly. Meir, inhaling the characteristic blend of Old Spice and medicine, was swept back into the tunnel of time and was again that seven-year-old boy shortly after he got off the plane. As a teenager, a college student, and a young man, that touch and that smell had always aroused the fear he'd felt when he landed in the too-perfect world, that all the abundance might disappear at any moment, as past experience had taught him. Arnie seemed to sense this, because he would always disengage gently and grip Meir's arms for a moment before he backed away a step to look at his face. This time, Arnie's glance lingered, as if he were searching for something new.

"You're not sleeping well, are you?"

"No."

"How about a cup of coffee or something stronger?"

They sat across from each other in the waiting room, quiet after office hours, and drank beer. Meir, as usual when he was with Arnie, dropped the defensive fortifications he normally hid behind in his dealings with the world.

"Do you think we should have told you about him years ago?"

"I don't know."

"Do you think it would've been easier for you at times, if you could've written to him, maybe go to see him?"

"I'm not sure. The problems I had over the years weren't because I didn't have a father, but first of all, because I didn't really have a mother."

"We've already talked about that, Meir. I explained her condition to you. She gave you everything she was capable of giving then. We all know that you were always important to her."

"I didn't feel that way. I felt completely superfluous. There were beautiful words with nothing behind them," he said. "There were days when there was no food in the house. Do you remember how you used to come every once in a while with a hamburger? Sometimes that was all I ate that day."

"I want you to know that usually she had called and asked me to bring a hamburger. That was all she could do. She was clinically depressed, and none of the medications helped her."

"I think that first with my father, then with her, I grew up with people who seemed fine and well-educated, part-Bohemian and part-bourgeoisie, but our life was not what it should have been."

"Do you know that most people think there's something abnormal about their lives? At least that's how it is with my patients."

"My life was abnormal, that's for sure. You were the most normal thing in it."

Arnie chuckled, raised his glass and took a sip.

"Can I ask you something, Arnie? For these last two weeks, I've been finding out things about my childhood, and I have many questions."

"Do you want to ask about your mother and me?"

"That, too."

"Your mother and I have been waiting a long time for that question."

"So now I'm asking."

"And the answer is that we couldn't get married because Martha wouldn't have given up Carol and Allison easily, and I wanted to raise them. I didn't want them to grow up with another man, and that's what would've happened if we'd split up, because Martha would've gotten married right away. She's not capable of being alone."

"So my mother waited for you until they grew up?" When he didn't have to, Meir avoided mentioning Arnie's daughters' names.

"No. There were no promises. But I took care of her and you. I made no promises, but I was committed to you both. Even more than just committed, I loved you and felt responsible for you because I wanted to. But I always remembered that you had a father who might be thinking about you and missing you, and one day, he might want to find out where his place was in your life. You could say I was saving his place."

"I'm a little afraid of seeing him," Meir said quickly, as if promising Arnie that he would have a place in his life forever.

"I imagine it wasn't easy living alone with him."

"He took me out of school and dragged me around to all kinds of places, all kinds of women. I'm starting to remember things that are still hiding inside me, I have no idea where. He may even have taken me with him to whores. That time in Tel Aviv, after my mother left, was completely crazy. We lived in the streets."

"Some people might say that's great material for a writer. One of the first things you told me was that you wanted to be a writer."

"Really? I don't remember that."

"That's what you said."

"Then you could say I pretty much failed. I wrote only one book before I turned thirty and I've had writer's block for the last three years."

"Every writer finds himself in that situation at some point."

"I'm not really a writer yet. One book doesn't make me a writer."

They fell silent.

"What I do remember is the first thing you ever said to me: 'Don't worry. Tomorrow is a new day.'"

"Yes," Arnie said and smiled, his face wrinkling. "You were a child with the most worried expression I'd ever seen. As if you were responsible for the whole world."

"Yes," Meir said, suddenly saddened. He had been a boy with an innate sense of responsibility, who'd been thrown into a life that didn't allow him to act on it.

**"Should I give you a few tranquillizers you can take before or after you see him, if you want to?" Arnie leaned toward him, and out of an old habit, put his hand on Meir's knee. Meir saw it less as the act of a doctor trying to ease suffering than as a kind of blessing given to him just before he left to see the father whose place Arnie had taken for all those years.**

"Yes, Arnie was always there."

"Very nice. . . . And they made you a bar mitzvah there?"

"Yes."

"Remember the synagogue near our boulevard, on the street next to Netzach Israel? You don't remember. There's a synagogue there with many steps leading up to it, and once, joking around, I told you it was named after you. There was a Meir Park that I also said was named after you. That's all I could give you then. So about that synagogue, if everything had gone like it should have, we would've celebrated your bar mitzvah there. . . . On the Saturday of your bar mitzvah, I thought about you a lot, whether you'd learned your *Haftorah* well, and how they do it there in America, in their fancy synagogues that look like churches, with organs . . . and in English."

**The building stood on the southeast corner of Second Avenue and Twenty-third Street. The door, like the doors of poor people's houses, opened onto the sidewalk, the wall facing Twenty-third Street was drab and windowless, and near the roof hung a verse from the Book of Isaiah: "For my house shall be called a house of prayer for all peoples." Inside, the soft light coming from the windows on other walls filled the hall, and Meir, almost choking with excitement, spoke in a voice that barely reached the ears of the listeners, and he kept a firm grasp on his thumbs the entire time.**

"There was a synagogue right across the street from the apartment house. It wasn't fancy at all . . ."

"Not fancy? In America?"

"The plainest synagogue in the area, lined up with the stores on the sidewalk."

"So you were still living in Manhattan then, right? And now you're living in your grandfather's house again."

"Yes. He left it to me."

"He actually left it to you? All to you? Not a part of it to your mother? Or to his other grandchildren?"

"All to me. In his will, in his own handwriting. And I think he was right."

His father suddenly burst out laughing and Meir was surprised to see that all the bad years hadn't changed this gesture of his, the one he used to make in the café, accompanied by his upright hand holding a cigarette, now only an imaginary one: he tilted his head back as if he were drunk, then immediately bowed it as if in mourning, laughing until he choked. Looking at him, Meir was suddenly frightened in retrospect: this was the man whose kindness and moods he'd been dependent on for five months that lasted an eternity when he was a child, and he was once again gripped by the old helplessness.

"What's so funny?"

"God's sense of humor," his father replied, lifting his head and looking into Meir's eyes, revealing tears in the corners. "For a boy who wandered around homeless, you have many homes now."

"I have one home."

"Yes," his father said, wiping away the tears of laughter and becoming serious immediately, as if they had been tears of weeping.

"So he left you a beautiful house in his handwritten will . . . That's a sign that he loved you very much."

"Or was very angry at the others," Meir said, finding himself angered by the inexplicable laughter. "Or felt very guilty toward me," he said, shooting a barb at his father.

"Yes . . ." his father said, ignoring the barb. Meir noted that what separated them was far greater than what united them.

"And you're comfortable in that house?"

"I love it. It's the first house I lived in when I got to America," Meir replied. "I have an open terrace where I can sit outside in the summer and there's a beautiful grove across the way, and fawns and does wander around my garden," he said, saying the names of the animals in English.

"Really?"

"Yes. And eat my flowers."

**For the first few months, he'd stand at the large window and stare unbelievingly at the miracle of the fawns and does grazing on the rosebuds, as if book illustrations had come to life before his eyes. And when autumn came and the leaves turned gold and drifted down from the trees, he'd play outside, make a pile of golden leaves in the middle of the garden, burrow under it and roll around inside it, unable to contain his joy. One night, in an epiphany, he suddenly knew for certain that in the denseness of the grove, hidden among the crowded trees, existed an Olympus that was twin to the Greek Olympus.**

**In the early evening, clouds would gather over the grove, and Meir saw clearly how they formed an arch, like the gate of clouds through which the gods entered. At the end of autumn, he would stand for hours in front of the trees that danced in the wind and search for Aeolus, the god of the winds. It was Aeolus who had given Odysseus a closed sack in which he had trapped the winds, forbidding Odysseus to open it. But the curious sailors did open it, and the wild winds burst out and blew their ship off course. When, a few weeks later, the winter winds hurled the treetops against each other, Meir clearly saw glittering eyes, the eyes of some of the hundred serpents that issued from the shoulders of Typhon, the flying monster, and then a bolt of lightning ripped through the dark sky: the fire spit by one of the hundred serpents that issued from Typhon's throat.**

**Even years later, after he was an adult, he'd find himself staring hard at the grove to perhaps catch a glimpse of Aphrodite, accompanied by Ares and the three Graces, doves circling above her head as she rode in her chariot harnessed to a flock of swans; or Diana and her brother, Apollo, going out to hunt; or Diana, accompanied by her nymphs, all virgins doomed to die in agony if they lost their virginity; or the insanely jealous Hera on her way to punish one of her husband's mistresses. And once, standing in front of a cascade of autumn leaves spilling onto the ground, Meir's heart stopped: there was Zeus, the eternal suitor, disguised as golden rain. Right there, before his very eyes, in his own garden.**

"I once saw photos of the house . . ."

So, he'd also been sent pictures of the house. Or maybe he had seen it in the background of the photograph of Eleanor, because then they all lived in his grandfather's house, together.

"A very beautiful house, and the fawns . . . the does . . ." his father said, using the Hebrew names of the animals.

He seemed to be straining his imagination to give life to the spectacular sight his son had been used to seeing since his childhood. Meir wondered whether his father was thinking about the sights he had seen during the long years in prison, while, far away, Meir was surrounded by all that beauty.

"I also had a dog."

"Really?"

"Yes. I called him Cerberus," Meir said.

"And did he have three heads, like the mythological Cerberus?"

"No. He was an ordinary, adorable dog."

"Did he like cake?"

"Why cake?"

"Because Hercules bought Cerberus off with a slice of cake," his father replied, then quickly added, "Sometimes I asked myself where you lived, what kind of home you made for yourself. You lived in so many places back in Tel Aviv." He sank into thought, perhaps seeing a particular home, room, or bed in his mind's eye. Then he asked, "You had your own room in your mother's house, didn't you? A bed, a closet, a desk. . . . Everything you needed?"

"Yes. I had everything I needed."

"That's good . . . very good . . . you had everything. . . . I'm asking because I know it's cold in Connecticut, like in Poland and Russia, no comparison to Tel Aviv winters."

"There are days in the winter when you can't even go outside because of the snowstorms," Meir said, fighting the urge to say: At least I wasn't homeless on the streets of Connecticut.

"So you had a coat, right . . ."

"I had a few coats and sweaters and fur-lined boots and gloves and even a special hat to keep my ears warm," he said.

"Very good. . . . And your mother made a good living for you? She worked?"

"Most of the time she worked in the office of a hospital on First Avenue, not far from the house, a Jewish hospital. There were times when she didn't work very much, and Grandpa must have helped her then."

"And you got along together, you and your mother?"

**Except for his grandfather and Arnie, Meir trusted no one, especially not his mother. After making the tiring trip to the airport in a wheelchair, she seemed to consider herself exempt from any further effort. In the diary he kept and found years later, he was surprised to discover that he never mentioned her with affection. He never forgave her for abandoning him in Tel Aviv, even though she told him several times how, to no avail, she fought the doctor who confined her to bed for the remainder of her pregnancy and forbade her to go back to Israel; how she didn't sleep from the moment she learned that the police hadn't found him until the day she saw him with her own eyes. And when Eleanor was born, it seemed to Meir that she showered all her love on the baby and there wasn't a single drop left for**

him. Eleanor's death intensified his anger. He didn't start loving her until after she died, remembering how she'd reached out to him whenever he passed her bed, how she pulled his hair with her tiny fingers. His mother had been depressed for several years after the baby's death, and they had lived in the house like two strangers. He spent most of the time reading in his room. He also developed nervous habits, tugging at the ends of his hair until he pulled it out and scratching his knees until they bled. He persisted in the knee-scratching for a long time, producing permanent scars. Sometimes he sat at the closed door to his mother's bedroom, ears straining to hear the sighs or sounds of crying she made, frightened when there was silence but then, reassuring himself with the thought that she was sleeping now and would get up soon to make him supper.

That was also when he perfected his habit of lying, not out of maliciousness or to gain something, but as a defensive weapon, out of the desire to extricate himself from the wretchedness of his real life and create a new life for himself. Even when his mother found him out, he insisted on the lie, not caring whether she raged at him, rebuked him in front of other people, or punished him. Later, throughout his college years, they hardly saw each other, except for the anniversaries of his grandfather's and Eleanor's death and Yom Kippur which, for some reason, she insisted he spend with her in her apartment and go with her to hear the Kol Nidre at the East End Temple across the street. But on Yom Kippur afternoon, she would ignore the sound of the door closing softly behind him as he slipped out for something to eat.

"We got along."

"Really? You really got along?" his father asked.

"Yes."

"Because at home, I mean at home in Tel Aviv, she almost never took care of you."

"In America, when she felt okay, she tried," Meir said firmly.

"So," his father said, "of all the things you don't remember, is the house on HaNevi'im Street one of the things you *do* remember?"

"I remember something about it, yes."

"The two of us left it after your mother went away. Do you remember that she went to visit her father, who was supposedly sick?"

"Why supposedly?"

"I thought it was an excuse, that she just missed America."

"He really was sick."

"But he lived quite a few years after that."

"Yes, but he was always very sick. Arnie took care of him," Meir said.

"She couldn't get married," his father said, "but did she have men . . . men who wanted her?"

"There was only Arnie."

"Well, Arnie's almost family," his father said.

What exactly was he aiming at? Meir wanted to know. Was he trying to find out whether, for Meir, there were memories of her men as well as the memories of his women? Was his father concerned for the boy or was he simply a jealous husband?

Someone was standing in the doorway, and Meir saw how his father's shining eye was drawn there. The patient's gaze was riveted on a long-haired woman, wearing a dress so thin it revealed her thighs, but the spark that had once flashed in his eyes when he saw a woman was gone. Meir felt a pang of sorrow when he saw his father lean forward, and instead of focusing his eye on her, he was sniffing as if to pick up her scent. The woman scanned the room, and when she didn't find what she was looking for, apologized and disappeared, but his father continued to stare at the empty spot she'd left.

"There are all kinds of new perfumes these days that I don't recognize," he said.

**One day, when they were sitting on one of the benches on the Boulevard sharing their one order of falafel, a woman walked**

past them, squeezing between them and a baby carriage, and his father abruptly raised his head.

"Do you smell it?" he asked, gesturing in the direction of the woman who was growing more distant.

"What?"

"The smell of a man."

"I don't smell anything."

"Half an hour ago, she was still in bed with a man," he said, as if amazed at his ability to get under her clothes, and a moment later, he regained his composure and realized that for the second time that day, he'd gone too far: "I was kidding, Meir, don't mind me. Your father's bored today."

Once—that memory stirred another one like a link pulling another link in a chain—his father had squeezed into his sleeping son's bed, a convertible armchair. Meir's stomach was pressed against the hard wooden arm and he woke up and said, "Daddy, there's no room."

His father whispered, "We'll manage till the morning. Here, move a little closer to me."

"Go sleep in the other room," Meir said loudly, and his father shushed him. "Don't yell. I can't sleep there. I can't stand her smell."

The next morning, walking down the street after they'd gotten up and left before their landlady had awakened, Meir said, "You didn't let me sleep all night."

"You asked me to sleep with you."

"No, I didn't."

"You said you were afraid."

"I was afraid in the house before this one because the window was broken. You came because of her smell."

"What are you talking about?" his father asked with a grin.

"You said so yourself."

"I never said anything like that. You dreamed it."

Several weeks later, they were trapped for quite a few hours in Berl's basement because a sewer in the yard had overflowed and was streaming past the cellar door, giving off a terrible stench. Meir went over to his father and asked quietly, to keep Berl from hearing, "Is it like the smell of that woman from Rembrandt Street?"

"I have no idea what you're talking about," his father said, laughing.

"The one you left to come and sleep with me," Meir said.

"I came because she talked in her sleep. She didn't let me sleep."

But for years, that memory, burned into his senses, haunted him: a man fleeing from the smell of a woman. His nose could pick up the faintest smell wafting from the women sitting next to him on the train, standing in front of him on line at the checkout counter, passing him in the street. The first test a woman had to pass before he slept with her, kissed her, or even shook hands with her was the smell test. He'd stop breathing for a minute, neutralize all his other senses and, like an athlete gathering all his strength before the starting shot, he'd focus intently on his olfactory sense, identifying the fragrance of soaps, body lotions and various flavors of mouthwash, the smell of chocolate, mint and raspberry, the scents of dozens of different perfumes, the odor of a recently smoked cigarette, light perspiration, an unwashed scalp, heavy perspiration, menstruation, feet—which were sometimes pleasant or exciting, and sometimes killed his awakening passion.

"Do you remember that we were together once in the hospital? I was hospitalized and the nurses pampered us. Maybe you don't remember, you were a little boy, but there were some beautiful nurses here then—beauty queens," his father said, then grew quiet, perhaps remembering their beauty, but then woke up from his reverie all at once. ". . . What were we talking about?"

"Arnie."

"Arnie, yes. . . . But there was something else I wanted to ask you before . . . before they interrupted us, yes, I remember," he said. "There was a time, you know, after we left the house on HaNevi'im Street, when we moved to a lot of different houses, and you slept in a different bed every night. You don't remember that either?"

**Once—he suddenly remembered with a sense of disaster—his father left him in a stairwell and went into an apartment with a woman who had a long braid and was wearing a transparent blouse over a black bra. A while later, his father came back very agitated, shoving his shirttails into his pants.**

**"Whore. All women are whores," he said, pulling Meir by the hand. "Come on, we can't stay here."**

**"I'm tired, Daddy."**

**"But we can't stay here."**

**"So what were you doing there all that time?"**

**"Trying to convince her."**

**"And she said no?"**

**"When she said yes, I didn't want to stay there anymore."**

**"Why not?"**

**"Because it took her too long."**

**"So what?"**

**"So sometimes, when things take too long, the best thing is to let go. Here's a mint candy."**

**"So what are we going to do now?"**

**"The café's closing soon. We'll go to Berl's place."**

"I don't remember," Meir said quickly. His father's voice was shaking. So this was the question he had wanted to ask first and foremost, the reason his father had wanted him to come. His father had been ready to pay for his flight so that he could look Meir in the eye, like he was doing now and find out what his son remembered about his women.

"I want you to know that every woman . . . I say 'woman' because those were usually women's houses. . . . You say you don't remember, but I want you to know in case you do suddenly remember—because it happens that memories come back all of a sudden after many years—with every woman I spoke to, even before she asked us to come and live with her, I'd ask if she liked children. It was important to me that you felt good, wanted."

Quiet tears began to form in the depths of Meir's body, at the bottom of his stomach, under the crushing weight of his diaphragm, and he breathed slowly to stop them before they found their way to his eyes.

**One rainy night, he was shivering with cold under an umbrella, watching his father talking in the café with a fair-skinned woman whose hair was combed in an upsweep. The rainwater, seeping into his shoe, had already reached his foot and he squeezed his eyes shut and prayed silently to God that his father would hurry up and take him to a dry place. When he opened his eyes, as if his prayer had just been answered, he saw his father taking leave of the woman with much nodding of their heads, then come out of the café and cross the street in a run.**

**"Who's she?" he asked when his father picked him up and they squeezed together under the rain-battered umbrella.**

**"A woman from Ben Yehuda Street."**

**"What's her name?"**

**"Liza."**

**"Does she have a son in the army?"**

**"No. She has a mother who lives there, but she's a very old lady and never gets out of bed."**

**That night, Meir slept on a mattress on the floor in the old lady's room next to the bed where she spent all her days and nights. He burrowed under the blankets and tensed the muscles of his neck tightly so it wouldn't sink into the quicksand of the down pillow, knowing in his heart that this time he and his father had fallen into a trap set by a woman sent to seduce men with small boys she could feed to her huge mother. Wide-**

eyed with fear, he stared at the white mountain on the bed, ready to scream the minute the old lady—an enormous woman whose head touched the ceiling—rose up at midnight and approached him to see what her daughter had prepared for her night meal. And his ears were cocked to pick up his father's familiar grunting and the woman's shrieks coming from the adjacent room.

The next day, his father found him shaking and red-eyed, pleading to get out of that house right away.

"You won't sleep in the old lady's room tonight. You'll sleep on the kitchen balcony. We'll set up a comfortable place for you."

"How many women were there, altogether?" Meir asked his first test question.

"Three or four," his father replied, his businessman's eyes alert, preparing to bargain. Meir wondered about the game they were playing: which of the things he said did his father believe? Which was he suspicious of? Did his father recognize the expression on Meir's face that clearly said: "Liar. I counted at least ten."

"And who were they, those women?"

The women, Meir had learned after he'd gotten to know many woman and many homes, adored his father at the beginning. Their faces glowed with yearning when they looked at him. They immediately volunteered to iron his shirts, laughed hard at his witty remarks, fulfilled his every request—but after a while, most of them got rid of him almost cruelly, insisting that he leave their homes within an hour, and when their hearts occasionally softened because of the boy, they postponed the decree until the next day. Meir's favorite time was the first two days in the women's homes. Usually, they would go to work in the morning and come back in the afternoon with delicious fruit and sweets. He and his father were masters of the house in the morning. His father would wash the dirty clothes that had accumulated in the blue bag and dry them outside or in

**front of the heater on rainy days. Then he'd sit down to finish writing an article or do his accounts, and the boy would splash around in the bathwater, cut letters out of the newspapers when there were newspapers or play with a puppy when there was a puppy.**

"Those were women I knew, good women who invited us to stay in their homes until we found a permanent place. You're asking who they were? One was a kindergarten teacher, one was a poet, one worked on a newspaper, but you say you don't remember . . ."

". . . I don't . . ."

"But you do remember Berl."

"Berl, yes."

"It's so mysterious, the way the memory works. . . . How some things suddenly disappear and others persist, as if history felt like reordering itself. . . . I myself. . . . During the trial and afterwards, when I was first transferred there. . . . I was completely blocked for a few months. I only remembered you, the way you only remember Berl. A few months later, the memories started coming back, but there were some that took years. You won't believe what I remembered a long time later: that I promised to buy you a magician's box with the first money I earned, but it didn't work out. I thought about that a lot. I had time to think, I was in prison. You know that, don't you?"

"Yes."

"But it wasn't all the time to think that made me remember. For instance, a few years after I got there, they changed cooks, and the new one made squash that had a certain taste. It reminded me of one house we stayed in where the woman used to make squash that had the same taste, with a little onion and dill. It was important for me to remember. My whole life was in the past. . . . I'm talking about prison. You say that you know I was in prison."

"Mom told me."

"She told me she did, but I wasn't sure . . ."

"And you really remember Berl's cellar clearly?"

"Yes. It was full of junk."

"Right. We spent many nights there. Sleeping on blankets on the floor."

"Yes."

"What else do you remember from there?"

"All kinds of things."

"Do you remember that he was terrified of the Gestapo?"

"Yes."

"Because a policeman came looking for us. Because of your mother. She filed a complaint through the embassy saying I kidnapped you."

"But a child belongs to his father just as much as to his mother."

"But you were already an American citizen. She got you a passport."

The whole time they were playing this strange game, neither saying what was on his mind, each wary of the other, his father examined Meir's expressions out of the corner of his seeing eye.

"Do you remember two sisters, actresses?" he suddenly asked, unleashing the storm. . . .

**A week before Passover, both of them tired from their wandering, his father found them a place at the home of two sisters, actresses, who were heavily made up and spoke with strange accents. The women had been sitting at Alterman's table in the Kassit when Meir's father—Aharon Rosinberg, Alterman told them—the handsome man who'd caught their eye a while ago, came in. Someone at the table saw him standing in the doorway and invited him to come and sit down across from the two women. From where Meir was standing in the street, he could see the women huddling together, whispering to each other like little girls trying to decide to do something, and then as if they'd made up their minds, they separated and raised their wine glasses as if toasting his**

father. A short time later, the three of them came outside and crossed the street toward Meir, holding hands as if they already cared very much about each other. Then the shorter sister broke the chain and opened her arms, and when they reached Meir, she hugged him and said, "This is the sweetest little boy I've ever seen, and of course he's invited to my house." The taller sister put her arm through his father's and tugged at the edge of the silk scarf he was wearing around his neck: "And you're invited to mine."

And so they went to the home of the actress-sisters, who had a calico cat, the last apartment they stayed in together, where the terrible thing happened in the bedroom with the blood-stained sheet, the place Meir was taken from by the police and, the very next day, sent to his mother in America. But before that, they spent many pleasant days in the ground-floor apartment that faced the street, long enough to restore routine and the old feeling of home to their lives for the first time.

It had been clear from the first minute in the café that his father favored the taller sister. He had raised his wine glass to her, directed his conversation to her, and had taken her hand when they crossed the street to tell the boy that they'd found a good place for the night. In the days that followed, when Meir lay half-asleep in his bed in the living room, peering through his closing eyelids at the cat curled up peacefully in his velvet-covered corner and the three adults sitting at a round table singing loudly or playing cards, a sparkling bottle of wine and crystal goblets always within reach, he'd see from where he was what the shorter woman wasn't able to see: his father's hand, the one that always had a life of its own, reaching under the table and meandering over the tall woman's knees. When the sisters had to go out to perform in the evening, the adults played cards in the afternoon, and Meir would sit between his father and the shorter woman, not knowing which of them he wanted to win. Occasionally, he'd wake up to the shouting of a neighbor who was banging on the door or yelling from the street, cursing and calling them drunken, dissipated Bohemians and threatening to call the police if they didn't quiet down right away. But most of the time, outside noises didn't disturb them. Inside the apartment crowded with furniture brought from Europe—velvet pillows, handmade napkins, countless tiny porcelain figurines—their lives began to settle down, suffused with a new tranquility. In the morning, Meir delighted in the sweetness of simple domestic moments: the intensifying whistle of the kettle heralding the approaching meal, the cat curled up in his lap, the trickle of the rain in the gutter next to the window, his father's humming coming from the bathroom where he was shaving in front of the mirror.

In the afternoon, they'd all meet again in the living room and Meir would pull the tip of the magic pencil his father bought him, again and again, turning it into a rope, to the repeated cheering of his audience. Then the sisters would sing a song or perform a dance from their rehearsals or from one of their old shows. Sometimes, the adults would carry on like children, fighting over a cookie, knocking each other off their chairs, hiding a shoe or an umbrella—as a prank—or pantomiming stories from Greek mythology: Agamemnon sacrificing his daughter, Iphigenia—his father standing erect as the king and the taller sister convulsing in death at his feet; Orpheus the piper making his way back to the land of the living, his beloved Euripides following him—his father looking straight ahead toward the hallway and the tall sister walking behind him, covered in a white scarf, but when his father stopped next to the armchair and turned to look back, the short sister, dressed as Hermes, leaped out from her hiding place, grabbed the tall, weeping sister by her hair and pulled her back to the edge of the armchair, which marked the kingdom of Hades.

As Meir watched them, wide-eyed, petting the cat on his lap, running his fingers along the cat's arched back to the place between his ears, he was flooded with a new, overwhelming happiness.

At night, Meir slept in the living room on the soft convertible armchair, the most perfect sleep he could remember, and while he slept peacefully, his father was in the bedroom with one of the sisters, sometimes both of them. The boy barely heard the night noises, but sometimes, his father would close himself in with one of the women during the day. By this time, Meir already knew what the couple was doing in the bedroom, and the sounds issuing from there were familiar. When his father was inside with the short sister, there was silence. When he was there with the tall one, moans and ringing laughter came from the bedroom. When his father was with the short sister, the tall one sat on the convertible armchair engrossed in reading or she ironed her dresses, ignoring Meir and the cat. When his father was with the tall sister, the short one would make jam in the kitchen or read Meir a story from his textbook, her entire body constricting when the sounds her sister was making grew louder. Within a few days, they had created a daily routine for themselves, as if they'd been living together their entire lives. As time passed—especially after they got slightly drunk from all the wine they drank at the Passover seder they celebrated together, when he had asked the traditional questions by himself—Meir felt the new stability in his life was good, and he thought that he could stay in this house forever. Now that they had a permanent address on a lovely street not far from the park that was full of babies, he wondered if he could also go back to his class at school, even though the school year was about to end.

"I don't remember two actresses."

"Their names were Ola and Pola. Two sisters. Actresses, and sometimes singers, too."

"I don't remember," Meir said, his heart jumping at the sound of the names, and a voice whispered in his ear: "Does Meir love Pola?"

"Pola loved you especially. She taught you to play the piano and she taught you the Bible."

When they sat at the piano, she couldn't stop admiring his fingers, which were so much like his father's. She taught him with passion, so excited that she sometimes uttered words in foreign languages, clapping her hands when he succeeded, wringing them when he failed.

When she wrung her hands, he said, "It doesn't matter. I don't have a piano anyway," experienced as he was in the disadvantages of the transient life.

"It matters very much!" she replied, drawing an exclamation mark in the air with her finger. "Music matters more than anything. Music and writing."

"I want to write," he said.

"I write, too," she whispered, as if it were a secret.

"About what?"

"About things that happen to me, but soon, I'm going to start writing seriously for our shows. Meanwhile, I'm looking for a subject. The hardest thing is finding a subject. Once you find one, things start moving quickly."

"You can write what you told me yesterday about that director from Habima."

"You can't write about the living. I'm looking for something about the dead."

"Why?"

"Because the living always get insulted."

"Maybe you can write about yourself."

"I can't write about myself without writing about Ola."

"So maybe you should write about when you were little."

"I'll tell you a secret," Pola said, leaning toward his ear. "No one would believe me if I wrote about that. Ola was a very bad girl. If they knew what she did, she'd have spent half her life in prison."

"What did she do?"

"Something disgusting."

"Does she do it now, too?"

"Yes," she replied quickly, scolding Ola from a safe distance. "People never change."

"But my father thinks she's nice."

"And you?"

"I think you're nicer."

"That's how it is," she asserted.

Once, Pola was so focused on her writing that she didn't notice him sitting quietly across the table from her, waiting for her to check his homework. When Meir said her name and she raised her head, she looked like someone coming out of a trance.

"Isn't this funny: you're sitting here while I'm writing about you."

"Show it to me."

"It's in Romanian, you wouldn't understand."

"So write it in Hebrew for me."

"I can't. The language closest to my heart is the language I spoke with my grandparents, and that was Romanian."

"So what are writing about me?"

"That you're the sweetest boy in the world," she said, moving her head so close to his that his vision blurred. Her hand, gripping the back of his neck, wouldn't let him pull away as she planted a long kiss on his lips, which contracted in fear as she crushed them with her own.

"You're going to be something special," she whispered, stroking his blushing cheeks with her cupped hands, making him quiver from his ears to his chin. "Do you know you're going to be the beauty king of Tel Aviv?"

"No."

"So now I'm telling you. There are people who don't have it and there are people who do, I can tell right away when I look into their eyes—and you definitely have it," she said seductively, looking even more deeply into his eyes. He tore himself out of her grip and stood up, pretending that he was going to look for a pencil.

"But even if you have it, don't be stuck up," she said, reassuming the role of his teacher. Her voice sounded normal again, too. "Some people, when they get ahead a little in life, stop saying hello to you. But in life, sometimes you're up and sometimes you're down, so you shouldn't walk around with your nose in the air," she declared.

Every once in a while, the sisters would argue. It surprised Meir to hear them fighting like children. He didn't understand what they were shouting because they slipped into Romanian after the second sentence, but he did recognize the taunting, insulting tone. When his father was home, he'd jump right in and get them back to Hebrew, and switching to a language that wasn't their native tongue was enough to halt the outburst. Then he'd placate them, reminding one sister of the other's generosity, and the other of how much her sister loved her, and his father would make peace between them. And like lovers after a fight, they'd have a sweet reconciliation: Pola would go straight into the kitchen to bake a cake and, when it was in the oven, the four of them would sit down at the table, enveloped by the baking smells, and laugh.

"Do you remember?" his father asked, looking into his eyes.

But Meir, lost in memories, didn't answer.

They went to the movies a few times, and Meir always sat between his father and Pola in the dark theater. Pola would stroke the back of his neck, her fingers leaving trails of fire on his skin. Sometimes, she leaned over and whispered in his ear, "Does Meir love Pola?" But most of the time, Meir and his father went to the sisters' performances. Bathed and perfumed, they crossed the streets, all four holding hands like a row of kindergarten children. When the sisters appeared in private homes or hotel ballrooms, Meir would sit in the audience with his father and wait for the moment they came onto the stage wearing the long dresses they'd ironed a short while before and brought with them in a suitcase. The minute they opened their mouths, his heart would leap into his throat and stay there until they finished singing their songs—most of them in a foreign language—in their shrill voices. His father would nudge him to applaud at the end of the show, and now that Meir's heart was lighter, because a performance had gone well and the sisters had remembered all the words and movements, he'd clap his hands together so hard that they hurt.

When they performed in large halls, his father sometimes slipped him into the dressing room with all its dazzling, bright lights multiplied in the giant mirrors. Meir would squeeze into a corner of the room so as not to disturb the actors dashing in and out, and stay there, intoxicated by the smell of the clothes, the makeup, and the pandemonium

As the days passed, a routine began to take shape. Pola would push open the shutters, proclaiming that the night had ended. The sisters would bathe first, going into the bathroom one after the other with unkempt hair, emerging later neat and tidy, exuding delicious scents. Then Meir went into the bathroom with his father. Sometimes, his father leaned over the edge of the bathtub and washed only his arms or his torso, and other times he undressed and washed his entire body, while Meir turned his head away in embarrassment. Meir bathed three times a week before going to bed, and every morning, he brushed his teeth and washed his face. Then they ate breakfast together and drank the coffee Ola managed so well to burn. Ola and his father usually left together, he to run errands and she to their manager's office, and Pola stayed home with Meir. Instead of a teacher at school, Meir had Pola. Every day, she would dampen a rag and wipe off the furniture, the nooks and crannies of the ornate picture frames, and the rows of delicate porcelain figurines that stood on the sideboard. Once she dampened a small rag for Meir, and they stood side by side like two servants in a nobleman's palace, wiping away indiscernible grains of dust, making his home shine. Pola explained that what they were doing was important. Some people thought it was a waste of time to clean all those little figurines every day, but if they knew how many invisible germs stuck to their intricate surfaces, she and Meir would be commended. She went on and on with her terrifying description of the imperceptible, hostile world they were now fighting with their damp rags. Right after that, came his daily piano lesson.

One day, Pola decided that the boy's studies should be more organized, and she hung an hourly schedule on the refrigerator. In addition to the piano lessons that had become routine, there were squares for arithmetic, French, and Bible lessons.

The arithmetic lessons bored them stiff, and they tried to find excuses to skip them or cut them short. Meir found French difficult, but Pola, who conspired with him about the arithmetic lessons, insisted on having the French lessons and wouldn't let him go until the big hand of the clock on the wall reached twelve.

"No one in my class is studying French," he said rebelliously. "I don't need it."

"Of course, you do. When you go to Europe, how will you talk to people? You know, only Israelis speak Hebrew, and no one will understand you when you go to Paris. Let's say you're thirsty, how will you ask for a drink of water? So that's it, we have to learn French."

"I don't have to go to Paris. There are lots of other places."

"But you need French in Belgium and in Canada, too.

"I don't want to go anywhere."

"You have to, Meir. This is not a good place. It's a place with wars."

"There are no wars here," he said, thinking about Berl.

"Not right now, but there were and there will be. You have to be prepared—and prepared means French."

But the Bible lessons were their favorite. Pola read slowly in a deep, resonant voice from the book of Bible stories for children, then acted them out in the living room, her eyes blazing with excitement. "The Garden of Eden," she said slowly, as if speaking from inside a lovely dream, and she stretched her arms as far as they could go to show the size of the place. Many trees: she whistled and, bending back at the waist, waved her arms to show branches rustling in the wind. The snake: she pressed her arms to her body, stood on tiptoe, then, swaying her hips, she lowered herself until she was lying coiled on the carpet. Eve: she proudly thrust her breasts forward and sunk her teeth into an apple, swallowing a bite of it, her neck taut, then she rolled her eyes and crossed her hands over her groin to hide it. Samson: she pushed imaginary columns to the right and to the left, then collapsed onto the carpet. Isaac: she held a kitchen knife close to her neck and went limp, as if she were fainting. And Abraham, she always left a great deal of time for Abraham. She wrapped herself in a white sheet, used a broom as a walking stick, and then played the role of God, saying in a thundering voice, "Get thee out of thy country" while she walked slowly from one side of the living room to the other, gazing at the walls as if they stretched all the way to the horizon.

"Do you remember a little bit now? There were two sisters. Pola was a pretty mediocre actress. Ola was better, both as an actress and a singer, but she was mentally ill, which I didn't know then. And Pola, I found out later, wasn't too stable either, but when we met her, she seemed perfectly normal. She was a little extreme, the way she took care of you and taught you, but it didn't bother you. And Ola wanted to marry me. I explained to her that I had a wife who was in America, but she wouldn't accept that. And when I told her my wife was pregnant, we had a big fight."

Meir looked his father in the eye. The big bang that turned his life upside down was close, and his senses sharpened so much that he could actually smell it. For a moment he thought his memories contained things he hadn't witnessed: Ola sits in front of the mirror brushing her hair in rapid strokes, looking at Aharon who is leaning against the side of the closet. He's telling her in a restrained voice that he has a wife; she keeps brushing her hair as if she hasn't heard. He tells her that his wife is pregnant; she hurls the brush at his image in the mirror.

"Is that why you killed her?" Meir asked in English.

His father grimaced suddenly and he asked quietly, "Why are you so sure I killed her?"

"Didn't you?" For a fleeting moment, Meir felt as if he were reading lines from a script.

"No," his father replied, his eyes narrowing in his tensing face.

"So who killed her?"

"She killed herself, apparently. She tried to commit suicide."

"How?"

"With a pair of scissors. She stabbed herself in the throat. Or maybe Pola did it. The police never found out exactly what happened."

"Why did they accuse you?"

"Because I was in the room with her and there was screaming that everyone heard because it was the middle of the night. She went berserk, started yelling in all kinds of languages, and ran to the drawer to look for something. She was standing with her back to me and I didn't realize that she was looking for the scissors. Then her sister flew into the room, ran over to her and grabbed her hands. Pola must have realized what Ola was planning to do, it probably wasn't the first time. When I saw blood, I rushed over and tried to take the scissors out of Ola's hands, and when the police arrived, I was covered with blood. I couldn't convince them that I didn't do it. Pola said she never touched the scissors, and I was completely confused. They asked me questions, and I didn't know what I was saying. I didn't remember what had happened. I think even the lawyer they gave me didn't believe me."

*   *   *

Meir awakened from a dream filled with motion and noise into an even greater tumult: Pola, wearing a bathrobe, sobbing and yelling, was sitting with her head down, pulling out her hair with both hands, then beating her thighs with her fists. A great many policemen were walking around the house, slamming doors, speaking in commanding tones.

One of them came over to him, bent down, and said as softly as he could, "What's your name, little boy?"

"Meir."

"Who lives here in this house, Meir?"

"What happened to Pola?"

"I'll explain everything to you, but first—"

"Where's my father?"

"Your father. . . . I'll explain it to you in a minute. Who lives with you and your father?"

"Ola and Pola."

"And where's your mother?"

"In America."

"I want to tell you a secret, Meir."

"What?"

"We have to leave this house right now."

"Who does?"

"You and me," the policeman said, reaching out to take him.

Meir straightened up and pulled quickly away from the policeman's grasp and threw himself into Pola's arms. He had never seen her so wild-eyed and red-faced. She gave him an inquisitive, distant look, and pushed him away with both hands.

"What's the matter with you, Pola?" he asked as large hands grabbed him and swung him in the air. Pola watched without reaching out for Meir or protecting him.

"I love you, Pola," he cried, trying to bribe her with the answer to the question she'd asked dozens of times but which he'd never answered before. Pola didn't respond.

"You're a naughty boy," the policeman said, putting him down on the carpet. "Sit here and don't move. We'll be out of here in a minute."

"Where's my father?"

"Your father is there already, Meir, at the place we have to go to."

"Why?"

"He'll tell you when we get there."

"Why is Pola yelling?"

"He'll tell you that, too. Do you have a bag, Meir, to put some clothes in that you'll need?"

"All my stuff is in my schoolbag and on the shelf."

The policeman took Meir by the hand, helped him put his workbooks, one textbook and his book of Greek myths into his schoolbag, made a small bundle of his clothes and swept everything else that was on the shelf into it: colored pencils, a key Meir had found in the sand, a pile of seashells. He gripped Meir's wrist tightly and led him to the door, continuing to ignore the boy's constant questions about his father and his pleas to go to Pola, whose screams were now filling the street. At the door, tightening his hold on Meir's small, struggling hand, the policeman said to one of the other policemen, "Don't touch the body 'til Nachmias gets here." Meir, catching sight of Pola's wild look, now began to cry and carry on, kicking the policeman's legs to extricate himself from his iron grip until the policeman scooped him up in his arms. Through the half-closed bedroom door, Meir managed to see the edge of the rumpled bed covered with a very wrinkled white sheet that had a large red stain on it. The apartment door slammed behind them, and Meir was dragged outside to the police car with its lights flashing, encircled by a ring of elegantly dressed passersby and neighbors in bathrobes.

Through the windows of the police car on the way to the police station further down Dizengoff Street, Meir suddenly saw the square of light of the Kassit café glow and disappear like a mirage. Then the officer handed him over, like a baby, to the policeman who was waiting outside and he was carried into a quiet room. There, a policewoman gave him hot chocolate and cookies, stroked his cheeks, and wiped away the tears that fell when she asked him about his father. She asked him many questions in her pleasant voice until he said he was very tired and asked her if he could go to her house to sleep. Surprised by the question, she chuckled and let him go to sleep on a mattress on the floor, covering him with policemen's jackets. In the morning, she woke him up and said in a cheerful voice, "Good morning, Meir. I have a surprise for you: you're going to America."

"I want my father," Meir said, clasping his hands together trying to stop his thumbs from shaking. Dropping the facade of cheerfulness, she reached out to calm the trembling thumbs, her starched policewoman's shirt brushing his face as she leaned to whisper in his ear, "Forget him, Meir. You have a mother. Just remember your mother."

"You're saying you didn't do it."

"I didn't do it, no."

"Why didn't you tell them that Pola was holding the scissors?"

"I did, I told them. But Pola said she didn't touch them. And they checked in their laboratories and found both our fingerprints on it. But the prosecutor said that Pola's prints had been there before because she used them when she was sewing, and my lawyer didn't fight her. He was sure I did it. And I can see in your eyes that you think so, too."

"I don't know what to say."

"Say what you feel, what you think. It's important for me to hear you."

"I think they don't put people away for twenty years for something they didn't do."

His father gave a bitter, sad little laugh, as if he already knew every step of this conversation. "Of course they do. The prisons are full of people like that. My fingerprints were on the scissors and I didn't know how to answer the prosecutor's questions. That was enough for them. They didn't investigate too much. When it was convenient for them, they quoted Pola, and when it wasn't, they said they couldn't accept the testimony of a woman in her state. She said that her sister loved life and would never have committed suicide. She didn't want to testify for me."

"Why not? Why didn't she want to help you?"

"That question has haunted me for all these years, and I have no answer. If she knows that she did it, then the answer's simple, too simple. But maybe she just went berserk or lost her memory. Maybe it had something to do with you."

"Me?" Meir asked, drawing back as if something had been thrown at him.

"Yes. She loved you very much. I thought that maybe, in her crazy mind, she hoped that if I was in prison, they'd let her raise you."

**Once their lesson schedule was on track, Pola decided it was time to take care of his clothes, to throw out the permanently stained items and the ones with worn edges that were unraveling from so much use and laundering, and buy him new pants and a few shirts, some underwear and socks, and a pair of new shoes, and in general—she waved both her arms as if she were onstage—to teach him proper hygiene habits. One day, in the middle of an arithmetic lesson, when they were alone in the apartment, she was suddenly in a frenzy. She rapidly wrote a few problems in his notebook, leaped up and rushed into the bathroom. While he was still trying to concentrate on the numbers on the page, Meir heard the water running, and before he could finish solving the problems, she called to him. He went into the bathroom, and found her on her knees, leaning over the edge of the bathtub, which was already almost completely full of water.**

**"We're going to take a bath now, Meir."**

"Why?"

"Let's say it's a lesson, too. A hygiene lesson."

"But I'm not finished with my arithmetic yet."

"A hygiene lesson is more important than arithmetic. Take off all your clothes," she said.

He hesitated. His father was the only person he wasn't ashamed to be naked in front of. In Berl's cellar, when he finished taking a bath in the tub, he even asked Berl to close his eyes until he was wrapped in a towel. He heard her determination now, and was afraid to hurt her feelings or to argue with her, but neither could he find the courage to take off all his clothes in front of her, so he remained standing there, his hands at his sides, watching her hands straighten the mat under her knees.

"Come on, let's go, there's no time," she said.

His fingers began to unbutton his sweater hesitantly, from the top button to the others. He prayed silently that a messenger would come and call Pola urgently to the post office or the medical clinic, or that his father would come home early and get angry when he saw what they were doing, he'd get angry that she was usurping his role as his son's educator. Or that a sudden bolt of lightning would smash the window. But when he got to the last button, neither a messenger nor his father nor a bolt of lightning had appeared. He stood, holding the sweater until Pola tore it out of his hands and gestured for him to take off his shirt. Once again, his fumbling fingers began the slow, tentative journey down the buttons until he'd taken off the shirt and handed it to her and she pointed to his shoes. He bent down as if getting into position to race with his friends, and took off his shoes, and under her stinging gaze, removed his undershirt and his socks and folded them neatly, gaining himself another minute, his eyes fixed on Pola's back as she checked the temperature of the water with her elbow.

"Are you finished?" she asked, turning her head and seeing him standing there motionless.

"I can take a bath myself, really."

"Take off your pants."

"I know how to bathe myself."

"You can bathe yourself starting tomorrow. I don't have time to do it every day. But today, I'll teach you how to wash yourself and shampoo your hair the right way."

"I always take a bath myself. Ever since I was little. And wash my hair, too."

"But today you'll learn how it should be done, and besides, it'll be nice, you'll see," she said, turning her attention back to the water that was already up to the rim of the bathtub. "Take everything off."

As he peeled off his pants, his fingers found the rip in the back of his underpants and he pressed himself against the wall to hide it. Now he remembered that his father had gone to Jerusalem and would be home late, and realized that there was no escape from Pola. Then, in a single sweeping gesture, as if he were committing suicide, he pulled down his underpants and went over to the bathtub to immerse himself in the water as quickly as possible. Filled with shame, Meir lifted one leg, and Pola glanced quickly at his small testicles hanging over the rim of the tub, peeking out from under his hand, which was trying in vain to hide them.

You don't have to be embarrassed in front of me, Meir," she said slowly.

"I know," he said, sliding quickly into the water.

"How did she think she could raise me if she knew that I had a mother who was looking for me?"

"She knew," his father said, "but you say you don't remember that. . . ."

Now they looked into each other's eyes like wrestlers a moment before one of them gets pinned.

"I'm really so confused about what I remember and what Mom told me."

"I know what that's like," his father said in conciliation, "People who don't have much of a present inflate the past. The easiest thing is to choose the memories you want. The easiest and the stupidest."

"First the head," she said, her face swimming over to him through the steam-filled room. She poured shimmering liquid into her hand as if it were liquid, put the bottle down, rubbed her hands together to flatten the hill of shampoo, and as if she were blessing him, ran her hands through his wet hair from his forehead to the back of his neck. Then she briskly worked the shampoo into foam, piling it on the top of his head and letting it slide in long white swirls down his back and along the sides of his face. Meir sat with his head tilted back, gripping the rim of the tub with slippery hands, his eyes squeezed shut, waiting uncomplainingly for her to finish washing his ears with her invasive fingers. Only after she had rinsed his hair and nape thoroughly did he open his eyes, proud that not a drop of shampoo had gotten into them, and she began to rub his shoulders with both foamy hands, sliding sensuously from the edge of one shoulder to the edge of the other, making his body tingle pleasantly. The pleasurable sensation intensified when her hand dropped to his left nipple and she pinched it and smiled. "This is where your heart is," she said. "You have to listen to it because the heart is the wisest part of the body." Her fingers slid to his stomach and washed it in a circular movement, drawing circle after circle around his navel. He abandoned himself to her touch, lying there and closing his eyes, giving himself up to the warm hands meandering along his body in the water, hearing the question that expected no answer: "Does Meir love Pola?" Air was trapped in his lungs as he stopped breathing, waiting for her hand to drop lower, but it skipped quickly along his thighs and calves and raised his foot above the water, surprising him, as if he'd been cheated, and he saw her smile at him over his extended leg.

"Does it tickle?"

"A little."

"I die laughing whenever anybody does that to me," she said, grazing his foot with the tips of her nails and starting to work diligently on his toes, sliding her fingers around each one and down to bottom of the spaces between them. He lay there quietly, completely relaxed under her touch. And then, with no hesitation or pause, she slipped her hand into the water to his small, limp penis, ignoring the shock that made his small body tremble. "Lie quietly. I have to wash you," she said, pushing a square of chocolate into his mouth as a bribe, and he wondered where she'd been keeping it. He felt her fingers sail around his soft penis, touching it as if by accident, busy outlining circles in the water, and very slowly drawn to touch it, causing sudden tremors in his body, pushing his slightly elongated penis away from his small testicles, stroking it teasingly, pushing it to the right and to the left in the water, rocking it as if floated back and forth until it began to come to life in her hands, growing and stiffening. The taste of the chocolate, sweet and heavy, seeped into his body and he tried to subdue his panting so Pola wouldn't hear it. He closed his eyes, and when he opened them, he realized that she'd seen everything, because she was looking at him, giving him a secret smile that didn't show her teeth, and he closed his eyes again to enjoy this new, furtive, forbidden pleasure.

"I have to bathe you like this twice a week," she said, shifting to relieve the pressure on her knees.

"Okay," he said.

A few days later, he was taking a bath in his grandfather's house in America.

"You know, I'm looking at you and I still can't believe you're here . . . that I'm here," his father said. "I still can't completely grasp that I'm out, free. When I was there, you know, in my cell, I'd picture you. On your birthday, I'd congratulate you in my mind, write you poems in my mind. In my mind, always in my mind. I never sent them. Once, inside, I went to a painting class and I painted pictures only of you, how I imagined you would look at that age. On September first—I didn't know whether school started on September first in America, too—anyway, every year on September first, I'd picture you going to school wearing that funny uniform, the suit and tie, like children dressed up as grown-ups for Purim. I asked for a picture of you, but I didn't get one. And that was my dream, that someday I'd be walking around a free man. I didn't know it would be in a hospital. I thought we'd go to a good restaurant and order the most expensive dishes, new restaurants opened here that we didn't have then . . . . That was my dream: that someday, we'd sit and talk. Put your memories in order."

So, his mother had sent a picture of Eleanor, but refused to send one of him. Did she send it after Eleanor died? Had she punished his father by sending a picture of the dead girl, then doubled the punishment by refusing to send a picture of the living boy? Why did she keep the photographed boy from the father if she didn't want the live boy herself?

"But you've been out of prison for a few years already."

"I'm out, but I don't feel like a human being. I didn't want anyone to see me in the condition I was in when I got out, so thin and with bad teeth. Not even Pola. People remember someone else . . . I thought that very slowly, I'd go back to being someone who resembled what I used to be. But after such a long time, people almost never remember who they were before. Right after I got out, I had plans to go to see Pola, to finally hear what she had to say, what she remembered, why she didn't tell the truth. But after a while, I changed my mind and had to go in and out of hospitals myself. And anyway, what difference does it make what she says now? She should have spoken up then."

"Where is she?"

"The last I heard, she was in a psychiatric hospital, some country place in the Sharon, not far from Netanya, called Pardessiya."

"But you must have wanted to hear her version of things."

"Hear it, not hear it, what difference does it make? I was in bad shape. I didn't want her to see me like that. I thought I'd get better, until I realized that I was getting worse . . . and then I wrote to your mother. Did she tell you about the letter?"

"She told me that you wanted to come to New York."

"Yes, there were a few months when I felt better, and I was on my way to apply for a visa. You know why I wanted to come?"

"To be treated in an American hospital," Meir said. It wasn't just chance that his father kept going back to the same point, gently probing around the painful place.

"Is that what she told you?"

"Isn't it true?"

"No, it wasn't because of that."

"Then why? Because you had no place to live?" Meir said, guessing out loud, then letting the thought flow forward silently: Like then, like always, your whole life. And today, you're too old to seduce women. And today, you don't even have the floor in Berl's cellar.

"I do have a place to live," his father said.

"Where?" Meir asked, defiantly.

"A one-room apartment on Dizengoff Street not far from the Kassit."

"It's yours?"

"I inherited it from Berl."

"Where did Berl find the money to buy an apartment?"

"He got reparations from Germany for what happened to him in the war."

"So he didn't die in the cellar?" Meir asked, his voice rising suddenly.

"No. He left the cellar a year after the Six Day War."

If so, it was a sweeter death than he had imagined: a room with a real window, a bed raised from the floor, a shower, maybe even a bathtub.

"I rented out the apartment all those years, and also the money left in Berl's account came to me," his father said, grinning mockingly at the confusion on Meir's face. "So I do have a place to live and I have something to live on," he said.

"So why did you really want to come?"

"Why do you think?"

"I have no idea," Meir said with credible seriousness, because after all he had been pondering that question himself.

"Think hard, maybe it'll come to you," his father said, pressing his lips together stubbornly.

"Because of Mom?"

"Because of her too, yes. I loved your mother very much."

If this were a movie, Meir thought, the flock of women would now come out of the café and the offices, emerge from random streets and move across the screen in a long line. If Meir hadn't said that his memories were gone, he would have dared to say this out loud.

"So, because of her?"

"A little bit because of her."

"And because of what else?"

"If I told you it was because of you?"

"I wouldn't believe you," Meir blurted out as if he were shaking off the responsibility.

"Then forget it," his father said. "You want to go now, don't you?"

"Yes."

"But we haven't finished our conversation. There are still things I want to tell you and there are things I want to hear from you. But you're tired, and anyway, we couldn't do it all in one sitting. How many days did you come for?"

"I have an open ticket. I told them at work that I was taking a month's vacation."

"You can't stay here for a month. There'll be a war in a month. But another few days is all right. So now you can go. I'll rest a little and then you can come back. Maybe you should go and rest a little in your hotel. You did say you found a hotel, right?"

"Right."

"I'd give you my apartment, but . . ."

"My hotel's fine."

"Not expensive? I know that hotels in Tel Aviv are expensive."

"Mine isn't."

"Because I didn't have time to straighten up the room . . . And there are things I wouldn't want . . . I'd like to straighten it up . . ."

"I understand."

"It was sudden, bringing me here . . . I fell in the street . . . I didn't have time to straighten up . . ."

"You fell in the street?" Years ago, Berl fell in the street, but then fate had sent him his brother-in-law and his little boy. This man had fallen in a street full of strangers, Meir thought, feeling the humiliation of the moment when his father hit the sidewalk, people's feet gathering around him or passing by him, someone bending over him, saying: "Don't worry, Mister, they're calling for an ambulance."

"I fell, yes," his father said, dismissively. "It's not important. I only told you that to explain why I didn't have time to get the room ready for you."

"When do you want me to come back?"

"In another hour or two."

"Another hour or two?"

"Why, do you have plans?"

"I wanted to see Berl's grave."

"Berl can wait another day. He'll understand."

"I'm not tired. I don't need that hour or two."

"But I do."

"Do you want to go back to your ward now?"

"I'll stay here a little longer. You can go. When you come back, look for me here."

"Visiting hours will be over two hours from now."

"They'll let you in. Ever since I don't have my eye, the nurses feel sorry for me."

"So goodbye," Meir said, getting up, trembling. The man still knew so well how to exploit his distress: in the past, it had been the motherless boy who didn't have a roof over his head.

"Go, go," his father said, waving the back of his hand at him, exempting him from a kiss or even a handshake. Then before Meir reached the door, he heard the shout: "Don't go! Don't go!" and when he turned around, his father said, "Maybe just let me rest for half an hour and then come back. Half an hour's enough. Go have a cup of coffee, eat something. In half an hour, I'll be like new. We'll continue our conversation about the good old days." He winked his blind eye and looked at Meir like a naughty boy who's said something clever and is waiting to be cheered.

Meir sat on a bench in the corridor, his strength drained. Deep, wounding sadness seemed to be making its way through a too-narrow passageway, seeping into him from the depths, and he suddenly knew that he couldn't write this story because it was too close and too painful. The range of possibilities for his writing had narrowed; he was able to write only about other people's sorrow or about his own happiness, which was nonexistent.

When he went back to the fern hothouse, his father's eyes—also the purple membrane—were red, and Meir wondered whether he'd been crying for the half hour he'd been left alone or whether he was just very tired.

"Do you want to rest? I can come tomorrow."

"No, no," his father insisted. "I have to ask you some more things, and I have to explain. too. First, the writing. Your mother told me that you write," he said, the words echoing through time and distance, like a refrain he'd heard in his childhood: your mother told me you drew a beautiful picture in her office; your mother told me how you helped her with the flowers; your mother told me that you added five pieces to the puzzle.

"I write. Yes."

"And that you had a book published," his father said, the ring of pride resonating clearly in the glass-walled room.

"Yes. One book."

"And that you also wrote a screenplay, and they made a movie of your book."

"Yes. They also made a movie."

"With famous actors?"

"Pretty good actors, young graduates of Yale Drama School. But none of them are famous yet, if that's what you're asking."

"So they're not famous!—After your movie, they'll be famous."

"That's what they're hoping."

"And the book, the screenplay—everything in English, of course."

"In English, yes."

His father suddenly smiled. "I think you're a little like me when I was your age. The writing you get from me, that's for sure. I'm glad, very glad. Do you have your book with you?"

"No."

"I'd like to see it, but if you don't have it with you, then you don't. The important thing is that you wrote a book. You're modest, and that's good. I have to admit that when a poem of mine was published, I used to walk around with the magazine and show it to the whole world. I didn't manage to publish a book. But you—the important thing is that you wrote a book, and you got good reviews, your mother told me that very proudly. Not that it's so important and not that the reviewers are so smart, but good reviews are better than bad ones, and the main thing is, there's a book . . . So all right, now it's your turn."

"My turn to do what?"

"To ask me your questions."

"About what?"

"About prison," his father said in a normal voice, but there was something pleading in his eyes, as if he'd raised the possibility so that it could be rejected.

Taking advantage of the opportunity, Meir said quickly, "Exactly how long were you in prison?"

"Eighteen years, three months, and four days. Exactly."

"And what did you do there all those years?"

"At first, I didn't do anything. I was in shock for the first few years. And depressed. Then I started to understand that even in prison, people live their lives, all kinds of things happen to them. Not like the things that happen to people outside, that's true. But

they can't imprison your imagination. And there were advantages.
I had a roof over my head and food on the table. I was tired by
then—you said you don't remember that time, but we used to
look for places to live when you were with me—and it was pretty
tiring in the end. So I had a roof, like I said, and there was a plate
of food on the table three times a day."

Meir's eyes grew moist as he thought of how life had dwarfed
the desires of the poet whose verse Alterman had read, the man
who had charmed women, of how his father had learned to settle
for a crumb of all the world's plenty, like a trained dog.

"And besides a roof and a plate of food?"

"Besides a roof and a plate, I started to build a library from
nothing, a pile of torn books, and in the end, I was in charge of a
pretty large, organized library and of classes for the prisoners."

"What kind of classes?"

"Some of them didn't know how to read and write, if you can
imagine that. I set up a study group for them, and then it developed into music classes, for example. A pianist came to give lectures on music. And there was a literature group. Writers came
to talk to the prisoners."

"Alterman, too?"

"No. Alterman died before I got my bearings in prison. But
even if he'd been alive, I wouldn't have invited him."

"Why not? Were you ashamed?"

"At first, yes. But later I asked other poets to come, and writers.
They were happy to. They also knew Ola and that she was unsta-
ble. They knew me, too. They knew I was in prison by mistake.
They knew I wasn't a murderer."

The casual way his father spoke the word *murderer* shocked
Meir. "So why didn't you try to appeal if you weren't guilty?"

"Because I didn't have a chance, that's what my lawyer explained to me. Pola was the only witness. Every few years, I'd write
to her, but she didn't answer, maybe because of her craziness and
maybe just out of malice. I asked every poet who came here to
talk to her. Two or three said they did, and she wouldn't help. And

her condition got worse and worse, so maybe her testimony wouldn't have been worth anything anyway. She was in that mental hospital, and then she got diabetes or something. Maybe they lied when they said they talked to her, I had no way of checking. Once, a woman who worked for the Writers Association—I had women friends in the Writers Association—asked their lawyer to take my case pro bono, and he really did come and ask questions and he went to see Pola—in his case, I'm sure he went to see her—and he said she was in bad shape and couldn't testify. Finally, he gave up, too. I could've hired a private lawyer again, but it wouldn't have helped. The Association lawyer—who I really think believed me—told me it was a lost cause and the sad and awful truth was that law doesn't always mean justice, that the only witness, who might be guilty, was mentally ill.

"And was she really guilty?"

"I don't know."

"You were there, weren't you?"

"Yes, but I didn't see exactly what happened between them. They were standing very close together. Who knows whether she really tried to take the scissors away from her sister to save her or whether she pushed them deeper into her throat. Only the two of them and God know that."

"But you were there. You heard what they were saying."

"I couldn't understand a word. They were screaming their lungs out in Romanian. Both of them were holding the scissors. And Pola went off the deep end, that's what happened."

"Was Pola mentally ill while we were living at her place?" A round face, he remembered, mischievous eyes, a pleasant expression, a generous laugh, an ample bosom. He liked to watch her put on her make-up and he'd imitate the contortions she made in front of the mirror when she opened her eyes wide to put on mascara and stretched her lips sideways to put on her shiny red lipstick. He also remembered her hands, white and plump like a baby's hands, offering food and cakes, ruffling the cat's fur, playing the piano, reaching out for his body under the water.

"To you she was wonderful. It's a shame you don't remember that. Of all the memories, that would've been a nice one to remember. She was mean to her sister, and sometimes to me."

But you slept with her, Meir countered silently as his voice said, "She definitely didn't hate you, if she let us live in her house."

"I had a lot of time to think about that. She probably thought, in that crazy head of hers, that Ola and I were planning to get married, even though she knew I had a wife. I'm telling you because I want you to know: that wasn't true. I was nice to a lot of women, but I never planned to marry any of them. I was just waiting for your mother to come back. But Pola must have been suspicious. So there was jealousy and also fear that if Ola left, then maybe there'd be no more work because Ola was more talented than she was. Pola couldn't have managed at work without Ola. It was very complicated between them. Maybe I should've realized that, maybe I wasn't careful enough. And now . . . I know you have a problem hearing this, but it's the truth: I wanted to go to America not because of the treatment. There are very good doctors here. I know exactly what my condition is," he said. He was silent for a moment. "I wanted to see you, to hear whether you remember, whether my mistakes ruined anything for you . . . I wanted to say I'm sorry. I had years to think about what that wandering did to you, our conversations on park benches, all the women. . . . You were a gentle child. I don't know why I didn't understand then . . . it was kind of insane then, and most of the time in the Kassit, I was a little drunk. I don't know whether you noticed, you were so young, and I don't think being drunk is a good excuse or anything to brag about, but it's true. I didn't want to send you to your mother. You were all I had. You know I lost my whole family in Europe, except for an uncle who came to Jerusalem before the war and Berl, who somehow got out of it alive. I didn't want to lose you, too. Your mother wrote that the doctor said she had a risky pregnancy and couldn't fly back, but I didn't really believe her. I thought she was using the pregnancy as a weapon because she'd started talking about going back to America long before that. She missed it and she missed her family. I hoped that in the end, she'd break down and come back. And if not—I took this into account, too—if she didn't come back, then I thought I'd eventually find a woman who'd be good to both of us and would stay with me. That's what they told me in the office. If I could prove that I could give you a normal life, she'd have to go to court to take you away from me, and she wouldn't have much of a chance. You were the most important thing in my life then. I couldn't let her take you away from me. I planned for us to find a woman, but it didn't work out . . ."

A wave of heat flooded Meir, like sudden desire. Sudden desire for the material of that life which, in his childhood, was flesh of their flesh. Was this the trembling that heralded his entry into the land of the living?

"But you say you don't remember, so maybe that's best. What you don't remember doesn't hurt, that's what Berl always used to say. But there were also good things, it's a shame you forgot those, too," his father said, a passion for life flashing suddenly in his eye. "It's too bad you don't remember how wonderful it was some- times walking around Tel Aviv."

"What was so wonderful?"

"We wandered around, free as birds, went wherever we wanted, met people."

"We met mostly women."

"You remember we met mostly women? It's true, we did meet mostly women."

"I know that from your stories. I don't remember anything, but what's that 'we'? You were the one who met them."

"We both did. In our wanderings, we met all kinds."

"I understand that you sat in cafés, but I was stuck next to a tree most of the time."

His father burst into mischievous laughter that lit up his face and restored some of the good looks of the young man in the photographs.

"Yes, there was a tree there," he said, adding quietly, "Not as beautiful as the trees in Connecticut. I saw a picture of the trees in autumn. Beautiful, very beautiful . . . I used to love landscapes. I also used to love being with people. . . . "

"And all those years that you were . . . locked up?" Meir's imagination had suddenly taken him back to the prison.

"What did I do with myself? I read. The truth is that except for missing you and your mother and thinking about the baby, I had some quiet time there, finally a permanent place to sleep. And I thought that maybe it was better for you in America, too. You had a bed and a room and books and toys and everything a boy needs . . . I had a lot of time and a lot of quiet. I even had a few friends, people who'd made mistakes in their lives, but there, they were my friends. And Berl came to visit me. He brought me my old glossaries and a few new ones. I don't know whether you remember that I had books like those for my editing and translating work. We took them to his cellar that day, and he brought me one every time he came to see me. I used to read them, I read all kinds of books, whatever they gave me, whatever I found."

"So you didn't suffer there?"

"I suffered because it was a long time, many years, and I was locked up, not free to get up and go. But I'd been through hard times before. I never told you about my childhood. I thought I'd tell you when you grew up. Polish neighbors murdered my grandparents when the Germans invaded Poland, and my father and I ran away to Russia. I stayed there until the war ended, always hungry, always afraid. . . . A year after the war—back in Poland—I found out that my mother was dead, too, and a few months later, my father died of pneumonia. So I was no stranger to hard times. Later, I came to Israel alone, to the kibbutz, and then, after I left the kibbutz, life wasn't easy in Jerusalem either because they wouldn't send me to school. From that history, you can understand that I was used to hard times."

"Did you write during those years? Were you able to write in prison?"

"It's really strange, you know. I actually did write there sometimes."

"Poems?"

"Poems, only poems."

"What kind of poems?"

"Without rhyme. Alterman used to laugh at me for not knowing how to write in rhyme. I didn't tell him, but I'll tell you, it's not that I didn't know how, but it was right for me to write without rhyme."

"What did you write about?"

"What do you think?" he asked, smiling, finding this amusing.

"Landscapes?"

"Why landscapes?"

"That's what I imagine a man locked up in a room would write about."

"I didn't write a single poem about landscapes. I wrote only love poems to your mother. We write about what we miss the most."

"Did you send them to her?"

"Some of them, yes."

"And she answered?"

"No. She never answered, but I knew she received them."

"Were they ever published anywhere?"

"Two or three poems were published in the Writers Association newsletter, but later I realized that they weren't taken seriously, that I fell into the category of the man imprisoned for murder, a kind of novelty, almost a circus, so I severed my ties with the Association."

A man convicted of murdering his lover, writing love poems to his wife, a subject with endless possibilities for a story—Meir tried to work up his enthusiasm—and he even published the poems to tell the world outside about his love.

"That was what you missed the most, right?"

"Yes," his father said before he could think through his answer and say, "You were the thing I missed most," as he had earlier. "Yes, I missed women."

*   *   *

Sitting together on park benches waiting for some office to open or for their appointment with one of the clerks, his father would tell him about women. He always talked about them with excitement in his hushed voice, as if he were telling a secret. First, there was his childhood sweetheart—he had kissed her for the first time in a dark alley in front of her house a minute before her mother ran out and dragged her inside, and that was the sweetest kiss of them all. Then there was his forbidden, teenage romance with a non-Jewish girl that had taken place under bridges. Then a teacher, for a few months before the war broke out. After the war, when he was fifteen, they had met accidentally in the street and the teacher invited him to the abandoned apartment she and her sister had taken over, and she seduced him there. One day she vanished without a trace, and only years later did he find out that she had secretly gotten herself a visa to the United States and left without telling her sister. Then there was a married kibbutz member whose husband was in the British army and spent months in Europe. She had asked to talk to him when she heard that he came from Poland. Sometimes his father would get carried away with detailed descriptions not meant for a child's ears, and sometimes he'd suddenly stop in the middle, as if he'd just woken up to this realization.

Of all the things his father told him, Meir remembered mainly the ones that were cut off when his father realized he'd gone too far. There are women, his father told him once, his eyes glittering, who have hairy bodies like men. Hair grows on their stomachs, their backs, between their breasts, and they're passionate and hot-tempered. You can find out the secret of a woman's temperament by looking at her palm— his father turned his hand over to demonstrate. If this hill that starts here at the thumb is high, that means the woman knows how to love; if it's flat, that means she's as cold as the North Pole and you can pass her up. Every woman is different, and the sweetest women are the pink ones, pink from top—he put a finger on his forehead as if he were saluting—to bottom. His fingers moved down to the opening of his pants, and he bent over as if he had a stomach ache. Sometimes the virgins—he said once, his eyes following two giggling high school girls—are the best in the world and sometimes they're a real disaster. Curly-haired women, he said, pursing his lips as if he were about to kiss them all, have the nicest hair to touch because it reminds you of the hair they have in another place on their bodies. The most pleasurable places to touch on a woman's body are hidden under her clothes, but of all the exposed parts, the most sensitive is the neck, especially the nape. And women love to kiss. Some of them like it more than anything, and some—he reached down and openly grabbed his testicles—know how to keep a man erect for hours. A real woman, he said, aroused, enjoys giving a man pleasure more than getting it from him. And this is something every man should know: women love to be conquered. You pretend to let them lead, but in the end, you master them by force. And here's something very important: you can't tell how big some parts of a woman's body are until she takes off her clothes— He stopped suddenly, pulled himself together. Many years later, the child at his side would still be puzzled by the bothersome riddle: How large are the parts of a woman's body hidden under her clothes?

"None of your girlfriends came to see you in prison?"

"Some did, at the beginning, yes. But it was awkward. Because I saw the fear in their eyes, and also because of the place—a disgusting room, an old table, and a policeman watching us. In the end, I asked them not to come anymore."

"You couldn't meet with them outside? Didn't you have time off?"

"After a few years, they started giving me short furloughs, and then I used to see people."

"Women?"

"Yes, women too . . . but it wasn't the same any more . . . I lived in Berl's room and . . . it wasn't like it used to be . . . "

Here's something worth a story, Meir thought, his imagination sparked. A man is on a three-day furlough from prison. He walks around the streets, hungrily breathing in the temporary freedom, and unused to the masses of people, he stares at them on the street or perhaps lowers his gaze to the sidewalk and hurries to his one-room apartment before someone recognizes him; unused to the sight of babies, his eyes linger on an infant sleeping in a carriage, frightening the young mother, or perhaps he walks through the city blind to babies and small children, who no longer have a place in his life; hungry for the closeness of women, he stares greedily at every passing woman, finding something seductive in even the ugliest ones, or perhaps he forces himself to look away from them, fleeing from temptation.

"And when you missed women, did you miss Mom?"

"Your mother was a woman, so I missed her, too. I loved your mother, I wrote her love poems—you're grown up now, so I can tell you and you'll understand—I missed women there," he said, then after a moment's silence, allowed himself to ask, "And you, do you write love poems?"

"No. I don't write poetry at all, just prose."

"Do you write prose about love?"

"I don't know what prose about love is."

"You mean you don't like women?"

"I don't know . . . "

"Are you saying you like men?"

"No . . . "

"I asked myself many times what it did to you, seeing the way I behaved with women. Most children don't see their father in situations like that."

"What did you think it did to me?"

"When all that was happening, I wasn't thinking at all, and for a long time afterward, my mind was completely paralyzed. Only years later. . . . Your mother told me that you're not married, but that you have girlfriends, women. She said you're having a love affair with a black woman."

"I wouldn't call it love . . . it's just . . ."

"You have problems with women?"

"I don't know what you mean by 'problems with women.'"

"Anyone who has them knows very well what problems with women are. But it doesn't begin with problems, it begins with a problem," his father said, his voice echoing the sound of the radio psychologist's voice. "You have to solve them one by one and you start with the most pressing one."

"It's not just her . . . I don't know how to talk to women," Meir said, shocked to hear himself say what he hadn't dared say even to Arnie.

"You just have to love them, and all the rest comes by itself. They say that a woman is a complex creature. I once read Freud's letters. When he was old, he confessed that he didn't understand women. If I'd met him, I would've said to him, 'Mr. Freud, you know what your problem with women is? You didn't love them.'—and I'm saying the same thing to you. There isn't much to understand, and you don't have to be a genius to do it."

"I'm not good at it," Meir said, the sudden, painful truth coming from his mouth like a cry for help, and his father heard it too.

"That's too bad," his father said. "You know, when you were little, I told you a lot about women. I hoped it would help you in life."

"Nothing I did with you helped me," Meir said, looking away, his pleasant voice clashing with the harsh words, but his father wasn't shocked.

"You knew things about women that very few boys your age knew," his father said, insisting on pursuing this important subject. "I let you in on all the secrets."

The women with hairy backs—Meir suddenly remembered the scratchy feel of the wooden bench in Meir Park, and how embarrassed he was by the thought of the grown-up world—the women, pink from head to toe, who were the sweetest; the virgins who gave the most pleasure or were a total letdown; the parts of women's bodies hidden under their clothes and the mystery of their size; the women who knew how to keep a man erect for hours.

"A seven-year-old boy shouldn't know things like that."

"So I take it that it didn't help you later with girls?"

"It ruined everything."

They didn't speak for a long while, and Meir, convinced that his father understood for the first time the extent of the destruction he'd sown in his son's life and was now busy trying to come up with a self-justifying remark or even a statement of regret, was stunned to hear him whisper, as if he were telling a secret, "I have a request . . ."

"What?" Meir asked, drawing back.

"Take me bowling. There's a bowling alley on Ibn Gvirol Street."

His ability to let his son's last remark pass right by him, to ignore the despair of the child whose fate he himself had determined—was that what helped keep his father sane in prison?

"I don't think you're allowed to," Meir replied, almost hostilely.

"Sure I am. For an hour or two. They won't even notice," he said.

Meir suddenly remembered, he'd once edited an article about a newly published book written by the head of a hospital geriatrics department. The writer talked about the moment when parents and children switch roles. In his department, the doctor said, children feeding their parents, combing their hair, and sometimes changing their diapers was an everyday sight. But there, Meir now argued with the quote in his memory, the children and parents have gone through the full cycle of life together, and the switching of roles is as smooth and as right as nature itself. But here, Meir had been forced to make the transition from a distance of half a lifetime and half the world, with only a few days' warning. He'd been made to look beyond the black pit of his life into eyes from his own childhood.

Soon, he'd wheel his father along Ibn Gvirol Street like a mother wheeling her baby, and then he'd sit and watch him bowl the way his father had sat years ago in the park and watched Meir scamper from the swings to the slide to the monkey bars. His father would bend over in his wheelchair, run his fingers over the ball, raise it to his heart, drop his hand to the floor and aim it toward the wooden pins lined up at the end of the lane. He'd throw it weakly and sway in his wheelchair from the force of the throw, holding his breath as his good eye followed the rolling ball, disappointed as it veered off to the side and touched only one pin, making it wobble but not knocking it down. Again and again he'd bend over and aim the ball, alternately disappointed and elated until he'd finished his round of throws, then he'd go over to the table where Meir was waiting and say, "You need two eyes to bowl, but it was fun."

Instead, his father said, "On second thought, I won't go bowling today. And I can see that you're not too crazy about the idea."

"I don't mind going—"

"So maybe a dance hall. There's a club where older people dance. That's something I'd like to see, just sit and watch while I still have my eye. Maybe the nurses know the exact address and the day and time. It's not open every day."

A while after they left the house on HaNevi'im Street, his father found a new place to meet women: a ballroom dance club with free admission for men on Tuesdays and Thursdays. Meir, sitting on a bench watching the circle of dancing women, who all looked alike, holding their partners' arms, would remember what his father taught him about the ways of women. "When a woman dances," he said once, "she reveals all her secrets without knowing it. When you look at a woman dancing, you can see how she does all kinds of other things."

"What things?"

"Everything she does with her body. The body has a language of its own."

Sitting on the bench, his head tilted back against the wall, Meir watched the dancing women pressed up against their partners and tried to guess what they were revealing about themselves. His father suddenly came into view and Meir was alarmed: he and the woman dancing with him were stuck together forever. His father, Meir thought in horror, wasn't his father anymore, but someone who had disappeared into this new creature that also contained the strange woman. Meir looked down at the creature's legs, made of a pair of woman's legs and a pair of men's legs, the four of them moving together in perfect synchronization. His father must have caught sight of the boy's frantic expression because he broke away from the woman and went over to him. "Is everything all right, Meir?" he asked.

"Yes," Meir blurted out, relieved to see that his father was himself again.

"Here's a mint. We'll go soon," he said.

And they did go, and never went back to that place again. "When you dance, you can't really talk," his father said, explaining his failure to find them a refuge with one of the dancing women, revealing that talk was the secret of his charm.

"I can see that this won't be the day for bowling or for dancing," his exhausted father said, giving up. "But maybe tomorrow. Will you come tomorrow?"

"I wanted to go to the cemetery—"

"To Berl's grave, I know. But you can't stay there all day. And we're still not finished talking."

"We're not?"

"No. I have a few more important things to say to you."

"Like what?"

"We'll talk tomorrow. They aren't things you can say offhand. So tell me, you weren't planning to visit me tomorrow, too?"

"I don't have any plans. I thought I'd go to the cemetery—"

"So come tomorrow, whenever you want. Just remember the cemetery's open until late."

"Okay. Do you want me to bring you anything?"

"I want you to come, that's all."

"So I'll come tomorrow morning."

"Morning is the best time. I feel better in the morning. Tell me, do you know the song, 'Don't say goodbye, just say so long'? No? It's a nice song, but if you don't know it, you don't know it," his father said and turned his wheelchair as if he was already busy with something else, and Meir got up, abashed, not practiced at goodbyes.

"And another thing," his father said, shifting his wheelchair abruptly, "If you talk to your mother, don't tell her about the eye."

Was he protecting her or did he want her to preserve the memory of the man he had been? First striding, then almost running, Meir fled the department and sprinted the short distance from the hospital to the boulevard of his childhood: down David HaMelech Boulevard, along Ibn Gvirol Street to the sign that said Chen Boulevard.

He sat down on the first bench, which had a view of the city hall building, and looked around, searching for the ghost of the boy he had been, and the ghosts of his father and mother. Perhaps he'd see them walk past: a young man and woman, their arms around each other's waists, their heads turned so their lips could meet in a kiss, the boy skipping along behind them; or a young man and woman waving their hands at each other and arguing in raspy voices, the mortified boy walking behind them. Then he began studying the faces of the people passing by: he might recognize a neighbor or one of the women who occasionally gave him and his father a place to stay; perhaps he'd recognize the man eating a falafel, who once walked past the tree across from the Kassit and stopped to tear off a chunk of thick, fragrant pita and give it to the boy. But the neighbors, his first-grade teacher, his kindergarten teacher—he could see their blurred faces in his mind's eye—were old now, and even if they walked past him right then, he most probably wouldn't recognize them.

Suddenly, like a flash from the future, he saw a scene in his mind. He looked in horror at the Tel Aviv city hall square after an attack of Iraqi missiles: the tall building had collapsed, and the rubble covered the tiled square and the iron sculpture. The apartment houses around the square and along the boulevard had caved in, too. The cars parked on the streets like strings of colored necklaces were crushed and most of the trees were lying on their sides, their clustered roots torn up. There were charred people everywhere: strewn like dolls amid the rubble, walking down the street alone or in pairs holding hands, trapped in their cars, standing at windows, sitting on their open balconies. An injured dog limped across what used to be a traffic island and collapsed. A last witness sat on a bench: a living man, elegantly dressed, photographing the surroundings with the concentration of a professional. When he rummaged around in his bag for a new roll of film, an American passport popped out.

Panicked, Meir jumped up, driving away the image of destruction and the idea that this was a hint that he should be writing futuristic fiction. His publisher would be happy about the decision. It was common knowledge that there was a large audience for that genre. Embarrassed by the thought that he was willing to exploit even destruction to make a name for himself, he decided to go right then to look for his childhood home and school, and the kindergarten on Netzach Israel Street.

He wandered, confused, from one end of HaNevi'im Street to the other for a long time, looking for the wall that had been built to keep shrapnel out of the entrance and for the little iron people that held the shutters open. The wall must have been taken down and the iron people ripped out, and Meir, stumbling with exhaustion, gave up on the school and the kindergarten because of the disappointment, the falling darkness, and the apocalyptic scene he still couldn't get out of his mind. He hailed a taxi.

The hotel was situated across from the dark beach in a long row of other hotels, all looking like sophisticated weapons of war in a science fiction movie, ready and waiting at the starting line. In the hotel restaurant, he ordered lentil soup, sat down next to the window and looked out at the sea glittering in the lights of the promenade like the ominous signals of a diver come to spy. He looked at the water rocking in the darkness and thought about the two young people who'd had their pictures taken so many years ago on this beach, the battlefield of his imagination, who might have stood on the strip of sand he was staring at now, over his bowl of soup, wanting to memorialize that good moment, believing in the power of poetry and their love. He thought about the boy who'd built sand castles on the beach, unaware of the intensity of the storm that would turn their lives upside down in only a few months. A bitter wind entered his conciliatory thoughts, and he could see the man who had wandered from Poland to Russia to Jerusalem, and the woman whose fate had carried her from her father's home in Connecticut to Israel. Whatever it was that had joined those two people would forever remain an enigma to their only son; he would never understand why they decided to have him, why they didn't split up of their own accord but instead let the whim of fate do it for them, leaving the boy alone, the small refugee of an unhappy history.

He made his decision right then and there: he wouldn't go easy on his father tomorrow, and he wouldn't lie or evade or blur the line between what he remembered and what he knew. Tomorrow he'd tell his father the truth.

Overcome by infinite sorrow, he got up, letting the heavy spoon sink into the untasted soup, and walked slowly to his room. It was as if, in only a day, he'd aged and erased the gap of years between the boy from Tel Aviv and the grown man.

*No matter how I look at it that was when fate itself stepped in after all those years when Ola and I were alone and never heard a good word from a guest and we were always fighting about men and none of them was worth fighting about with my little sister but the great big truth is that Ola's men were nothing but garbage and besides they were married. I told her I didn't want her to bring them into my bed because every ten days when we changed the sheets we also changed beds, ten days she was in the big bed in the big bedroom and ten days she was in the small bed in the small bedroom, but when she found one of her men she'd ask for the big bed and didn't even change the sheets and I wouldn't sleep on the same sheet a married man slept on because who knows what kind of dirt and invisible germs he brought into my bed from all his women. Ola and I have been fighting since we were little girls because she likes to fight but the fights about men didn't start until we came to Tel Aviv. I don't tell anyone about her men so they won't say ugh we're disgusting but I mark down numbers and she already brought twenty-five men to the big bed since Purim last year when we got dressed up like nurses from the hospital and she brought the man from the party home after they both drank straight from the bottle and she shoved her hand into his pants and said he was a really tough case and she had to take care of him like the head nurse of the clinic and they laughed and I went into the small room and started making the signs for numbers and I wrote him down number one in my little book. He came a few more times after that but I wouldn't write him down again because he had a number and that was that and once in the middle of a fight she kissed me because that's how it is with Ola when you start something you never know how it'll end so she kissed me and told me that she would pass the men on to me and it was about time I acted like a real woman because I wasn't a little girl any more and it didn't matter what kind of stupid little-girl dresses I wear she knows exactly how old I am and she knows I'm the big sister and it's not normal for a woman my age not to want to be with a man and I told her that all those twenty-five men she brought home since Purim I wouldn't let any one of them touch me with the tip of the nail on his pinky ugh they're so disgusting with their dirt and germs and she said Pola Pola a normal woman's body wants a man's body every few days like she's hungry when she doesn't eat and it's about time you act like a normal woman and that same evening we met him and the boy and a man with a boy was a completely different story without another woman's dirt and without another woman's talk and we started living a normal life. I told all that to Dr. Susskind in his office today and I started to cry and couldn't stop because he asked me what I would do if I could pick a profession for myself and all of a sudden I thought about how Ola's life was wasted and mine too and how we could've opened a candy store or a kindergarten because I really love children and we could've done a lot of other things with all our talent and our looks instead of singing to people and being dependent on the invitations and having to be nice to them and listen to their complaints and Ola and I could've traveled to far-away places that not a lot of people go to for instance India to see the beautiful building that a rich man built for his beloved and thinking about that love and how she went and died on him in the middle of giving birth. I cried even harder and Doctor Susskind gave me a tissue like in the movies and I wiped my eyes carefully because I put on mascara for him today like I used to do in the mascara days but we didn't have to travel so far we could've traveled somewhere closer for instance Greece and climbed up Olympus and seen the place the boy used to tell me about where the gods lived and did all those ridiculous things but we didn't go to India or Greece or anyplace else and that's why I cried and couldn't stop even though I knew that besides the mascara, every time I cry like that I get hungry and that's the end of my diet which I just started today and that's how all my diets end and end and end and I can barely get into a size forty-eight and people look at the picture next to my bed. And I can't believe it's me in my stage clothes with Ola who looks like a real queen on a night I remember very well because we sang Natan Alterman's new songs and when I tell people that I knew Natan Alterman the important poet and I used to sit with him back in the café days then people start to understand something about my history and even Dr. Susskind said that's wonderful Pola and he said I could write the story of the café but I only want to write about Abraham from the Bible and now I'm really in love with the goats' eyes and most of all I love describing the goats' eyes. I look into their eyes like I'm looking into the kaleidoscope my father gave me when I was a little girl and my little sister and I used to fight over it all the time and I see shapes and colors in the goats' eyes like nobody would believe. I told that to Dr. Susskind and when he asked me why goats' eyes, I explained to him that you can see right away in people's eyes when they did something bad, and with the goats you can see right away that they didn't and he asked me to give him an example of something bad and I didn't have an example I don't know about anything bad and he asked what about your fights with your sister and I said there were fights yes mainly when we were little but I loved my little sister and there was never anything bad between us—*

The burial society people at the Kiryat Shaul cemetery, trained in the unpleasant aspects of human existence, listened patiently as he explained with uncharacteristic effusiveness how he'd gone that morning to see his father, as they'd agreed, and even planned to take him to a bowling alley or a dance hall for older people. But the nurse told him that his father had died during the night, and among the words of consolation and the compliments she showered on the European gentleman—that, it turned out, was what the nurses called him—she said that many sick people delay their deaths until their loved ones come. It was a fact, the nurse said, that many of them actually die on Sunday, after weekend visits. The burial society people bowed their heads as the words streamed from him, not wanting to disturb the flow, and when he finished, they confirmed what the nurse had said, telling him of the large number of funerals held on Sundays, and said they were surprised that apart from him, no one else had come to the funeral. They quickly gathered a minyan of ten men to take the place of mourners and hinted that dollars were preferable to shekels.

Watching a crowded funeral procession in the adjacent row from the corner of his eye, he was sorry he'd never know what his father had wanted to say to him. Still exhausted from the flight of only a little more than a day ago and a bad night's sleep, Meir trudged along the path crushed by thousands of shoes, carrying seven bouquets of roses, surrounded by strangers. He thought about the fate of the man whose body was now wrapped in a prayer shawl, swaying on the stretcher in front of him, about to be dropped into a freshly dug pit along with his secrets and the important things he'd been about to tell his son and now never would. He thought about the man's wasted will to live and the poems that had remained locked up inside him. His son would repeat after the cantor, saying in as clear a voice as possible the words of *Kaddish Yatom*, the orphan's prayer on his parent's grave that he'd heard spoken with a different accent at other funerals, and then he'd go home with his unanswered questions about his childhood and those five months and all the years he hadn't known his father was alive. No one but himself, his mother, and Arnie would think about the handsome man who was so attractive to women, whose life was ruined in a single moment, and who died with the riddle of his guilt unsolved. Perhaps a stranger, looking for a relative's resting place, would occasionally pass by and stop to read the sentence Meir's father had asked to be inscribed on the headstone that would be placed on his grave thirty days after his death: "The song of his life was silenced too soon," and the passerby wouldn't know that the man buried here had continued to live for twenty-three years and eight months after that song was silenced.

As they plodded along, it began to drizzle, and out of nowhere, Meir suddenly had a vivid memory of drowning. His arms open as if to embrace, he abandoned himself to the gentle waves, rocking pleasantly with them, until suddenly, he was inundated and, terrified and feeling betrayed, he kicked his feet as hard as he could, struggling to rise. He managed to get his nose above the surface of the water and breathe in some air, and he swallowed a huge amount of salt water before he sank and again fought to push the water away with his legs, but it refused to retreat, and he was swept into the depths, flipping over and over in the current, propelled into it, too weak to stop the wild jerking of his body. In the turbulence of the water that pounded him, he heard the distant sound of human voices and he began to sink like a weight into the cold, sucking abyss. Then silence subdued the echoes of the war going on in his body, soothing and consoling the way sleep assuages overwhelming tiredness. Suddenly, the water was pierced by a blinding light and a hand pulled him upward and pressed him against a warm, living body, and his father wrapped his arms around him and said, "Everything's fine, Meir. Daddy's here now."

The strangers placed small stones on the mound as proof that they'd been there, and left. As Meir bent to spread flowers over the fresh clumps of earth strewn with stones, it occurred to him that the man who loved women, the man women loved, had been carried to his grave by a group of men, and not a single woman had accompanied him, either with her presence or in her thoughts. As for the woman he'd written poems to, she didn't even know he was dead, and was most probably asleep now—three o'clock in the morning in New York—in her bedroom overlooking Second Avenue.

Meir had not yet laid down the last flower when he stopped musing and began of think about what he would do now. First of all, he'd ask in the burial society office where Berl's grave was. He'd hire a cantor to say a prayer in Berl's memory and he'd put the bouquet he'd saved for Berl on his grave. Then he'd order a headstone in one of monument-maker's workshops right outside the cemetery and write the inscription for them to carve on it. He'd ask for the headstone to be placed on his father's grave in his absence and pay in advance, for the cantor, too. Then he'd find a taxi and go to the apartment on Dizengoff Street; a nurse had given him the keys, together with his father's belongings and a will in Aharon Rosinberg's handwriting, signed by a lawyer and two witnesses. In it, he had bequeathed the apartment on Dizengoff Street and the money in his bank account to his son, Meir Rosinberg, and the last clause had asked for an inscription on his gravestone that would read, "The song of his life was silenced too soon." If there was a working phone in the apartment, he'd find the number of the hospital in Pardessiya and call to ask if Pola was still a patient. From there, he'd go back to HaNevi'im Street to look for his childhood home, and maybe, in the light of day, he'd recognize his elementary school and the kindergarten on Netzach Israel Street. Later, he'd go to the Beit Ariella public library where, the nurse had told him, there was a newspaper archive, ask for the May 1967 volume and read the newspaper reports of Ola's death and what they said about his father.

Then he'd work up the courage to go to the Kassit.

Berl's grave, reached through muddy paths, was at the far end of the cemetery, adjacent to the military section. A simple headstone

his father must have ordered bore his name and the dates of his
birth and death and the inscription: "In memory of his family
who perished in the Holocaust." Meir brushed away the years of
dust lying on the bare stone, placed the bouquet gently over the
words "perished in the Holocaust," and stood there for a long
moment, his throat choked with tears. It occurred to him that
there was no one left in the world, except maybe Arnie, whose
memory filled him with warmth and moved him as did the memory of Berl. He had a clear vision of the first time he saw Berl
when he collapsed on Allenby Street and the shaking hands that
reached out for Meir's face when he came out of his faint. As if he
were assuring Berl that someone he loved was nearby, Meir
looked over the rows of headstones to where his father had just
been buried. When he turned and left, it was still drizzling. His
hair and coat were wet. Meir walked quickly toward the main gate,
where he would order a headstone for his father, then look for a
taxi to take him to the apartment on Dizengoff Street.

At the door to the apartment which, by law, now belonged to him,
his legs stopped moving of their own accord and refused to go
any further. From where he stood, his eyes could take in the entire
small room: a tiny kitchen on the right, a gas range so shiny that
it looked newly purchased, a small toy-like refrigerator, a clean
and bare marble counter and next to it, a small table with two
chairs facing each other as if to proclaim that no more than two
people could visit here. On the left was a floor-to-ceiling, built-in
closet, and standing next to it was a convertible couch covered
with a blue blanket his father had folded in crisp army style, a
habit that must have been instilled in him in prison. A very small
table with slender legs, usually meant to hold a plant or a radio,
was where he ate his meals. The floor was bare and the walls
empty, the apartment of someone without a past, who possessed
only the necessities: gas range, refrigerator, bed, blanket, sheet,
table, chair, plate, cup, pot, fork, spoon, knife, towel, and a few
items of clothing.

Surveying the modest apartment, Meir suddenly thought that this room was the most reliable witness of the transformation his father had undergone. He had left behind the man who wore silk scarves and carried mints in his pocket, who was always ready to plant a kiss on a woman's lips, who moved elegantly even when sitting alone, reading a book at his desk. He had once been a man who wouldn't have lived in this Spartan room for even one hour, without the familiar accoutrements of comfort. But when he was released from prison, he must have been very much like Berl after the war, who could totally blend into his furniture and tools and almost become one with them. And there, for the first time, standing at the open door to the ascetic apartment over a sooty bus stop on Dizengoff Street, Meir mourned the man from the cafés and the man from prison, both of them his father, both of them unknown to him. Gripped by that feeling, he remained standing in the doorway for a long time, just as he'd stood there as a child when the Memorial Day or Holocaust Day siren sounded—it had seemed like an eternity then –after which his father explained in the simplest words that it's important to remember the dead not for their sake, but for the sake of those who remained and retain the memory.

Now he remembered how his father had avoided giving him the key to the apartment by claiming it was messy, and he wondered what he'd been trying to hide. The sound of squealing brakes and car horns came from the street, and Meir quickly pulled the key out of the lock, closed the door behind him and walked to the tiny balcony overlooking the street, and then—his eyes wide and his heart overflowing—like someone finding his lost love in an unexpected place, he saw the elegant desk from the apartment on HaNevi'im Street standing now on the balcony on Dizengoff Street like an aristocrat fallen on hard times. Though it was warped by sun and rain, it still retained a hint of the former splendor Meir remembered, and it was piled high with books and papers here, too. When he was a baby, he'd been photographed sitting on one of those unsteady piles; this was the desk where his father sat writing in the quiet hours after midnight, especially frightening hours, because, as the religious neighbors' son told him, that was when evil ghosts rose from under the gravestones in the cemetery on Trumpeldor Street and wandered through the city, satisfying their hunger by eating little children who weren't yet asleep; this was the desk his father, Berl, and a porter had moved, and he himself had been recruited to participate in that "man's job," holding up one of the corners when they carried it down into the cellar on Shlomo HaMelech Street.

Meir ran a soothing hand over the exposed strip of the desktop that had once been polished: here was the most reliable witness to his childhood, this desk that had been moved from one house to another, waiting patiently for the baby that had been seated on it so many years ago to grow up and come back, and to decide that, as soon as he could, he'd move the desk inside and cover it with a layer of protective lacquer.

Shouts rose from below, and he looked down at Dizengoff Street, where he'd so often trailed after his father, both walking along it like beggars in their wrinkled clothes and underwear they hadn't changed in three days. What a transformation: now wearing a Calvin Klein jacket, Meir was looking down at a soot-blackened bus stop, at a sidewalk stained with the detritus of crushed ficus fruit, seeing the street through eyes that were accustomed to viewing the Manhattan skyline and the Connecticut foliage.

Some papers flew off the desk, as if trying to escape, and Meir picked them up from the corner of the balcony where they'd fallen onto the others lying there: a letter from the city regarding property tax, an invitation to a fundraising event for soldiers, a flyer for a new café opening in a bookstore on Dizengoff Street. At the top corner of the fourth page, in tiny handwriting, was: "To My Wife," and in the middle of the page was the title of a poem. Meir's lip curled involuntarily in astonishment and revulsion at its brazenness: "Sperm."

Looking up *stardust* for the night-lit sky
My finger stops at *sperm*.

*   *   *

He didn't want to read any more than that. Agitated, he put all the papers back on the desk, turning that one over, regretting that he'd been tempted to look at something not meant for him, refusing to learn more about his father than he already knew.

Books were piled up on the corner of the desk. With a pounding heart, Meir recognized the old glossaries that had been his father's most devoted escorts, moving with him from his house in Jerusalem to his apartment on HaNevi'im Street, to Berl's cellar, to the prison—where he'd looked through one of them for *stardust*—and to this apartment on Dizengoff Street. An intriguing, stuffed envelope sat between the pile of books and the unopened official letters. He found pictures of women in it, some of them wearing dresses and some in their underwear. He flipped through them, afraid he'd find one of a naked woman. He didn't find a naked woman, but it was obvious that the women, apparently photographed by his father, had been naked not long before or not long afterwards. The clothed women were posing seductively, the women in their underwear shyly. One was hiding her crotch coyly, clearly toying with the photographer. And in one of the pictures, a beautiful woman leaned against the desk on the balcony, her hands crossed over her wide-strapped bra.

Carefully, Meir returned the package of photographs to its place next to the business envelope that had slipped to the side, as if to say now was its turn. He picked it up and took a few newspaper clippings out of it. It took a while for him to realize that now he didn't have to go to the Beit Ariella archive and think up an excuse for the librarian about why he was interested in newspapers from May 1967. With trembling hands, he arranged the clippings according to date and read.

On May 10th, between an ad for smoked goat's cheese and one for Berlitz and a picture of King Faisal of Saudi Arabia sitting beside Queen Elizabeth in an open carriage waving to the crowd, the newspaper, *Ha'aretz,* had printed an item with the headline:

"Murder or Suicide in Tel Aviv—Actress Dead; Sister and Poet Friend Arrested." Under the headline were two pictures, one of his father standing next to an official car, and the other of the sisters singing together on a stage, their heads meeting over the microphone, wearing long dresses, one dark with white sleeves, the other white with dark sleeves, reverse images. From their height, he knew which was Ola and which Pola. The text of the article said: "Last night, the police were called to an apartment on Dubnov Street in Tel Aviv. In the bedroom of the apartment, they found the dead body of Ola Metkovitz, 28. Her sister, Pola Metkovitz, and their friend, the poet Aharon Rosinberg, were in the apartment at the time. Both were taken in for questioning. The police still haven't reported their version of events because of the sister's unstable mental state. The sisters, actresses and singers, performed in bars, small halls, and at family parties."

Meir's eyes skipped to the last two lines: "The police later released for publication that when the murder or suicide was taking place, the jailed poet's seven-year-old son was asleep in the living room of the apartment."

So that's how it was, Meir thought. Here was the secret stripped of its mystery, exposed to the eyes of the Kassit patrons, who would have passed the newspaper around, and also exposed to tens of thousands of other readers. Perhaps in the evening, women had told their husbands about the Tel Aviv murder or suicide that took place while the suspect's seven-year-old son was asleep in the next room, and with a compassionate click of their tongues, had served the smoked goat's cheese they bought that day after seeing the ad on the same page.

Meir felt an unfamiliar emptiness inside him, not the barrenness that had been part of him all those years. Now, the space inside him was filled with an aching sorrow it was futile to feel because it was too late. It couldn't be remedied and there was nothing to learn from it. He picked up the clippings, even the ones he hadn't read, pushed them all back into the envelope and secured the flap firmly, as if he were closing a chapter of his life.

He decided right then not to open the closet doors, afraid he'd find the ghosts of his childhood there, the tin cup Berl had brought from the concentration camp, and other objects his father hadn't had the heart to throw away when he moved from the cellar to the new apartment: Meir's cloth lunch bag that had wandered with him from school to school—four, altogether— his old notebooks, a half-term report card he'd stayed in one school just long enough to receive, his seashell collection.

Suddenly, Meir was utterly exhausted, as if part of him had been standing guard for all those twenty-three years. With leaden feet, he walked back into the room, shook out the carefully folded blanket and without changing the sheet, sprawled onto the bed.

This was his father's bed, which might have been Berl's before that, and now he was embracing them both under one blanket, almost the way he did back in the days of the cellar, when they had huddled together to the sound of the rain hammering on the wall. Had women ever lain in this bed? he wondered suddenly, the women his father met on his furloughs from prison? And after his release, could his father still seduce women, even though he was sick and unattractive, and apparently depressed? Had one of them been a woman looking for a place to take a break from the rat-race of life and rest a while with her small son? Had they made a mattress of blankets on the balcony floor for that boy, too, until they finished their lovemaking? Was the boy as frightened as Meir had been when he heard those hushed voices? Had they taken the boy into their bed after their passion was spent? Meir suddenly remembered being placed carefully on the bed, like a fallen chick being returned to its nest by a kind hand. Instead of falling asleep, the boy had been shaken into intense wakefulness by the steamy, living, new odor rising powerfully from the sheets, and he shoved the pillow aside and buried his face in the heart of the elusive, insinuating odor that held the secret of life.

When he woke up, Meir saw that night was falling and it would be dark in an hour. The time had come to do what he'd been putting off until the end of the day. He refolded the blanket neatly, as if that was his father's last request: to preserve the little he'd bequeathed him. Then he went out and turned left toward the café. Like a refugee returning to his home after the war, he was afraid that he would find only buildings in ruins and fruit trees torn from the ground. The closer he came to the café, the clearer it became to him that what he feared was the encounter with himself, with the child whose life had stopped at the tree across from the café, whose shadow had been sent to America and who grew up to be a thirty-year-old shadow, while for all those years, the real him was staring fixedly at the windows of the café. Most of the patrons, cheerful, drunk, or sad, poets and actors and the cliques of their admirers, had all grown old, some were ill, some had died—even Natan Alterman and the owner had died—and others had come and gone, except perhaps for one man sitting alone at a table, who would grin at him and say, "Here's Aharon Raisin-Mountain's poor kid." Only seven-year-old Meir Rosinberg had remained as frozen as a statue, as eternal as the circle of sand around the tree where he used to stand, waiting quietly for his salvation.

The boy's eyes that once observed his father work his charm on women suddenly became the eyes of the man sitting inside the cube of light, knowing that his young son was standing across the street watching everything he did. The father didn't want to disappoint the son, but was afraid that the woman—a bad choice this time—would certainly reject him, and he was already thinking up a cheerful explanation for his humiliation as he went out to the boy and said, "Tonight, the mice return to Berl's den."

Buses pulled up next to him and spread the wings of their doors at him in invitation, then closed them, but Meir stood rooted at the side of the shelter, never taking his eyes off the nearby tree.

Only when it was dark did he slowly approach the tree. Reaching out tentatively, he ran his fingers over the rough bark, then touched the thick knob he used to rub his neck against while he was waiting;

it was at the level of his waist now. He pressed his back to the trunk, facing the café, and slid down slowly, his legs folding under him until his rear end touched the ground, compressed like a rubber man in a circus. The enormous vacuum of his missing childhood left him only with defiant words that refused to come.

He suddenly felt the ancient desire to be a magician, the desire to bring things to perfection. He focused all his powers on the café across the street and watched the vision that was revealed to him, as if a curtain were rising on what had always been there, camouflaged. Meir clearly saw a halo poised like a large bell above Alterman's table, made of diagonal rays like the sun's rays he used to see in his childhood coming through the slits in the shutters held open by little iron people. Then slowly, the bell of light descended until it touched the tabletop and stopped.

Meir stood up and, without brushing the sand off the seat of his pants, crossed the street slowly and went inside, as if fulfilling a prophecy. He sat down at the illuminated table, ordered a bottle of orange juice, and asked the waiter, "Do you by any chance know how far it is from Pardessiya to Natanya?"

"Never heard of Pardessiya. Ask at the taxi stand, they'll know." And as if he weren't seeing a miraculous vision, the waiter asked casually, "Want to order anything else?"

"Yes, a little later."

Meir sat there for a while, seeing the people around him through the glow of the bright but not blinding halo whose light did not go beyond the table. A strange peacefulness lay heavily on his eyelids and filled the spaces between the walls of his body and the crevices between his blood vessels. It stopped the trembling and numbed the yearning that had been throbbing within him for twenty-three years.

Closing his eyes, he sat with his face to the source of the white, diamond-like light, trying to decipher his past, what he hadn't experienced at all and what he had experienced without understanding. He didn't know how long he sat there motionless, his thumbs lying solidly in the cradle of his fingers. For the first time in his life, he knew that something right was happening, that this time, everything around him was right: the burning emptiness inside him settled down slowly like an animal that had eaten its fill; the flooding light and the deep calm were like the moment of breathtaking silence before falling in love; the endless yearnings repressed in his depths rose and evaporated in the open air; he was certain of the knowledge that tomorrow would be a new day.

Meir opened his eyes and took out of his bag the smiley-face notebook he'd bought at the airport newsstand and the pen he'd been given on the plane to fill out a form before landing. Then, as he moved his chair to the center of the halo, he could feel something growing inside him, a burning passion for life that was both tranquil and clear. Aware of its power pulsing in his veins like new blood, infusing him with boldness, his hand sailed across the page, line after line:

"All the years that my father was dead, I had no memory of the first seven years of my childhood, especially of the five months when my father and I wandered among his lovers, as if those memories had been buried with him . . ."

# Part Three

December 20, 1990

PARDESSIYA

Sometimes I have so many thoughts all jumbled up in my head that I'm so dizzy I have to sit down. Dr. Susskind says that first thing every morning I have to get my thoughts organized and because I'm such a good writer maybe I should write down my thoughts in the right order first the important ones and at the end the ones that aren't important and now the most important thing is my guest and the second most important thing is the eyes of Abraham's goats. My guest is someone with a gleam. The gleam is always something you see right away and the minute I saw him from the side and a little bit in the dark I knew right away he has the gleam and even from the side and a little bit in the dark I saw it clearly because there are people whose gleam hides deep down and there are people whose gleam isn't even there and they can stand on their head and yell cock-a-doodle-do and it won't help them because they don't have the gleam and that's that and with him I saw the gleam right away from the way he was standing at the door of the café straight and tall like a soldier the way soldiers used to be and looking at the people as if in another minute he'll go and conquer the world and you just want to fly over and be near him to get a little of the sweet taste of his victory and when I said that to Dr. Susskind he was very interested in the gleam and the truth is that Dr. Susskind has it too and I told him how the first time he didn't even see us because when we came in he was busy talking to some opera singer's widow and then we went and sat on the other side of the café with an actress who got a small role at Habima and ever since she was stuck up like it was such a big deal and he only looked at us over the widow's head when we left and smiled that charming smile of his and then we saw him a few more

*times sometimes with a smile and sometimes without a smile but
we never met I told Ola that here was a person with a gleam and
too bad we never get a chance to talk to him until one day we were
sitting at Alterman's table because we sang a few of his songs in our
show and we met him and his young artist lover so we already had
a few drinks when he came into the café and Alterman got up and
shouted to him that he'd read a very nice translation he did of a
poem by Anna Akhmatova and asked him to sit down and poured
him a cognac and he sat down across from me and Ola and looked
deep into our eyes like Rudolph Valentino and picked up his cognac
and said "Lovely, gracious ladies, I drink to your health" and he
sent us that gleam and I saw that Ola was getting an electric charge
from him too because she put her hand on his sleeve like she wanted
to tell him something but anyone who knows Ola knows that she
likes to touch even when she was a little girl she liked to touch and
we used to fight all the time because I don't like people touching
my things and everything she touched I had to wipe five times to the
right and five times to the left and while I was busy she would play
the piano and that's how she learned to play and I didn't and later
I had to appear with her even though my voice was better than hers
but she could play better and Dr. Susskind said that from a young
age I wasn't independent and that's why I remained childish and
that was the beginning of all the problems and all of a sudden Dr.
Susskind asked what about my fights with my sister and I said there
were fights yes especially when we were little but I loved my little
sister and there was nothing bad we had our games and there was
nothing bad about them either but Momma didn't like our games
and she'd catch us in the middle when we were little my sister and
I had games that drove our mother crazy for instance there was the
color game that was a game for people with strong nerves like we
had then and you play it like this you take a really strong short strip
of rubber and tie it tight around your throat first you turn white
then red then blue and the winner is the one who stays blue the
longest and when you take off the rubber strip it's like your head is
dancing and it's a nice feeling and the prize is chocolate and we*

*had another game we used to switch hearts back then I still didn't know that the heart is the stupidest part of the body and I was willing to take her stupid heart. The scariest time was when the heart came out of my body and wasn't in hers yet and we used to stand really really close so the heart wouldn't fall and we'd say one two three and I'd feel my heart rip out of my body and run away and in one minute another one sneaked into my body like a thief and took its place. When I had my own heart I was always happy but when I had her heart I was sad sometimes and sometimes not depending on what I found out she was thinking about me and sometimes I was sorry I gave her my heart because she would find out all my secrets and as soon as I got my heart back I erased all the old secrets and started making up new secrets and sometimes it was hard to make up new secrets and I'd say let's stop playing this game because Momma'll catch us again and put us in the closet but we liked it so much that we used to play it a lot. When I was her I was braver and not ashamed to talk in front of the class and I ate everything so Momma loved me and sometimes I'd do stupid things because my sister was good at doing stupid things when my heart was in my sister's body I didn't feel it at all and when I got it back I checked to see what she did to it because sometimes when it was inside her she'd try to ruin it and once she really did manage to ruin it and I told her to take it back because I gave her a perfectly good heart and she promised not to ruin it any more and it really did get better a few minutes later and she didn't ruin it any more so we played our game until we were big and then later every day between breakfast and the twelve o'clock pill or between the occupational therapy and the twelve o'clock pill I walk closer to the gate carefully so I won't see them slaughtering a goat again and my knees won't start shaking again and I faint and they call Dr. Susskind just for that so I walk closer to the gate carefully and look at each one of the goats and write down a description of each one's eyes but I'm so excited today because my guest is coming soon and I combed my hair especially and put on bright red lipstick because he remembers me very beautiful from the lipstick days. People who don't know goats think that all goats' eyes are the same and what is there to describe here but anyone who cares knows that it's a whole world and every goat has different eyes, this one has slightly larger ones or that one has slightly rounder ones or another one has eyes slightly closer together and some goats have eyes with mixed colors and there's even a goat with blue eyes and dots that I told Dr. Susskind about and he believed me and said that it's the same way with goats as it is with people the most interesting things are the differences. Sometimes that man from the closed men's ward comes here to take a walk and then I go right back to my ward because he's a horrible sex maniac and he loves to pester me and ask me hard questions. If I was good at painting I would always paint goats' eyes but I really love to write I already have twelve goats' eyes and the shortest is five lines and the longest seventeen those goats are going to be in Abraham's herd in a very beautiful story about Abraham that I started to write and I already have seven pages and I still didn't get to the story of Hagar but that part's so sad that I don't know how I'm going to write it. Today I put on my orange dress with the rosebuds and I hope all the buttons are okay and I don't know if I should watch the parking lot or the bus stop because I don't know whether my guest is coming in his car or on a bus. When that whole thing happened with my little sister I'm sure he didn't have a car but maybe he has one now because it suits him to have a car. Dr. Susskind gave me permission to walk near the part of the gate between the main entrance and the occupational therapy room and look at the Bedouins' goats and I always look at their eyes and sometimes I bring them cabbage from the kitchen so they'll come and I can look into their eyes up close. I'm making very beautiful rugs in the crafts room and even in Dr. Susskind's office there are two rugs I gave him as a gift for letting me write my stories on his computer one is yellow and full of shapes like the sun with straight rays coming from them and one is green with shapes like bananas. At rug time I sit with everybody and work on my rug and we listen to very pretty Hebrew songs about the old Israel and my favorite singer is that Yemenite woman with the strong voice but when the sewing hour starts I run out of there and go to write my story because ever since that whole thing with my little sister I never touch a scissors and I can't look at a scissors. In the evening sometimes Dr. Susskind asks me to read everyone what I wrote that day and some of them say it's very beautiful and some of them fall asleep because of the pills and once a woman they transferred a long time ago carried on and started to cry and wouldn't say why. My guest is supposed to come today and I'm so excited that I'm afraid I'm going to do something I'll be sorry for later and I'll have to apologize too. Once a very famous writer who they wrote about in the newspaper and printed her picture came to the literature class I go to sometimes and she said that the most important thing in writing is first of all inspiration and then you need a story and a sense of mission and then the most important thing is the little details so now I'm working on the details of Abraham's goats' eyes and I've had inspiration ever since I was little and I have a sense of mission straight from the Bible. I remember she came at the beginning of the year because she said happy new year and I was right in the middle of a very bad time when my inspiration was gone and I couldn't write and the words rattled around in my body and couldn't get out and I told Dr. Susskind that I have word poisoning in my body and he said that the best way is to take them out in writing and I could write without inspiration too and why don't I try and it took me a long time till I found the goats' eyes and the words started to come out of me. The truth is that Dr. Susskind isn't too happy with the idea of the story about Abraham and he wants me to write a different story and he tells me that someone who lived thousands of years ago when Abraham lived should write about him but I'm better off writing about what happened to me in the twentieth century we live in because I had a very interesting life and things happened to me that don't happen to many other people and I have material from life that I know better than anyone and I don't have to read other books or the Bible and I told him interesting yes but I didn't have goats and I just started describing the goats now and he said okay you're free to create whatever you want here and I told him that's why I'm staying in his ward because of that freedom to create and I don't ask to be transferred like that woman who lives in my room and when she was little her parents had a fish store and forty years later her hands still smell of fish. I'm excited about my visitor but the truth is that I'm a little worried too especially because they said it would rain today and I still can't see his car if he's even coming by car. When Dr. Susskind told me that someone called just to ask about me and he was planning to come and visit me I told him I don't want any visitors. My friends here get sad sometimes after they have visitors and besides I don't know how to talk to them anymore because I haven't had a visitor for so many years so the best thing is not to have any but Dr. Susskind asked me to see him as a personal favor because he promised him and now I'm glad he talked me into it and then we talked about the problem I'm going to have with my story when I finish with the goats which I'm really worried about but I'm more worried about the story of Hagar and I have no one to ask my problem is that Abraham wanted to kill Isaac like God asked him to and I don't want a story about murder because I want to write stories that make my readers feel good and besides I don't talk about murder since what happened to my little sister and if it's going to be about someone getting murdered then it shouldn't be someone from the family because the worst thing is when it's someone with the same blood and Dr. Susskind said I could make up someone else from the time of Abraham if I want to write about that time so much maybe I'll write about a woman from then because it's easier for a woman to write about a woman than about a man so I said that a woman isn't the hero of that story and a story has to have a hero so if I need a woman from that time then I should write about Hagar and not Sarah because I feel better with the weak women and Hagar is the weakest the way they threw her out into the desert with Ishmael and Dr. Susskind said that maybe I should write the story of Ishmael and I said don't be silly Ishmael became a Muslim and now those Palestinians are giving us a hard time on TV because of him and then there's that Arab from Iraq who's making war on us now with that gas and everything—I won't waste my writing talent on him so Dr. Susskind asked why don't I make a dramatic change and write a story closer to my own life and I said that I used to work in the theater and I'm all for dramatic changes but when it comes to my life I don't—and then I see him.*

*I see him as if all those years hadn't passed and now I also know that he has a car in a very pretty green color I didn't notice his car coming into the parking lot but I hear the door slam and I feel like I'm going to have heart palpitations like I did once and I see him get out of the car and I recognize him from the way his leg comes out of the car and the way he moves his hand when he closes the door because it's exactly the same way he closed the door to the café as if he's sending the door forward and leaving his hand in the air like in a samba when the woman spins around and he really looks exactly the same as if all those years and wars and tears and illnesses and fat never happened as if the whole world didn't turn upside down over and over again and only he stayed the same with his beautiful Apollo head and the lovely way he moves and now he's reaching down and locking the car and looking around and I wave at him with my whole arm high over my head like I used to do in the café days when he came in and he recognizes me right away as if all that time hadn't passed and he picks up a bag and puts the strap on his shoulder like a girl and comes over to me in that walk of his with his head slightly to the side as if his thoughts are heavier on one side and his face is very serious and here he is standing in front of me and I see the brown eyes with the gleam and his first question is whether the gate is locked and I tell him it isn't that it's the gate to the open clinics and he can come right in and he comes right in and only now does he say hello and reach out a hand and say is it really you Pola? I laugh and say did you think I was Ola because I know I changed since he saw me last but not so much that he'd think I was Ola because he knows very well what the difference between us was even though once he mixed us up and he was naughty with me and my hand in his is reveling in the warmth and he says I'm very pleased to meet you and lets go of my hand and says that he talked to Dr. Susskind and they told him he could visit me and he's very glad and I say that I'm very glad too because it's nice to have someone in the world who comes to visit you and I'm also very good at receiving visitors and he says they told him there's a special room for visitors where we can talk quietly because it's cold today and it's going to start raining soon and we shouldn't stay outside and I laugh and tell him that he changed a lot that there was a time when he talked about flowers and butterflies and poems and now he's all direct and matter-of-fact like a lawyer but it really is a good idea to go inside because all I need is for that man from the closed ward to come over with his questions. We start walking and he walks straight and tall and fast like he used to and I'm walking behind him and he turns around and asks do I need help and I say that he probably didn't recognize me with all the fat that settled on my knees and doesn't let me walk straight and fast and he says no problem we can walk slower and that's what we do we walk very slowly across the yard like a king and queen in a play or like a bride and groom that's a very nice description too and we sit down in the visitors' room and I look at him how handsome he is and if I was a painter instead of a writer I'd want to paint him just like he is now in profile with the tree swaying outside and I tell him that and I'm sure it'll make him laugh like he used to but he stays very serious and asks me how long have I been here and I tell him I don't want to talk about that we have more interesting things to talk about and I want to talk to him about the creative process and he looks very surprised and asks what do I mean the creative process and I tell him that he writes even though he doesn't know how to write with rhymes and that's the highest form of writing there is and I write too and that's a very interesting subject I have no one to talk to about and I tell him about the writer who came to talk in our literature class and said that when she starts writing she has inspiration and a sense of mission but even so she doesn't know where the story will go because it still hasn't decided where it wants to go and I want to ask him because I felt uncomfortable asking in front of all the people in the class and mainly in front of that writer who vol-*

*unteered to come and give us her time that's what she said instead of staying home and writing herself so I want to ask him what she meant by the story hasn't decided and how can I know when it does decide and what should I do in the meantime and he says that he's also heard writers say that and he thinks they mean that their story progresses as they write and they have no idea where it'll end up and I'm very excited because with Abraham's story I have a sense of mission but it has an ending already so how can I change his story now because it's written in the Bible and the whole world knows it and he asks me if it's true that I once lived at 8 Dubnov Street and I ask him what does that have to do with my question about my story and he says that he went to that address but it didn't look familiar and he must have made a mistake and maybe it's a different street or a different number on Dubnov Street and he thinks I remember the address because I lived there and I ask how it would help him to know the address because Ola's gone and I don't live there anymore and he can't go and live there any more like he used to and he says he knows that he just wants to check details to find out the truth and I see that it scares him a little when I yell what truth and what's he talking about and who even knows the truth except for God and maybe he does and maybe he doesn't and he should stop right now because there's no way of knowing the truth and he looks like he's going to cry and says that we should at least aspire to the truth and I tell him that aspire is a nice word that I'll use in my story and it fits because Abraham had aspirations and he says that sometimes there's one truth that's righter than others and I tell him that he can even ask Dr. Susskind who says all the time that everyone has a different truth so how can you know that and anyway life is so hard the way people are ready to suffer so much without doing anything about it and he probably decided not to cry because he puts his bag on the table and takes out a small box wrapped in paper with hearts on it and a ribbon around it and gives it to me and I feel like I'm going to cry myself because no one gave me a present for a long time except for the notebook with the drawings the staff and my friends in the ward gave me for my birth-*

*day and he says it's for me and I can open it and I try to take off the wrapping paper slowly but it tears and I open the box and there are balls of chocolate inside each one in a little paper basket like eggs in a nest and he says he remembers that I love chocolate and all of a sudden I remember the hiding place for chocolate I once had in the closet and I ask him whether I told him about my hiding place for chocolate and he says that everyone once had a hiding place for chocolate and I say that it's no accident we fell in love with him and you could fall in love with him easily just for that sentence even before he wrote those wonderful love poems of his and I offer him a chocolate ball but he says they're all for me and I take one and put it in my mouth and the taste fills my whole body from head to toe and I give him a big thank you and close the box and put it on my notebook with the story. We never invited anybody to our house not even for a cup of coffee and definitely not to live with us but in his case we fell in love and when you're in love you do things you don't do with other people and he asks me what love poems he wrote and I remember poems he sent me in the mail and I used to show them to Dr. Susskind because there were poems there that I thought were vulgar and I wanted Dr. Susskind to tell me if they really were vulgar and if I should be insulted or not and he asks me if I remember a few lines and I don't I only know for sure that there were a lot of them with the title Sperm and that's why I didn't know if I could even call them love poems because love is one thing and sperm is something else and he asks where are the poems and I tell him I threw them right into the wastebasket after Dr. Susskind returned them to me even though he said that you don't ever have to feel insulted by a poem because every poem has a lot of meanings and one of them definitely isn't insulting but I don't keep dirty poems like that in my closet and he asks if Ola received love poems too and I actually laugh at him as if he doesn't know and he asks what happened to Ola and I tell him Ola's dead and he asks do I know why she's dead and I say that everyone dies in the end yesterday a goat died before I could write about her and now I can't and besides I don't want to control myself anymore because after all he himself was there with Ola so he should know better than anyone and besides no one's allowed to ask me about Ola because I get very upset and I'm not supposed to get upset because of my blood pressure pills and I'm really sorry he reminded me about the poems about the sperm they're disgusting and especially now when I still have the taste of chocolate in my mouth and he asks me if it's possible that Ola committed suicide and I ask him where he got such an idea no woman in the world loved life like Ola did and she had a special talent for life a real inspiration for life and he says that he knows that the person they said killed her didn't do it and he was in prison for many years for nothing and his life and his family's lives were ruined and that made me really laugh and I say why are you asking me so many questions as if you don't know very well what happened there so why is he asking like he's half policeman and Dr. Susskind can tell him that I have nothing to do with that whole business and he looks out and the air outside is gray now as if it really is going to rain in a minute like he said and he gets up and says he has to go back and I tell him not to go yet because it took him so many years to come and visit me and I still have a lot of things to tell him and secrets too and I want him to meet Dr. Susskind and a few people here who think I don't have anyone in the world so let them see that someone came especially to visit me and besides he still didn't tell me if I should ask to be transferred to a place that has a bathtub but he takes his coat and says thank you very much for agreeing to see me just like a gentleman from the movies and I say what do mean agreed I've been waiting for you so many years that I'm out of my mind from waiting for him to come and I want him to stay because apart from the secrets I still haven't told him about the goats and I want to read him at least a few pages from my story and he puts on his coat and says that he wants to get back before dark because he doesn't know the roads here because he doesn't live in Israel and I ask him how he managed to arrange a place for himself in another country and he says that he has to go back to Tel Aviv and then I have no choice and I have to tell him the secret I've been keeping all these years and never told anyone not*

*even Dr. Susskind the secret of why I was there with him and my lit-*
*tle sister in the bedroom because in fact I was always there with*
*them and they never saw me but that time I came out of my place*
*behind the closet and I held the scissors and I saw the blood run*
*out of her throat onto the beautiful imported sheets that we loved*
*and just like I planned he doesn't want to go anywhere now and he*
*just sits down again without taking off his coat and asks which*
*night I'm talking about and I say he shouldn't think I'm so stupid*
*because I have a good memory and I remember that night very well*
*when the police came and my little sister was lying on the bed with*
*the scissors that were red with her blood and he asks whether I killed*
*my sister and I laugh what are you talking about she was my little*
*sister and once I used to give her my heart so how could I want to*
*kill her and he asks why didn't I tell the police the truth and I tell*
*him that I already said there's no such thing as the truth and he*
*asks why I didn't tell the police that I was holding the scissors and*
*I tell him why should I talk to the police I never talked to any police*
*in my life and I give him a big smile like he was a photographer to*
*show him that everything's fine and tell him that I want to read*
*him the story I started to write about Abraham and he gets up and*
*takes his bag and hurries outside and I run down the open ward*
*hallway after him because I'm still not finished telling him every-*
*thing I have in my heart but he's walking quickly and I run after*
*him and he's already at the door and I'm afraid that if he goes out*
*it'll lock but I manage to open it and run after him with the weights*
*on my knees and he's already at the main gate on the way to his car*
*and I yell at him as loud as I can that next time he comes he should*
*bring the boy with him and as if I said the right magic words he*
*stands still and even turns around and walks a few steps back and*
*asks what did I say and I say it again I want to see the boy and he*
*asks what boy and I tell him he shouldn't think I don't remember*
*his sweet little boy who didn't go to school because the police were*
*looking for him and I myself used to teach him how to play the*
*piano and once we sang "Frere Jacques" together the little boy he*
*used talk about who was almost completely blue and half dead*

*when he saved him on the beach in Tel Aviv and all of a sudden it started to rain but we didn't move and I suddenly wanted so much to read him just three lines from my story and I remembered that I left my notebook back in the room and someone could find it and even steal the box of chocolates and say he wrote it and how would I prove he didn't and he's looking at me with eyes glittering like glass and I tell him we'd better go back to the room now because it's raining and he tells me he's not going back but he says that maybe I should go back because it's cold and I'm all wet and I shouldn't get sick and all of a sudden a zigzag of lightning flashes across the sky like in paintings and it's right behind his head at the level of his eyes and he asks what the boy's name was and I say are you kidding me you know very well what his name was you're the one who made him so crazy with all that running away and the police the wandering around from house to house and with your women and how you made him stand and wait for hours next to the café you yourself told us that and I don't believe you saved him from drowning you wanted to drown him and he was blue and you thought he was already dead and that's what happened so the one who drove him crazy should at least remember his name and he turns his back to me and almost runs to his car and I yell that I have something else very important to tell him about the boy but maybe he didn't hear because of the rain and I don't move because maybe he did hear and maybe he still wants to hear the three lines from my story and he'll come back but he gets into the car and slams the door shut and he won't hear that the boy was a terrible sex maniac and I'm all wet now and wave goodbye to him but he isn't looking at me and his car splashes mud and drives away and my body is all wet but I suddenly understand something very important and I couldn't care less about the rain and how wet I am because I know that I have a wonderful story from life about two sisters and I still don't know whether I'll finish it with or without the scissors because maybe it'll develop in a completely different direction but the way he sat down when I told him I touched the scissors that might be an interesting story and maybe I should put it in but I still have a lot of time to decide and the most important thing is that now I know that I have a good beginning and it's his eyes when he turned around near the gate and looked at me and I'll write exactly how his eyes opened in his white face and looked like the glass eyes of a doll I had once when I was a little girl and Ola stole it and all of a sudden there was lightning and it was like his eyes were lighting up the sky and first I have to tell Dr. Susskind right now that I'm not writing a story about Abraham any more who cares about Abraham and his goats and I'll be a wreck if I happen to see the blood of the slaughtered goat again now I have a story from real life and I'm so happy and I stretched out my arms to the side like in the show where I played a princess and spin round and round and while I'm spinning I see the car at the end of the road and in the next spin it's gone but I don't care and I'm still happy because I have a good story from the twentieth century and I have a good beginning the description of the look in his eyes and who needs goats' eyes if he has a person's eyes and it's going to be at least six or eight lines and mainly it's that I feel that sense of mission already starting in my body—*

# A NOTE ABOUT THE AUTHOR

Savyon Liebrecht is one of Israel's most respected and popular authors. She was born in Munich in 1948, the daughter of Holocaust survivors. The family left Germany and moved to Israel when she was a young child. Liebrecht studied philosophy and literature at Tel Aviv University and began to publish in 1986. She is the author of six collections of short stories, including the critically acclaimed bestseller *Apples from the Desert* and the award-winning *A Good Place for the Night;* two novels, *A Man and a Woman and a Man* and *The Women My Father Knew;* as well as essays and plays. Her books have been translated into English, French, German, Italian, and Chinese. Among her many honors are Israel's Playwright of the Year award in 2004 for *I Am Speaking to You in Chinese* and again, in 2006, for *Apples from the Desert.* In 2009, she was awarded the WIZO (Women's International Zionist Organization) Prize, in France. Savyon Liebrecht lives in Tel Aviv, and is a frequent visitor to the Unites States, where she reads and lectures widely.